The Unnaturalists

THE UNNATURALISTS

TIFFANY TRENT

SIMON & SCHUSTER BFYR

NEW YORK   LONDON   TORONTO   SYDNEY   NEW DELHI

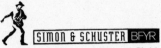

An imprint of Simon & Schuster Children's Publishing Division

1230 Avenue of the Americas, New York, New York 10020

SIMON & SCHUSTER BFYR is a trademark of Simon & Schuster, Inc.

For information about special discounts for bulk purchases, please contact Simon & Schuster Special Sales at 1-866-506-1949 or business@simonandschuster.com.

The Simon & Schuster Speakers Bureau can bring authors to your live event. For more information or to book an event, contact the Simon & Schuster Speakers Bureau at 1-866-248-3049 or visit our website at www.simonspeakers.com.

Book design by Chloë Foglia

The text for this book is set in Weiss.

Manufactured in the United States of America

10 9 8 7 6 5 4 3 2 1

Library of Congress Cataloging-in-Publication Data

Trent, Tiffany, 1973–

The unnaturalists / Tiffany Trent.

p. cm.

Summary: Vespa Nyx wants nothing more than to spend the rest of her life cataloging Unnatural creatures in her father's museum, but as she gets older, the requirement to become a lady and find a husband is looming large over her. Syrus Reed's Tinker family has always served and revered the Unnaturals from afar, but when his family is captured for refinery slaves, he finds that his fate may be bound up with Vespa's—and with the Unnaturals. As the danger grows, Vespa and Syrus find themselves in a tightening web of deception and intrigue. At stake may be the fate of New London—and the world.

ISBN 978-1-4424-2206-3 (hardback)

ISBN 978-1-4424-2208-7 (eBook)

[1. Fantasy. 2. Naturalists—Fiction. 3. Animals, Mythical—Fiction. 4. Witches—Fiction. 5. Courts and courtiers—Fiction. 6. Sex role—Fiction.] I. Title.

PZ7.T73135Un 2012

[Fic]—dc23

2011033262

FIRST EDITION

To Tricia Scott, the Queen of Art

"As the voice of Science increases in strength,
the horns of Elfland blow ever fainter and fainter...."

—Elizabeth Robins Pennell

Chapter 1

The Sphinx stares at me from her plinth. I edge closer, daring her to open her mouth and enspell me with her riddles. She crouches, eyes a-glitter, teeth gleaming through parted lips.

But she never moves.

She can't, trapped as she is by the paralytic field that holds her suspended. Once, the Museum of Unnatural History stuffed specimens of the Greater Unnaturals instead of presenting them like this. There are a few of them still in odd corners of the Museum, but they never fare well. Most have crumbled into dust. Decades ago, the paralytic field was developed by a Pedant working for the Raven Guard, and we use it to hold the larger specimens we otherwise couldn't. Only the Lesser Unnaturals—sylphids and the like—are stuffed and mounted now, and I do most of that work.

Which means, basically, that the Sphinx crouching just beyond the pulsing blue light is alive, even if she can't move. I'm certain she would eat me if she could.

I like leaning in toward the field, tempting her, tempting Fate. (Though the saints know a devotee of the Church of Science and Technology should not even think of temptations or Fate). I like the way the etheric energy buzzes and tingles just at the edge of my skin.

A patron—some dowdy woman with a whimpering babe in a perambulator—makes disapproving noises. I lean closer to the field, so close the energy leaks into my nose and the corners of my eyes. I look over at the woman and grin while my hair crackles.

We used to do this with the little kobold on display at Miss Marmalade's Seminary for Young Ladies of Quality. None of the other girls thought anything of it, until I told Effie Lindler how to trip the field.

I didn't think she'd do it, of course! But when she did, it was quite possibly the best day of all my sixteen years.

The kobold wreaked havoc, cursing Miss Marmalade with the Malodorous Slime and turning Effie into a cow. For some reason, he left me unharmed, even giving me a slight nod as he leaped from the dance hall window. I don't know if the kobold was ever caught, but the upshot was that Father and some junior Pedants were called in to clean up the mess, I was expelled, and I've been here in the Museum working for Father ever since.

That was almost a year ago. I'm very nearly seventeen now, and those days of fun are over. Besides, this field is much stronger than that at Miss Marmalade's. One would have to be as powerful as a witch or warlock to trip it, much less survive trying. Since all magic (except that sanctioned by the Empress) is heresy, there's nothing to worry about there.

But I can't resist teasing this woman just a bit more. I spread my arms as if hugging the wall of energy to me. She gasps. The needling oddness hovers at my fingertips.

Then, the unthinkable happens.

Someone pushes me hard in the back and I pitch forward.

The woman's scream follows me through the pulsing curtain.

The etheric energy zips across my eyelids, my wrists, slithering down my stockings into my boots. I am suspended in the crackling field for several seconds before my palms and knees hit the floor.

I breathe slowly, afraid I'm nothing more than a cinder. But cinders don't breathe. Nor do they think. It's impossible, though, that I'm still alive. I should be burned to a crisp.

The field is down. Somehow, I've tripped it, though that, too, should be impossible.

The Sphinx's claws splay before me, five perfectly curved scimitars. One lifts and ticks against the marble plinth as the beast stretches her toes.

I may not be alive for long. Lucky for the screaming woman that she's managed to faint dead away.

I probably should recite Saint Darwin's Litany of Evolution now, but the words of my patron saint escape me. Something about all of us being tiny twigs on one small branch on the Tree of Life, et cetera, et cetera. I can't remember. Terror dissolves whatever words lurk on my tongue.

I hear a sound, as of a thousand buzzing bees. The sound might almost make words, except that I know Unnaturals cannot truly talk. Oh, there are stories, of course—the Riddle of the Sphinx, for example—but it's been definitively proven by our Scientists and Pedants that Unnaturals are dumb, irrational creatures. Like dogs or horses, only perhaps a bit more cunning and certainly more deadly. Because they have magic.

"Be still!" someone shouts through the sudden silence.

I'm trying to place the owner of the voice—someone male and educated. And youthful.

"And do not look into her eyes," he says, coming closer.

I search my memory as to why I shouldn't look into the face of the Sphinx—isn't it the Basilisk one is supposed to avoid?—but that information is as inaccessible as the Litany. So I don't look up. I look aside at the owner of the voice instead. He wears the teaching robes of a Pedant, though he isn't wearing a wig. He's so young that I check to make sure he isn't wearing Scholar robes. But no. He has the braid on the collar and the long, colorful tassels, even if his garment looks a bit ragged.

He isn't particularly handsome. Something about his face looks wrong, but I can't tell if that's because I've been nearly blinded by falling through the field or . . . It's as though he's blurred at the edges. I blink, trying to place his shifting features as he signals to two Scholars to remove the petrified woman and her babe. I know every Pedant here, but I have no idea who he is.

He crouches at the burn line that used to be the edge of the field. He holds out a hand, his easy smile betrayed by the concern in his eyes. For one second, I think I see his face clearly, like sun breaking through cloud, but then he speaks.

"Come to me slowly."

I focus on his eyes, blue beyond all Logic. I am terribly annoyed that I've even noticed the color of his eyes. I turn from him, trying to stand on my own. The Sphinx's gaze catches mine. And then I'm frozen, unable to feel my cramped toes in my too-small boots anymore.

The buzzing grows louder, almost intolerable. The Sphinx is so close I can smell her breath—metallic and dry as an iron desert.

The Pedant whispers something I can't hear, pulling me by the wrist and thrusting me behind him. He steps between me and the

Sphinx, breaking her hold. The buzzing seems to migrate from my ears into my limbs.

The Sphinx turns, intent on this Pedant who has placed himself literally in the jaws of Death to save me.

I take two more trembling steps backward, but I can't look away from the Sphinx and the new Pedant. A strange glow, like the faintest of fields, dances across the man's fingertips. All sound drains away. It's as though we three are indelibly etched on the air of the hall—girl, man, and monster—and everything around us has faded into ghosts and shadows. The Pedant retreats slowly so that the burn line is between his scuffed boots and the Sphinx's claws.

"Raise the field!" someone cries. The silence shatters and there's movement in the alcove where the rusty field box hangs. The switch is thrown and the blue wall rises between the Pedant and the Sphinx, trapping the Unnatural again just before she can leap.

The young Pedant approaches me, and I try to stop gaping, to breathe through my nose again. The crowd surges closer, except for the woman I teased who pushes her baby out of the Grand Hall as quickly as possible. I'm acutely aware that I'm not wearing gloves, that my laboratory apron is stained, and that my hair is probably a sizzling halo around my head from contact with the paralytic field.

"My apologies, miss, for my rough treatment," the Pedant says. There's a glint of humor in his eyes that I mislike. "Do you require further assistance?"

I draw myself up and look him fully in the face. "I thank you, sir, for aiding me"—I cannot bear to use the word "rescue"—"but I require nothing further at present."

There are gasps from the crowd. I suppose I've insulted him, but there's something about his manner that's far too familiar for my liking. Much as Aunt Minta and Father might want me to think differently, I prefer the life of a Scientist, working here at the Museum with Father. It is my most cherished, most secret dream to be the first female Pedant—well, the first in several generations—and no man will overshadow that.

He has the nerve to smile, an infuriatingly charming smile. "Very well, then. Until we meet again, I advise you to be more careful where you step, Miss . . . ?"

"Nyx," I say. His eyes widen as he realizes whose daughter I must be. I will not give him leave to be even more familiar, and I do not ask his name in return.

"Miss Nyx." He bows just as Father arrives, pushing through the crowd.

"Vespa!"

Father takes my hands in his gloved ones. He's wearing his traveling coat and has replaced his teaching wig with a traveling wig and tricorn. I would ask him where he's going, but my teeth are suddenly chattering so much that I can't form words.

"I am grateful to you, Pedant Lumin." Father says. His gaze is filled with concern, but his flat tone surprises me. He dislikes this new Pedant even more than I do. Why?

Etheric energy from the field courses through me, unbalancing my humors, jarring my nerves. I grip Father's hands tighter to stop my fingers from trembling. I try to assess the new Pedant covertly while he and Father make small talk. The glow I saw has faded from him; I'm not sure it was ever there. Perhaps it was a trick of the dim light that sometimes filters in through the skylights. I shake my head. My wits must be addled by the power of the field and the dangerous magic of the Sphinx.

"I'm afraid we must be off," Father says, nodding so sharply that his tricorn almost slides off. He releases my hand to right the hat before it can do so. The pressure of his fingers tells me we will speak of this incident later.

Pedant Lumin's gaze lingers on me. I meet it with raised chin, clamping my lips shut to hide my teeth chattering, as he says, "And I, as well; it would be impolitic, I think, to be late for my first lecture."

"Indeed," Father says. His storm cloud brows descend. I am reminded that, doddering as he may sometimes seem to me, Father is still the Head of this Museum. Pedant Lumin is very aware of this as well, for he bows and hurries off, his considering glance flitting across me one more time as he passes.

I look up and see Father's odious assistant Charles moving toward us through the crowd. He's carrying a giant, iron-sealed trunk. I have no idea how he lifts it with his spidery arms and legs. Utter loathing for Charles replaces my irritation at Pedant Lumin's familiar manner. His dull eyes meet mine—his regard is akin to having a chamber pot poured over one's head.

"Are you well?" Father says. His fingers relax somewhat.

I nod at him.

"Vee, I thought we came to an understanding after the incident at the Seminary."

"Father . . ." I do not wish to discuss this in front of Charles.

I use every bit of Logic and Rationality I possess. I must remain calm. He will never believe me otherwise, even though this time

I'm telling the truth. "Father, I promise I didn't trip the field intentionally. I was *pushed*."

Father frowns. "By whom?"

"I don't know. I didn't see. But somebody had to have done it. I couldn't have just fallen on my own."

"Mm-hm," Father says. He releases my hand.

"What's this, Miss Nyx?" Charles asks, obviously trying to pretend the strongbox isn't nearly tearing his arms from his sockets. His last name—Waddingly—suits him very well. He has a waddish soul, like a lump of something one can't shake off one's boot. I secretly call him The Wad.

The trunk emits waves of dark energy. It's not just nulled to mask the magic of whatever is inside; it's nevered. A nevered object has such negative power that it has the potential to burn souls, so Aunt Minta says. I don't know how Charles is holding it without pain, except that I'm fairly certain he has no soul anyway. I can't bear to get near it. Not that I'd want to be near The Wad anyway.

"Did you not hear the commotion as you came in, Charles?" Father says. "Vee very nearly set the Sphinx free in the Great Hall. She says that someone pushed her through the field." Charles looks around, as if both relishing the mayhem that might have ensued and regretting that he missed it.

"You could have died, Miss Nyx." I can't tell whether he's disappointed or incredulous that I didn't. To Father, he says, "Everything is in readiness, sir. The carriage awaits."

Father nods, but his dark eyes are trained on me. "I'm afraid you'll have to come with us, Vee. I'm worried about leaving you alone after such an encounter. Thank Saint Newton you survived it!"

"But, Father . . ." I begin. The trembling starts anew. I'm not sure I can manage the delicate work required to mount the new sylphs in their cases in my present condition, anyway. I allow him to escort me from the Museum by the elbow while Charles leads the way with his infernal trunk.

My fancies must be getting the better of me, for I'd almost swear the trapped Sphinx's grin widens as I pass her.

Chapter 2 —

Syrus Reed sat by the wheel of his clan's rusting train car, cleaning an old music box he'd found in the City refuse pile. It was an antique, something that worked under its own power, rather than the mysterious *myth*-power of the Refineries. If he cleaned and replaced the missing parts, he was sure he could get the music box working again. Chickenfeet stew bubbled above the nearby cookfire, setting his mouth to watering. He hoped it would be time to eat sooner rather than later, but he didn't dare steal a stewed foot for himself for fear of a sharp rap from Granny's cooking spoon. Somehow, Granny always knew what he'd done no matter how he tried to hide it.

Inside the decaying passenger car, Granny tended to the fussy new baby just brought in from the roadside. The New Londoners abandoned any child who resembled a Tinker or had been born under odd circumstances—children whose laughter moved toys through the air or whose cries caused little rain clouds to form inside the City-dwellers' lush townhouses before their talents could be squelched by nullwards. Anything that stank of illegal magic was left outside the City gates. Syrus wasn't sure who would ultimately take the baby—he knew his Uncle Gen and Aunt Jaya had asked for another child whenever one became available.

Syrus sang a charm-song in the sacred language of their people. It was low and soft and sad, but it carried the sound of another world that Syrus could just barely envision through the train car's open windows. High mountains, tall forests in which strange animals moved through the mists, and glacial plains where flowers bright as stars nodded. A world lost to his people now, but so rich in memory and song.

The baby quieted at last.

Syrus half-smiled. Of all the clan members in Tinkerville, he still had the strongest touch of the old ways. When he sang, even the shyest of Elementals drew near. He could speak to and understand them better than anyone, and he alone was bonded to one of them—the hob Truffler—as all Tinkers had once been bonded to Elementals of old. Such understanding was a dangerous talent that was best kept hidden, especially from the brooding New Londoners who sometimes took it into their heads to Cull the trainyard for new workers for their Refineries. In the last Cull twelve years ago, they'd taken Syrus's parents. He had been barely two, and their faces were a distant memory to him, kept alive only by Granny's tales. They had been victims, like every Tinker, of the Cityfolks' fear and greed.

If the New Londoners discovered one thimbleful of talent among any of the clans, they stamped it out as quickly as you'd behead a poisonous snake. Even though the talents weren't exactly the same as the magic they so dreaded and feared, even though they most often faded once the Tinkers reached adulthood, the Cityfolk were terrified of the Tinkers who were gifted with them. Granny said that the reason Tinker talents never developed anymore into full-blown magic was because of the disease in the land. Until that was healed, the talents would continue to flicker like candles about to go out. Still, the Tinkers refused to give up teaching their children the sacred language or the old ways, even if they never spoke it aloud where a New Londoner could hear.

Syrus often wished his talent was more useful for something besides speaking to Elementals. If he had real magic, what he would do with it! He imagined tearing down the Refinery and freeing the parents he'd barely known, if they were still alive. Tearing down the walls of the City, even. He imagined the white fires of magic burning through the Refinery smog and the Empress's Tower opening like a dark flower to the light. . . .

A small, hairy hand pinched his arm. Truffler glared at him. "Such bad thoughts," he said.

"C'mon," Syrus said, "don't tell me you wouldn't bring the City down if your people could!"

Truffler shook his head. He was hairy all over except for his startlingly bald crown. He came only to about Syrus's chest, so it was always hard for the boy not to think of him as an odd little child, even though he knew Truffler was older than anything he could imagine. Like most of the Lesser Elementals—trolls, kobolds, hobs—Truffler found mortal speech difficult and spoke in halting phrases.

"Not our way," Truffler said. "Peace."

"But the City doesn't even belong there!" Syrus said. "It's only there because of one Scientist's big mistake!"

Truffler looked at him down his big nose. "Peace," he said stubbornly.

Syrus knew it was disrespectful to argue, so he just shook his head and turned back to the music box. He reached for another tool, but Truffler anticipated his thoughts and handed him the tool kit and a bottle of turpentine.

Granny emerged from the passenger car then, her worn shoes and faded skirts almost noiseless on the iron stairs. "I didn't just hear ye arguing with Truffler, did I, boy?" Granny asked.

Syrus kept his eyes lowered on his work as she bent near him, inspecting the stew.

"No, Granny," he said.

"Because it'll be lessoning time, if that's the case."

Syrus glanced up at her. Her dark eyes twinkled above weathered apple cheeks. She pushed aside one of her gray braids to reach into her patched coat and draw out her pipe.

"You know that isn't really much of a threat, *Nainai?*" He said her title low in the old language.

She tried to look threatening, but a grin split her face after only a few seconds. Syrus loved her stories more than anything; it wasn't a chore for him to listen as it was for some of the other children.

Granny lit her bowl with a taper, and her whiskered chin puckered as she sucked at the long-stemmed pipe.

"Did I ever tell ye about the man whose arrogance cost him his entire life?" Granny asked.

"No," Syrus said.

Granny chewed on her pipe stem a bit. And then she began. "In a green country far from here, a man of the Feather clan found a box washed up on the riverbank. When he cleared the mud and reeds away, he read these words carved in the old language on its lid: *Only the one who is strong enough can bear the weapon inside of me.*

"There was no lock and no seal on the box, just that warning.

Now this man was the pride of his clan—he was their war leader, because it was back in the days of fighting, and he had forced the rival clan's daughter to be his bride. He had killed a fierce creature called a bear and wore its teeth around his neck. There was nothing he believed he couldn't do or withstand. And he had big dreams for the clans. At the time, in that far country, our people lived under the boot heels of warlords who came into the mountains to steal our sheep and our women. This man hoped to rise up against them and throw them out of our land. He was ready to fight, and as he bore the scars of the bear on his chest, he was sure that he could stand up to anything.

"He didn't even wait to get the chest home. He opened it right then and there, sure that the weapon inside would help him on his quest."

Granny paused, drawing deeply on the pipe before exhaling a cloud of smoke.

Syrus remembered the bits of the music box that had some-how drifted out of his fingers and into his lap. Truffler grunted at him. The smell of turpentine from the opened bottle was almost as strong as Granny's pipe smoke.

"And then?" Syrus finally said. Because he knew she would expect him to.

"The weapon for which he was so eager was no more than a tarnished mirror. He very nearly threw it into the mud in disgust, but then couldn't resist looking at his own proud, handsome face. Do you know what he saw?"

Syrus shook his head, though he had his guesses.

"He saw the truth. He saw that his plans for battle would destroy our people. He saw that his wife was sleeping with another man.

He saw that everyone thought him a blowhard, a bully, a person of ugliness. But he also saw the man he might become."

"And do ye know what he did?" Granny asked.

Syrus waited.

"He repacked the chest carefully and took it home. He gave away the bear claw necklace to someone in need of its power. He told his wife she was free to go to her lover. And he sent the chest to his enemies with a note that said: *Let there be peace.* He went on to become a great leader, and when we needed shelter, the Elementals heard his pleas and granted it to him. He was the first to enter here, and he saved our lives by the way he changed his own."

Syrus snorted.

"What?" Granny asked. "You were expecting something else?"

"Something more interesting. More dramatic. Like he killed himself there on the river and his blood turned into something horrible. Or—"

Granny clucked at him like an aggravated hen. "That wouldn't serve the lesson."

Syrus looked at the bits of music box as Truffler spread its pieces on a little cloth on the ground between them.

"The lesson is this," Granny said. "Arrogance destroys the future and masks the truth. Let go of your pride and learn who ye truly are."

Syrus nodded, feeling chastened. It was as though Granny had again read his mind and found the thoughts there just as disturbing as Truffler had. And yet it was difficult to unthink them. Even though he hated the City, he was always the first to volunteer to help on Market Day. Something about it fascinated even as it repulsed him. He could have said it was because of many easy marks he found to pickpocket, but it was more than that. There was a mystery buried at the heart of the City that he longed to open wide.

Granny blew smoke into his face to get his attention. She laughed when he coughed and squinted at her through watering eyes.

"And learn the lesson within the lesson," she said. "There's more than one way to defeat an enemy. Sometimes the best attack is no attack at all."

From within the train car, a thin wail rose. Granny frowned. "That didn't take long," she said. She rose, still surprisingly spry for however old she might be. Syrus wasn't sure of her true age, but she had been old for as long as he could remember.

A disturbance at the far side of the clearing drew their attention. A runner came through, pushing past metalworkers and women at their cookfires, nearly tripping over a group of children playing tiles in the dirt.

"Headwoman Reed!" he called.

Granny peered at him, taking the pipe out of her mouth and holding it in a gnarled hand.

The runner skidded to a stop next to Syrus, and the boy was glad that all the music box parts were on his other side. The pieces would have been scattered beyond recall otherwise.

"There's a fine carriage on the old Forest Road," he said. "Gen thought you'd want to know."

Granny smiled. "He's right."

"They're carrying a box of the Waste."

Immediately, everyone of the Reed clan was at attention. Syrus's cousins Raine and Amalthea came from around the train car, their sleeves and patched aprons sopping from doing laundry.

"What?" Granny said. All the joy was gone from her face.

"Gen's group saw them collect it. The fools are actually taking it into the City with them."

"I don't know whether to let them take it inside or make them put it back where they found it," Granny said. Murmurs rose among the clans—who would be stupid enough to try to carry a box full of the Waste around? Especially when everyone knew of its destructive power? Only the Cityfolk.

"Come along," Granny said at last. "Raine and Syrus, bring whatever supplies we might need. Amalthea, you stay with the baby."

To the runner she said, "Send someone back to Gen to tell him we'll be there directly. Rest yourself here by the fire."

She clamped the pipe back between her teeth and waited, her eyes glimmering with impatience. Syrus rolled up the music box parts in the cloth and shoved them at Truffler. "Guess we'll worry with this later."

The hob nodded.

Then he leaped up the rungs of the passenger car ladder to gather his things.

As the Reed clan tromped through the Forest toward the old Euclidean road, Syrus hummed a song of hopeful victory—of bulging pouches and chests full of jewels, of rich foods and warm coats. Not that the Tinkers would keep such things for themselves. But they would bring excellent prices in the market and hexshops of Lowtown, which would allow for necessities they'd been unable to afford in this lean year. It had been a long while since anyone had been foolish enough to travel along the old road, much less carrying a box of the Waste. He hoped what the runner had said wasn't true. It had to be impossible—what box was strong enough to hold the Waste, much less keep it contained?

Syrus thought about Granny's story as they marched, especially the lesson within the lesson. *Sometimes the best attack is no attack at all.* She was telling him to think differently about the City, about the problems between Tinkers and Cityfolk, but how? The Tinkers supplied the Cityfolk with workers, with knowledge of old-fangled machinery. The Cityfolk barely tolerated the Tinkers in their derelict trainyard, keeping them close only because they were useful. Syrus had often wondered why his people didn't just leave. Even if they couldn't return to their old home, they could at least move somewhere else. He had asked Granny that repeatedly a few years ago until he'd seen the Manticore for the first time.

And then he'd understood.

The Forest touched him gently with fiery, dreaming fingers. The rest of the year, the tree faces were obscured by leaves, but through the falling golds and scarlets, he saw the sleepy faces of a dryad or two curled behind the bark. A few fairies peeped out at him as he passed, but there were not as many as there had once been, so Granny said. Through the Forest came a humming heartbeat—the Manticore. Her life was bound to this Forest; she was the source of all that dreamed through the winter and woke to blossom in the summer. Without her, the Creeping Waste would swallow this place whole.

She was why the Tinkers stayed. Why they continued to observe the old rituals and forms despite what the Cityfolk did and said. The Tinkers were the Manticore's and the Forest's last defense. They stayed as a diversion and prayed that they would never have to fight openly ever again. They had done so once and lost horribly, Syrus knew. That early war with the First Emperor was when the Culls had started. And they had continued off and on up until Syrus's childhood. There hadn't been one since then, and Syrus hoped there would never be another one.

Uncle Gen signaled up ahead for the rest of the line to quietly fan out and take positions. Voices along the road filtered through the trees. Syrus crept up through the dried leaves and ferns without a sound. Truffler squatted next to him. Syrus was wishing there had been time for stew when the carriage came around the bend.

Then his uncle gave the signal to move forward, but the line of Tinkers stopped almost as soon as they'd begun.

Syrus watched as an old highwayman and two rotten-toothed accomplices stepped out from the opposite side of the road, halting the carriage in its tracks.

Uncle Gen *humphed* and leaned on his bow.

Granny chewed on her pipe, then said softly, "Well. Ain't this interesting?"

Chapter 3 ━

Every bump and rattle of the carriage makes me grit my teeth. Considering that such things are the natural order of most carriage rides, my jaws begin to ache.

I'm annoyed that I fell asleep. It appears I've missed everything—the onion domes of the Night Emporium spanning the bridge over the River Vaunting, the glimpses of the Empress's Tower with its ever-circling ravens, even the seedy yet strangely alluring rag-and-bones shops of Lowtown.

"Where are we going, Father?"

I still feel groggy. Almost as if someone drugged me.

Then again, falling through a field of that magnitude could also be the reason my limbs still feel stuffed with bricks. And the reason why I pretty much fainted once Father dragged me into the carriage. I scrub at my cheek; my skin is imprinted with the pattern of the carriage upholstery.

"I would reckon," Father says, "you mean where have we been? We're returning to the Museum now. And home, for you."

I don't follow. "What?" I stare at the box at my feet, wondering what's inside, why it's so strongly nevered that my toes tingle.

The Wad chuckles at my consternation. "You needn't worry,

Miss Nyx. It isn't as if there's a bomb in there that will go off at the slightest provocation."

I repress the urge to make rude faces at him.

Father smiles sidelong at me. He's obviously quite proud of himself. He wraps my hand in his. "All I'll say is that we've been on a mission of vast importance. All will be revealed when the time is right, you'll see."

It's utterly unfair that I missed everything. Before Charles came along a few months ago, I was Father's assistant. I helped him with all his important work. Now I've been shoved aside, relegated to the Cataloguing Chamber. Though I do love my work, the knowledge that I've been replaced—and especially replaced by The Wad—still stings. What does Father see in him? Is it just that he's male? I am determined to prove that I can be a Pedant too, but . . .

"But, Father . . ." I begin.

His gaze, so warm a moment ago, freezes me now.

"What we carry is of the most secret and delicate nature, Miss Nyx," Charles says as if he's speaking to a petulant child. "Your father is showing you a kindness by not involving you inasmuch as he is able."

I say nothing. Instead, I finger the curtain, wanting to raise it and see where we are.

Father tightens his grip on my hand. "No one must see us," he says.

I look at him, trying to gauge his response. His demeanor worries me. This is a man I've never seen.

His face softens a little as if he senses my concern.

"I wouldn't have brought you except that I feared you might be ill after your encounter. I couldn't very well send you home by

yourself nor leave you. I'm trusting you to keep silent about this. One day you will be able to tell stories about how you rode with us on this august day!"

I nod slowly and bite my questions back. I've found that the best way to get what I want these days is to outwardly comply. Later I will look in Father's files or his laboratory and discover whatever it is I wish to know.

The carriage judders wildly over the road. If the driver isn't careful, he could easily break a wheel or axle.

Then, the carriage stops.

The driver's voice is muffled and tinny as it comes through the speaking tube. He's not talking to us, but to someone outside. The horses stamp and their harnesses jingle. The carriage creaks as I hear the driver get down and again when he unfolds the steps and climbs up them to open our door.

"Ye must come out, gentlemen, lady," he says.

"Whatever for?" Father says.

But the driver just shakes his head and disappears back down the metal stairs.

"Not a word about the box," Father whispers to us.

The Wad and I both nod and follow him outside. Trees rustle their flaming robes along the road. We're in the Forest. Instinctively, I make the sign against irrationality to protect myself from pixie infestation. It's all I can do, since we've had no time to don nullsuits, if Father and Charles even remembered to bring them. Most young ladies my age would be terrified if they found themselves so unshielded on a Forest road that's likely teeming with Unnaturals.

But not me. I look around in unabashed wonder at the sun in the autumn leaves, the endless march of trees. I'm more interested in what sort of sylphids inhabit this stretch of road than in the three men with yellowing lace cravats and rusty-looking swords advancing on us.

They're perhaps the most pitiful excuse for highwaymen I've ever seen, except that I've never seen a highwayman in the flesh before. When ground travel between New London and Scientia became nearly impossible due to the Creeping Waste, most of the brigands disappeared or took to the skies. But now they're here, looking hungry and, if anything, bored.

"We'll have your valuables now," says a man with a ratty wig and bad teeth I can see even from here.

Father coughs. "We have no valuables to speak of, sir. But our purses are yours."

The highwayman frowns. He gestures with his rusty blade toward the carriage, and one of his men climbs inside.

"A strongbox, boss!" the man says as he backs out of the carriage.

I look from Father to the Wad to the driver. All of them stand still, barely daring to breathe, like Museum specimens caught in a paralytic field.

"Bring it out," the boss says.

I move forward. "Touch that box and we'll all die!" I shout. I have no idea whether it's true or not, but it has the desired effect.

Everyone looks around. Father's mouth forms a tiny *o*. The Wad's eyes narrow.

The brigand snarls at me and moves again toward the box.

"I mean it!" I say. "If you want us all to die in a blaze of etheric energy, by all means, continue." I make myself look as tall as I can and fold my arms across my chest.

The boss glares at me, and his lackey looks back and forth between us, trying to figure out what to do.

A voice comes from the trees.

"She doesn't jest, highwayman."

Several people step out, thin and stocky, boys, men, and a few girls. All I can see in the gathering gloom are their patched coats, their fur-lined bandoliers. The girls in their checkered headbands hang back. The chicken feather on one old granny's hat licks the dusk like a white tongue.

Tinkers.

I know of them, of course. I've seen them from afar in the markets, selling their mechanical wares from bright-painted wagons. But I've never been allowed to do more than watch them covertly from a distance. Aunt Minta always sends the maid to buy from them. For while their wares are reliable, they themselves are not. Or so Aunt Minta says. She's sure they all carry pixie infestations or sylphid sickness, though I've reminded her often enough that they must pass under the wards of the City gates before they can enter. The wards should clean them of any such contamination.

But Aunt Minta always sniffs and reminds me that she knows more than I do. "After all," she says, "if they weren't all heretics, why would they have been sent beyond the walls in the first place?"

Effie Lindler used to tease me unmercifully that I was of Tinker descent because of my pig cheeks and cat eyes. (Which was part of why I was immensely if secretly gleeful when the kobold at Miss Marmalade's turned her into a cow.) As I watch the Tinkers come closer, though, I really don't think I look anything like them. My hair is auburn and my eyes are hazel, after all, while the Tinkers are mostly dark-haired and dark-eyed.

One of them—a boy with unforgivably mussed hair who looks to be around thirteen or fourteen—casually loads a blow pipe with feathered darts. The older Tinker who spoke catches and releases chains that chime in his palm. Others withdraw curved daggers or strange throwing instruments from the pockets of their coats. Even the granny has a wicked little blade in her hands.

Most City people hate the Tinkers, but their stealth and facility for making whatever they need out of virtually anything are reasons for all but the strongest or most foolish to leave them alone. There is often talk of ousting them from the derelict trainyard, but it never comes to anything. In the past, Tinkers were Culled to help fill the Refineries, but I'm fairly certain that doesn't happen anymore.

The Wad's lip curls as he looks at them, but I'm merely curious. Almost everything I know about them is hearsay. I wonder how they see themselves. I wonder how they see us.

The highwaymen understand they're outnumbered. The leader spits into the dirt. He and his men melt into the scrub along the abandoned tracks.

But that leaves us with a new problem.

I move closer to the stairs. I don't want to put myself in the way of that leader and his chain or the boy with the blowpipe, but someone has to stop them.

The leader laughs at me, however.

"We know what's in the box, little lady. We saw your men take it. We reckon the Cityfolk are more than welcome to the Waste, if you're really bent on taking it there."

I struggle to keep my face composed. I was only bluffing about something being in the box. Is he bluffing along with me or is he serious? I can't imagine the latter at all. It's first of all impossible.

No one can get near the Waste without dissolving into black sand. And, though that strongbox is nevered beyond all reason, I've been told that nothing can hold the Waste. Nothing. Surely it must be the former. Surely he's bluffing along with me, just so he and his people can scare the highwaymen and take what they want for themselves. Isn't he?

My Father's face hardens. He clears his throat to lecture the man, but the Tinker leader is having none of it.

"No need, Pedant. Unlike those other fools, we really do just want your purses. As payment for your rescue."

"Rescue?" the Wad splutters. "This is a rescue?"

"I don't think you want us to call it anything else," the leader says, tossing the chain from hand to hand.

Charles's face looks darker than the dusk, if that's possible. He steps forward, whispering words I don't understand. His hand lifts. What is he doing? I recall warnings from Scripture. *Ye shall know them by their gifts.* If such a thing wasn't utter heresy, I would almost think he's about to throw curses at the Tinkers. That, too, is impossible. I'm beginning to wonder if anything can happen. That is a frightening thought indeed.

And then Charles melts to the ground, a feathered dart sticking up over his collar. The boy lowers the pipe from his lips. I can't help but match his wicked grin, though I smother it quickly, because Father is sputtering in shock. I'm not sure he even noticed Charles until he slid to the ground.

The boy slips the pipe back into his patched coat and comes closer. He takes a few coins out of the driver's purse. He stoops to take Charles's. After he takes Father's, Father kneels next to Charles, checking his breathing.

The boy stands in front of me. I glimpse dark eyes under even darker tousled hair. I hold my purse out toward him, and he undoes the strings with a deft twist of his fingers.

As soon as the purse strings fall open, regret sours my mouth like preservative acid. Nestled amid the coins is my little jade toad, the only thing left that belonged to my mother. Father gave it to me when I was five, as a reminder of the mother I never knew. There are no portraits of her, only this, a thing she carried with her for luck just as I carry it now. I wish fiercely that I had never gotten in the habit of carrying it with me everywhere. I'm not really a sentimental sort of girl, but it's the one thing (aside from books and the displays I've made at the Museum) that I hold dear.

Its carnelian eyes wink at me and I want to snatch it away as the boy inspects it.

"I wouldn't take coin from a lady," he says. "But I'll have this toad here for my troubles, if it's all the same to you." His eyes meet mine. I catch a glint of gold in all that dark. I'm taller than him and I do my best to seem as formidable as possible.

"It isn't," I say through gritted teeth. I see the leader and his chain out of the corner of my eye, the way some of the other men point their weapons so casually in our direction.

"Good," the boy says. He plucks the toad from its small nest of coins.

"Syrus!" the leader calls.

The boy grins at me and returns to the Tinkers before I can do more than splutter my protests.

Then, Syrus and his people melt away into the Forest. Charles sits up with Father's help, clapping a hand to his swelling neck. His tongue is mercifully too thick to talk.

At last, we climb back into the carriage—bereft of all, it seems, but our box and whatever it contains. I shake my head again at what the Tinker leader said. Impossible. Nothing can contain the Waste.

Two resolutions fill my mind as the carriage crawls back into the city.

I will have that toad back.

And I will find out what is in that box.

CHAPTER 4

As the carriage departed, Syrus's clan gathered round to see his haul. They exclaimed over the coins and his cousin Raine announced proudly that this was dowry enough for her to marry her sweetheart for certain.

Syrus laughed. "Who said I was giving any of it to you?"

Raine slapped him on the head and stomped away, pouting.

Rubbing his crown, Syrus gave everything over to Granny Reed, as she would distribute the wealth among her clan as she saw fit. Granny touched the toad with her forefinger and frowned at her grandson. "You shouldn't have taken that, boy," she said.

"Why not?" he asked. "Bring a good price in the hexshops, I'll bet."

"We don't deal in this sort of thing no more. Best get rid of it quick," she said. "It'll bring bad trouble, if you don't."

"What do you mean, *Nainai?*" Syrus asked.

Granny smiled at him, her wooden dentures almost invisible in the dark. "You get to Gather tonight, for starters," she said. Gathering Night came before Market Day. Some unlucky soul was chosen to gather whatever he could find of value in the Forest to take to the City markets the next day.

Syrus's shoulders slumped, but he knew better than to complain out loud. He'd really hoped to be rewarded for bringing in such loot—getting to sleep a full night closest to the potbelly stove, for instance. Instead, he'd now be up until the wee hours, digging in the cold forest loam for night-blooming phosphors, midnight morels, whatever he could find that the Tinkers could sell.

While it was true that he was one of the best Gatherers, it certainly wasn't something he enjoyed doing in the cold.

Granny rounded up everyone else, including the still-pouting Raine. They said quiet farewells before they disappeared back down the road toward the trainyard. Tonight, he knew there'd be roasted apples and dancing. Granny would probably tell one of her clan stories by the light of the stove as everyone bedded down for sleep. A story of the World Before or how the Manticore stole the Emperor's Heart or . . . maybe even the story of how Granny had found him floating in the river, which Syrus thought was the best story of all. He kicked at a white pebble and sent it skittering off into the dark.

Then he sighed. Best get started. Perhaps if he hurried he could get back early.

He sang a soft calling song in the old language and soon Truffler appeared. The hob's nose was the real reason Syrus was such a good Gatherer. He could sniff out the best mushrooms from miles away.

Syrus trudged along, complaining to himself about the dew-dampness, the necessity of wandering mostly in the dark, the possible things that might eat him without anyone knowing what had happened to him. "When you're wailing 'cause I'm nowhere to be found," he grumbled to his absent Granny, "then you'll change your tune about sending me off at night."

Truffler turned and made a hissing noise to silence him. The hairy little hob alternately walked or crawled over the ground, his giant nostrils flaring like a bellows. Sometimes he resembled a dog or pig, but was never clearly one thing or the other. Often, though, the outline of his big nose was all Syrus could see of him in the dark.

Truffler turned and pointed at the dirt. Syrus dug in with his rusty trowel and thrust the morels Truffler had discovered into his sack, except for a few which he gave to the hob as payment for his work. Syrus also always made sure to leave behind a bit of whatever it was he took. Greed didn't pay the Gatherer, so Granny said.

The mid-autumn chill stiffened his fingers as they worked their way to the river's edge. Virulen Forest snaked in a long tentacle between the wreck of Tinkerville, where Syrus and his people lived in the ancient trainyard, and the River Vaunting that slid from under the Western Wall of New London. Beyond the Wall, the City Refinery coughed out streamers of phlegm-colored smoke, and the river that rolled past it was slick and shiny as snot. Syrus never swam here, but it was narrow enough that it would have been easy to cross had it not been so very swift and deep.

Something caught Truffler's attention on the other bank. "Bad. Things," he said in his halting, gritty voice. The hob crept back toward the trees.

"Wait," Syrus said.

Truffler stopped, crouching in the cattails at water's edge and clapping his hands over his ears.

Syrus heard the song before he saw the singer. A prison carriage bearing a Harpy between iron bars and drawn by iron horses rattled toward a gate in the wall. Like most things from New London, the horses were powered by *myth*, the mysterious dust that provided the city with heat and light, among other things. The Cityfolk claimed there were *myth*mines far to the north in the Myth Mountains from which the dust took its name. Raw *myth* was brought to the Refineries, which then distributed power via steam conduits or delivered blocks of refined *myth* throughout the city.

Or so they said. Granny Reed said that the story of *myth* itself was a myth. That somehow the Cityfolk captured the souls of Elementals and bound them to their iron or ground them into dust to power their infernal machines. Syrus couldn't believe anyone could be so cruel, so blatantly unaware of the sacredness of all life, especially that of the Elementals. And yet he knew that the City Lords still occasionally hunted and ate what Elementals they caught. He knew there were places where Elementals were held as curiosities for the Cityfolk to look upon, as though they were lower than beasts.

The Elementals his people served could be dangerous—the Manticore who ruled this Forest was a case in point—but they were the lifeblood of the land. And if you knew the proper forms for dealing with them, there generally were no problems. His people had been visiting here for as far back as they could recall; the Elementals referred to them, in fact, as the Guest People. It was only when the City suddenly appeared by the river, slamming shut the doors between this and the World Before, that the real troubles began.

Syrus still couldn't believe what Granny said was true, though. How could the Cityfolk treat the Elementals as if they were little more than livestock? Why did the Elementals allow it? Surely they could defend themselves if they truly wished.

And yet the *myth*work horses drew the Harpy onward, their eyes pulsing with *myth*light.

At first, he saw only the Harpy's talons gleaming as they reached through the bars of her cage. They gripped and retracted; the bars must be nevered to counteract her magic. But the bars couldn't stop the Harpy from singing. Her voice fell through the night, a descant of loss and abandonment intertwined with the whisper of river reeds. She told of the lonely mountain crags where she and her kind soared. Of sunlight on dark wings, of snow falling between her talons and the ground. Of flight and freedom and the eternity of wind across the peaks.

And then Syrus understood why *myth*work horses drew the carriage. Real horses would have been driven mad by the Harpy's song. It took every ounce of his strength to stand still. The clear rapture of her voice pierced him to the core. Her song confirmed what the Manticore had told his people long ago. When the Greater Elementals were killed, the land and all the creatures they had once protected would be consumed by the Creeping Waste.

Syrus knew what had to be done. The Harpy must be freed.

Syrus moved toward the river. A long, hairy arm grabbed the edge of his patched coat. The boy looked down and saw Truffler trying to cover both his ears with his free arm. The hob shook his head.

The door in the wall opened. A crowd of sexless people in hooded cloaks and goggles emerged, escorted by floating everlights. They were Refiners, the engineers who kept the City Refinery running day and night. A strange machine rolled out with them, its black dome mounted over a nest of hoses and wiring. They also carried thunderbusses—long guns that shot a blast of energy at any Elemental—or human, for that matter—who defied them.

All of this should have frightened Syrus enough to send him skittering back to Tinkerville, but the Harpy's song sheared him to the bone. Somehow he had to get her free before anything happened to her.

"No. No," Truffler said, grasping at his coat. The hob hated water with a passion and he groaned as Syrus stepped into the river. Then the hob's hairy weight nearly pushed Syrus under as the creature clutched him around the crown of his head, trying to keep from getting wet. The River Vaunting was freezing and swift, and it occurred to Syrus only now that perhaps something might be living here, another Elemental that would happily suck him down to the bottom and devour him.

Luckily, there was nothing but the current to fight against. He pushed hard until he managed the other side without drowning or dunking the terrified hob. When Syrus emerged, he was covered with the gooey, cold sludge that rode the rapids. He gasped at the awful smell—like burned bone.

Truffler made soft clucking noises and shook his head as Syrus crept toward the cage.

"Foolish. Foolish," he whispered.

Syrus was close enough that he could see the Harpy's sad eyes through the cage. She had the feathered feet, body, and wings of a giant owl, but the head and shoulders of a beautiful woman with straggling, dark hair. Power radiated from her in waves so strong it lifted his hair off his neck. He had never been so close to an Elder Elemental—serving the Manticore had always meant that his people kept a respectful distance from her den.

The Harpy watched him. Her song trickled to a melodious, insistent hum.

The time was now, but Syrus wasn't sure what to do. The Harpy might very well eat him when she was free. She might scoop him up with her talons and carry him off to her mountains, break his body on the crags, and pick his bones. He didn't care, though, and not just because she'd enspelled him with her song. The world would be sadder and smaller without her. What was his life compared to that?

Pick the lock, the Harpy hummed.

Truffler put his hairy hands over his eyes and peered between his fingers.

The cage was between Syrus and the group of Refiners, and he was able to sneak close to it without being seen. He could feel the dark magic infusing the bars and the lock. He had half-hoped he could sing a charm of opening, but if the Harpy couldn't open it, he knew he couldn't. He'd have to do things the old-fashioned way. He didn't have his lockpicking tools with him, but he drew a thin, sharp bone out of his sleeve, which had a number of potential uses. His hair fell in his eyes and he pushed it away with fingers clammy with green Refinery-slime.

Hurry, the Harpy sighed, her mournful eyes trained on the approaching Refiners.

Syrus shrugged off Truffler's imploring fingers. It was going to be difficult with just one bone. And since the lock was nevered . . .

Syrus heard shouting over the Harpy's humming. The iron horses stood still, the *myth*light in their eyes dimmed to pale flickers.

He crept under the cage and peered around one of the spoked wheels.

Mist uncoiled from the trees and slithered toward the Refiners. It grew into a swaying snake of darkness and the Refiners fell back before it, raising their thunderbusses.

Syrus clutched at Truffler as the snake split into five people hooded in shadow. The Harpy hummed to herself above them.

"Architects," Syrus hissed. The Architects of Athena were an ancient fraternity devoted to the destruction of the Imperial order ever since the execution of their founder, Princess Athena. He'd never seen them before; wild stories were told of how they fought their enemies with dark magic. Certainly, the Empress blamed them whenever something went wrong.

"Watch this," Syrus said.

Truffler shook his head and squatted under the cage, covering his bald pate with his hairy arms again.

Free me, the Harpy sang above him. Her talons thrust through the bars and retracted quickly as the nevered poles sparked.

"Let the Harpy go," one of the Architects said. His voice was a rich tenor that Syrus felt he would know anywhere if he heard it again. It sounded very Uptown, very posh. How did a man with such a recognizable voice keep himself disguised?

"You have no authority here, Architect," a Refiner sneered.

"We don't need any," another Architect said.

While they quibbled, Syrus rose and started examining the lock. Out of the corner of his eye, he saw the Lead Architect's hands shape the air into a globe of swirling mist.

Syrus levered the thin end of the bone into the lock.

The Refiner's thunderbuss ejected a gout of energy.

The Architect didn't move. He lifted the globe, and it caught the energy until it blazed. Then he threw the light back in the

Refiner's face. Goggles burning blue, the Refiner fell to the ground.

The lock shuddered to life. Iron teeth splintered the improvised lock pick and tried to bite Syrus's fingers, too. Tiny iron arms sprouted and seized his wrists. The Harpy's dark eyes held his. Her serrated tongue rolled over three rows of teeth.

Syrus screamed.

Everyone turned.

Before he could blink, the Lead Architect was beside him. Syrus smelled strange things—mushrooms, crushed roses, tarnished silver.

"Foolish Tinker," the warlock said. His voice wasn't unkind. The Architect rubbed his hands together, energy crackling between his gloves. He touched the lock, wincing at the nevered iron, and the warlock sent a burst of energy through it that made Syrus's teeth buzz and his eyes burn. His wrists were free, but the lock was also broken.

And the Harpy knew it.

Open the door, she sang. *Come closer.*

"Get underneath, boy!" the Architect shouted. He clapped his hands over Syrus's ears and pulled him down off the cage.

He crowded in beside Syrus and nodded to Truffler, who was still hiding and moaning near the back wheel.

The Harpy threw herself against the door so hard that the carriage nearly tipped over. A rush of wings, a foul odor of carrion and feathers, and the Harpy's talons hit the earth near Syrus's hand.

He snatched his fingers back, wondering if they were really all still there.

A wild, gold-ringed eye peered at him.

Come with me, she sang, sweeter than songbirds.

Syrus couldn't help noticing that she also drooled.

"Enough!" the Architect said. "You have your freedom, Harpy. Take it while you can!"

It wasn't the proper form of address at all, Syrus knew. Not by a long shot. But he was so stunned that his stiff lips couldn't make the words.

The Harpy bowed and lifted off, her owl-wings carrying her into the night.

The only sound now was their breathing and distant moans from injured Refiners. The other Architects had already vanished. Syrus shifted away from the warlock. The boy could just make out the edge of a bone-white mask under the man's hood.

"Good thing she didn't have arms," Syrus said, to break the silence.

Truffler snorted.

"Indeed," the Architect said.

Syrus felt the Architect's gaze on him even if he couldn't see it. "You were very foolish to attempt what you did. That Harpy would have polished you off as a midnight snack and thought nothing of it."

Syrus began to protest, but the warlock stopped him. "But you were also very brave. We Architects are remarkably fond of this combination. Perhaps you might aid us every now and then in our work?"

Syrus didn't know what to say. An Architect—one of the most powerful, devious, and wanted sorts in all the Empire—asking him to help them? What could he really do?

And then he thought about what Granny had said. Maybe this was the no-attack she was talking about. He nodded. Any road, he wasn't sure he wanted to know what would happen if he refused.

"Very good," the Architect said. Syrus heard a slick smile in the Architect's voice. Apparently, he'd been thinking the same thing. "We will let you know should the need arise."

Syrus tried to keep his jaw from dropping. Truffler covered his face with his hands and shook his head.

"Well, then," the Architect continued, watching the Refiners collect themselves and their broken machine. "You should be off before they take it into their heads to catch you."

He pressed something round and flat into Syrus's palm.

"Here is our token. If you have dire need of us, clasp it and whisper this spell: *Et in Arcadia ego.*"

"*Et in—*" Syrus began.

The Architect clapped a hand that smelled of lizard skin over Syrus's mouth. "Not now, boy! Dire need! Dire!"

Syrus nodded and the Architect dropped his hand. "Dire need. Yessir."

"Good. Now off you go. I'll keep watch until you're safely across the river."

"Thank you, sir," Syrus said.

But the Architect had already turned his back and was peering beyond the carriage wheels to make sure no one was creeping closer to them. He signaled that Syrus should make haste.

Syrus scuffled out from under the carriage, shivering in the chilly night air. Truffler leaped on his back and climbed astride his head as he waded into the river.

"*Nainai* will never believe this," he muttered, as the icy water clutched at his waist.

Then again, he thought, she just might.

CHAPTER 5 ⟵

I dislike when other people work in my laboratory, particularly when that other person happens to be Charles Waddingly. The Wad's at the other bench now, puttering about, watching me like a hawk. Somehow, he's convinced Father I need help cataloguing Pedant Simian's latest collection, which the good Pedant brought to me because he knows I'm better than anyone at identifying the lesser sylphids. Since the incident with the Sphinx, I'm more than happy to occupy myself with this task, though I'd much prefer to be doing it alone.

I don't need Charles to tell me how to do my work, but I'm quite certain that's not what he's here for anyway. He's watching me to make sure I don't go poking around, looking for the strongbox he and Father brought back to the Museum. It's the only thing that could possibly lure me away from the lab, but Charles knows me less well than he thinks. I'm waiting for Father to relax, for the furor about the Sphinx to die down. I have time.

I try to ignore Charles by burying my nose in a catalog called the Ceylon Codex. The pictures are oddly drawn, brushstrokes rather than the usual illumination. There's one that fascinates me— it looks like a bearded, horned Dragon. I try to decipher the characters next to it, odd shapes that no one can read. One of them reminds me of the characters inscribed on the bottom of my toad. The toad I no longer have.

I clench the book a little tighter and then remind myself I'll get it back. Even if I have to sneak off to Tinkerville and rifle through every one of those rusting trains to get it.

I trace the edge of the Dragon's scales with a fingertip. If only I could see an Unnatural like this in the wild. If I could have one wish, I'd be off in an airship tomorrow, mounting my own expedition. There are still so many Unnaturals we don't yet understand. Yet the life of a Pedant is not mine to choose.

Unless I somehow take it.

For a moment, my fingers are still on the page. I no longer see the sylphid sprawled next to me, its tiny arms obscenely limp, but a feverishly green jungle filled with living Unnaturals. Perhaps I witness Wyverns in their mating dance, or see a Giant wading over distant hills. Perhaps I see this long-bodied, golden-horned Beast. Greenmen and dryads peer at me from their trees. The air is thick with sylphids floating around me like clouds of butterflies. . . .

Charles shouts. A golden fog buzzes in front of my face. I can barely focus before a sharp pain at the tip of my nose sets my eyes watering. Before I can swat it, something darts away, twittering madly.

"What did you do?" the Wad screeches. When he gets excited, his voice sounds more like a girl's than mine does. I strip off my gloves, holding the end of my nose in my bare hand, dashing the tears out of my eyes with my other hand.

A flock of sylphids flits around madly. They try to escape

through the skylight, tossing curses down at us that manifest as tiny darts.

It's then I understand why Charles is so upset. He's closest, and he's hopping around, waving his arms around his head, literally on pins and needles.

I cover my mouth with my hand so he won't see my grin.

"Don't just stand there gawking! Get your father and a containment unit!" Charles yells, as he crawls under the bench for cover.

"But, Mr. Waddingly," I say, mostly to prolong his obvious consternation, "could we not simply use that ladder and one of those butterfly nets to catch them? Perhaps then we could subdue them just enough for observation. . . ."

"What? And have them blind us with curses? You sound like a bloody Architect," he says, almost spitting the name. "We don't need to study them! Just get your father—he'll know what to do! And see you don't let them out the door, either!"

I don't like being ordered about by the likes of the Wad, but he has a point. If the sylphids get out on their own, they could truly wreak havoc. Not on the order of the Sphinx, of course, but still. They're small and obviously adept at cursing things. As a group, it's possible they could do a good bit of damage.

Of course they may just find a way to escape and have done, like the kobold at Miss Marmalade's. Or the Grue. The Museum lost him not long after I came here, and such a creature is very, very bad to lose. No one knew exactly how it had all happened, but of course the Architects of Athena were blamed. Anything that goes wrong is always blamed on the Architects.

Or Athena herself, though saints know she's been dead for five hundred years. She was a Princess, the only female Pedant. She was also a witch. Unfortunately for her, her father the Emperor happened to dislike witches quite a bit. He took to heart the saints' old maxim, *Thou shalt not suffer a witch to live.* He had her hauled out to the Creeping Waste and executed. Practically every household with a daughter has the painting called *The Chastening of Athena* hanging somewhere. It shows Athena dissolving into salt, looking back mournfully at our great city of New London. It's a warning to us all.

Of course, in my typical stubborn fashion, I rather see it as a challenge.

"Miss Nyx!" Charles shouts from under the bench. I realize I've been daydreaming again.

I make certain the sylphids are still occupied with the skylights, and then I slip out the door.

I hurry down the corridor to the emergency closet, remembering just as I pull it open and find no containment unit that the old unit was sent out for repairs. The only unit we have left right now is in storage below the old observatory.

I run past a series of dour paintings, the founding Pedants of the Museum and the University of New London. The last one is of Athena, but I've never seen her face in this portrait, because it's draped all in black.

I want to pull it down and look on her face, to see the one whose footsteps I'm following when she's calm and serene.

Mind, I'm not interested in her because of the magic. No, I follow her because I'm determined to change history. We have an Empress now. Why can we not have a female Pedant? I've heard there was also an Empress in Old London. Surely there were female Pedants there, as well.

It's hard to know. History begins with Saint Tesla and the

experiment that brought us here to found New London. That's the only history for which there are more than whispers and rumors. The rest of history before the New Creation is as shrouded as Athena's portrait. We find rumors of it in antiquary shops, in the codices we use to identify Unnaturals and the Holy Scientific Bible, but Old London simply isn't spoken of in polite conversation. One mustn't dwell on the past. Or so Aunt Minta says.

I'll take the old lift on the way back, but the stairs are faster right now. I hurry down them into the darkness; my boots echo on the worn marble.

Two floors down and the storage corridor greets me with its moldering damp and flickering everlights.

Right as I come alongside another stair barred by an iron gate, all the lights go out. I stand still, holding my breath. If the lights are out, that means that everything's out—the paralytic fields, containment units, water closets. I can't help but think about the other day when someone pushed me through the field and nearly let the Sphinx loose. Who did it? And why?

The Architects cross my mind again, and I'm not sure what to do. We're trained upstairs to lock ourselves in safety closets until help arrives. But it's pitch dark and there are no safety closets. No one knows I'm down here. Leave it to the Museum designers to assume no one would be in storage during an emergency.

And then I hear it—a deep inhalation, a vast purr. Something is breathing down here. Gooseflesh raises on my exposed skin as I think of the Grue again. Pedant Mervold managed to collect it on his expedition in a Southern stinkswamp. It was a dark and mysterious creature—couldn't bear being exposed to light. Supposedly, it ate people's hearts and lived inside their skins, stashing the bits of their organs in little caches here and there. Father wasn't sure it belonged on display, but Mervold was so proud of capturing it and it truly was fascinating. It was on exhibit for a little while, trapped in a field like the other Greater Unnaturals. And then one day, it vanished without a trace. The entire Museum was scoured for bodies or bits of bodies, but the search turned up nothing.

Rumor has it that it's still hiding in some dark corner. And no one knows how long a Grue can go without eating.

Another deep breath. Can it hear me? Is it stalking me even now in the dark?

Something floats past my fingertips—the ghost of scales, the tickle of phantom claws.

I can't help it.

I scream.

I scream so loud I think it scares the lights back on.

They flare again along the corridor, brighter than they were before. The Museum above me hums and whirs to life; the pipes along the ceiling clank with steam forced from the *myth*furnaces deep below.

I still think I can hear breathing under the murmur and hiss, but Father would say it's just my foolish fancy, and that I should be careful of my fancies getting the better of me.

I shrug and move on past crates and leaning, canvas-covered paintings, past the dark mouths of rooms filled with dusty specimens. Things shimmer in the gloom—glass eyes and scaled wings. I look carefully to see if anything has gotten loose in the power drain, but storage is empty of any living thing except me.

The closet is unlocked, thanks be to the saints, because I forgot my keys in all the kerfuffle. I drag the unit out of the closet, and its wheels squeak behind me all the way to the lift. I'd swear the breathing noises hitch as if I've disturbed something deep in a dream, but again, I am nothing if not fanciful.

I slam the lift door closed as quickly as possible, just in case the Grue is on my heels.

Upstairs is a madhouse. Scholars and Pedants are dashing everywhere, casting disdainful glances at me as I struggle to get the ancient unit over a crack in the tiles. I'm considering leaving it so that I can go find Father more quickly (though the thought of the Wad impaled by sylphid curses is pleasant), when Pedant Lumin enters the Museum through the University archway and comes to my aid.

"Let me help you, Miss Nyx," he says in that low, steady voice.

He mistakes my frown for annoyance at him, but I'm thinking of how I once again look just as I did the other day—wild hair, stained apron, ungloved. I look down and see my left boot is also unlaced and my face flames. Why do I care this much about appearances?

I hear the smile in his voice as he says, "Unless you'd rather keep dragging that heavy thing along behind you. Where are you taking it?"

"Upstairs."

He raises a brow. Again, I feel as though I'm looking at him through a cloud. He's not handsome, but certainly not unhandsome, either. And I definitely don't feel as though someone's dumped a chamber pot over my head when he's looking at me.

I stammer a bit before I can think what to say. Finally, the words push through my teeth. "I have to find my father; there's been a slight accident upstairs in Cataloguing. Charles requested that I bring Father along with the unit."

Pedant Lumin's lips quirk, before he says, "Would you like me to take the unit upstairs for you?"

Normally, I wouldn't allow anyone to do something like this for me. I don't like showing weakness. But in this case, the sooner the unit gets upstairs the better.

I nod. "Yes, thank you."

Pedant Lumin makes sure the hoses are secure and then starts hauling the ungainly thing back toward the lift. I hurry on to Father's office, grateful that at least someone with manners stopped to help, even if said mannerly person annoyingly seems to find me a consistent source of amusement.

I'm slowed by Father's new clerk, a boy younger than me who refuses to listen when I say that there's an urgent need for Father up in Cataloguing.

"He's in a meeting, not to be disturbed," the boy says. His nose is so far up in the air I can see his walnut of a brain. Father keeps saying he'll buy a reception wight to staff this desk, but he never has. Too expensive, I imagine. But a wight would be so much easier to manage than a person. They speak only when spoken to, don't put on airs, and do exactly what they've been manufactured to do.

"Do you know who I am?" I ask.

The boy glares at me, ignoring my questions. "He said he was not to be disturbed, miss."

"Look out there—can't you see the Museum's in chaos?" The clerk looks away from me. He's not to be reasoned with. I turn swiftly and march straight through the arched corridor to Father's office door.

"Miss!" the boy shouts behind me. "Miss!"

I knock, boldly and loudly. I glance back and see the boy's head in his hands.

No one answers. I put my hand on the doorknob. Father hasn't locked it, so whatever he's doing can't be that important.

I open the door. A small assembly of Pedants and Museum Directors turn and glare. Father looks up. I know it's him only because his wig, which I secretly call the Sheep of Learning, cascades in white locks over his shoulders. His face is mostly obscured by nullgoggles over his eyes and a nullmask over his nose and mouth. He's wearing thick gloves and holds a dropper in one hand, a beaker in the other. The gloves, dropper, and beaker are outlined in shadow—they must be strongly nevered for the shadow to show so boldly.

The mysterious strongbox is open. The gentle breeze from where I've pushed the door open stirs grains of black sand. The Waste. The Tinker was right—the box was indeed filled with a sample of the Creeping Waste. Stares of irritation, horror, and fear turn on me through several pairs of nullgoggles.

"Father." My breath is a whisper, my gaze held by those gently stirring grains of sand. It's as though we're frozen in one of the Church's instructive paintings, like *The Chastening of Athena*. I cannot help but wonder if someone will call our painting *Curiosity Kills the Cat*.

If anyone survives to paint it.

Will I feel myself turning into a pillar of salt as the Waste touches me? Or will it happen so fast I'll feel nothing? One moment, flesh. The next, salt blowing across a desolate sea of black sand.

It occurs to me, too, that I might just have destroyed New London because I opened a door hastily.

"Vespa," my Father says. His voice is muffled, but it's so calm and toneless that I understand him perfectly. "Shut the door very carefully. I will find you later."

Everything I was about to say dies at the back of my throat. I nod. The grains are settling, and if I am as careful as he asks, they will stay in the box. Sweat glimmers on his brow.

I close the door slowly, oh so slowly, and back away from the alcove as if even the sound of my boots could stir the Waste. My face scalds with embarrassment as I pass the desk clerk. But I put my nose in the air just as high as his and march past.

I am full of questions, but the one that will not leave my mind is this: What is Father doing with the Waste?

I climb the stairs slowly. I'm not looking forward to being in that room with Charles again or listening to his recriminations. Or having to apologize to Father later. I just want to be alone in my laboratory, dreaming over the Ceylon Codex again. Is that so much to ask?

When I enter, I'm surprised. The Wad is nowhere to be seen, but Pedant Lumin is still there. I seem to have caught him in the middle of something. He swiftly puts a hand behind his back. Something shimmers at the edge of his arm.

He edges toward the door, clearing his throat. "I sent Mr. Waddingly with the unit back to storage. It unfortunately isn't working properly," he says.

I stand in front of the door. My heart's fluttering in my chest, still thinking about what I almost did, but I force myself to speak. "Really? That's the last working unit we had, as far as I know."

"I shall speak to your father about it."

I nod. Father doesn't like this new Pedant. There was some grumbling over dinner the other night about being forced to make appointments to unsuitable candidates, and I'm guessing he was referring to Pedant Lumin. The Board must have appointed him without Father's full support.

I decide to focus on the issue at hand. "What happened to all the sylphids, then?" I ask.

I look around the room. All I see is a pile of dust glimmering on the laboratory table, a pile I don't recall seeing before. Is Pedant Simian's entire collection gone? That, I'm quite certain, will be enough to banish me from the Museum forever.

"All the sylphids?" Pedant Lumin asks. "I don't know what you mean." He's still edging toward the door, but I'm between him and it.

A sweet smell wafts to me over the scent of preservative spirits and moldering tomes. Like plums and confectioners' sugar . . .

There's a soft plop on the floor behind Pedant Lumin. I step around him and see wadded paper wrapping and crumbs of jam cake. Something burrows inside the rubbish.

"Is that . . . jam cake?" I ask. Jam cake is my favorite.

A bright little head emerges. It's a sylphid, cheeks engorged with cake. It tries to curse me, but only manages to spit crumbs.

I draw back, but Pedant Lumin scoops up the mess and stuffs it in his pocket. The little head pokes up again, unrepentant.

"Pedant Lumin," I say, "why have you got a sylphid eating jam cake in your pocket? And where did the other sylphids that I'm to mount go?"

"I don't know," he says almost sheepishly. "I found this one and coaxed him out of his hiding place behind a cabinet."

The little sylphid starts squeaking again, pointing and spewing crumbs.

"Perhaps Charles found a way to dispose of them," I say.

"Perhaps." Pedant Lumin's hands move, shifting so that they look like they're cradling a ball. One hand is still sticky with jam cake. I see a blue glow on the edges of his fingers, like what I thought I saw the other day during the episode with the Sphinx.

I swallow hard and back toward the door. I don't know what Pedant Lumin's doing or why, but I think it best if I retreat. "Shame," I say, keeping my voice as steady as possible. "I should have liked to study them. And Pedant Simian will be furious at the loss." *And I will most likely be dismissed.*

Our eyes meet. He's looking at me in such a peculiar way, as if he expects something to happen. Nothing does, except that the little sylphid continues to glare at me from his pocket. He swallows and resumes his miniature tirade.

Pedant Lumin's eyes narrow. His hands drop, one of them covers the sylphid's head and gently pushes him down into his pocket. He brushes his hands along his robes, leaving a trail of crumbs and jam.

"His name is Piskel. I've made peace with him," Pedant Lumin says.

"Peace? With jam cake?" It's an interesting concept, one that would certainly work for me, but the door handle is at my fingers now. I've only to slip out in one swift motion.

Before I can, Pedant Lumin's gloveless fingers slide along my temples. His grip is strong but gentle. I sense he could break me, but he holds me as if I'm fragile as an egg. His brilliant eyes bore deep into mine as he bends closer. I can't look away, and for a strange moment I fear he might kiss me. Except I have no fear at all; in fact, I think I might like it. He smells of crushed roses and jam cake. I'm utterly terrified.

"Who are you?" he asks. His voice is less sure than usual; there's a tremor in it. Hope? Uncertainty? Fear?

I might ask the same of you, I try to say. But I can't. Blue light fills my peripheral vision, and an odd pulse of energy courses through me, holding me still and silent. It's like that moment again of falling eternally forward through the paralytic field. Only this time, there is no screaming, no smiling Sphinx, only his steady breathing and his mind fluttering soft and golden through my own.

I stiffen. If he doesn't let go of me in approximately two seconds, I will kick him in his well-shaped shins. My cousin Manny taught me that trick long ago.

"Unhand me, sir," I say, with as much icy calm as I can manage.

He does so, albeit reluctantly. My left temple is sticky with cake. I wipe it with my gloved hand, but I think I only succeed in smearing jam everywhere. I feel a terrible strangeness, as if he knows exactly what I'm thinking.

"How dare you treat me so?" I say. I'm suddenly furious, but I'm not sure if I'm more furious because he didn't kiss me or because he seized me so rudely. I've never had thoughts like these before. Never. I don't want to start having them now.

He grins and, bowing, hands me a handkerchief from another of his robe pockets.

"I had to be certain," he says. "Forgive me."

"Certain of what?" I ask. I refrain from using the handkerchief to clean off the jam cake. Instead I draw myself up as tall as I can. My eyes are almost level with his.

"Miss Nyx, I do believe you are a witch."

I stare at him. I don't know what I thought he was going to say, but that certainly wasn't it.

"How do you know?"

His lips twitch. "I think that will be obvious to you soon enough. I will keep your secret. I trust you will keep mine." He bows again and leaves me standing there with jam and crumbs drying in my hair, his handkerchief clutched in my hand, my nose throbbing again where Piskel bit me.

I look down at the handkerchief. Embroidered in the corner are two *A*'s linked at the center in a cross-hatched diamond.

The Architects of Athena.

I stare at the closed door in shock. Pedant Lumin is an Architect. And he has revealed himself to me. Not only that, but he is also under the delusion that I'm a witch.

At least one thing is certain.

The world has gone mad. Absolutely and utterly mad.

CHAPTER 6 ▬

The need for the stone came sooner than Syrus could have imagined.

Two nights after his encounter with the Architects, he settled gratefully into the nest of old quilts between uncles, aunts, and cousins. Granny Reed was at the rusting potbelly stove, feeding it carefully gathered wood and pony dung. As it often did when winter approached, the passenger car smelled of bodies that hadn't been washed in a while. But Syrus didn't mind so long as everyone was warm.

The summoning stone was secure in an inner pocket of his jacket and he patted its hard circle one more time just to be sure it was there. In a family of pickpockets, he'd be an absolute idiot to keep the stone where it would be easy for one of his cousins to steal it. He hadn't told anyone about his encounter for just that reason. He was hoping to be able to tell Granny when all the others weren't around; he just hadn't found a chance yet. Perhaps tomorrow.

Evidently, Granny hadn't told the story of the Manticore's Heart last night because he heard her say, around her corncob pipe: "It was quite some time ago that a Tinker witch made a bargain with a Scientist from a City in the World Before. He asked her to steal something very powerful for him. And what he asked her to steal was none other than the Heart of Tianlong, the heavenly Dragon that rested on the banks of that river yonder. For it was said that the Heart of Tianlong was a well into the Universe, and if a man held that—well, then he held the power of the Universe in his hand. But only a powerful witch could remove the Heart.

"So, she took the Heart and sold it to the Scientist who in turn used it to bring his City here. And one of the Scientist's followers called himself Emperor, and his descendants still rule to this day.

"At the time, the Emperor had only one daughter, a Princess named Athena. And Athena was as wise and just as her father wasn't. She knew that magic is the lifeblood of this world, and she was determined to use her knowledge to keep magic alive.

"In his dungeons, the Emperor experimented on Elementals, stealing the secrets of their magic when he could. He had discovered that when he used their magic in conjunction with Tianlong's Heart that his mortal life could be extended. But not indefinitely. Occasionally, he needed to recharge the Heart, so to speak. That didn't satisfy him, though. He wanted a direct way to absorb the Elementals' power and live forever. And so he tortured and maimed and killed the Elementals in service of that desire.

"The Princess came to understand the truth of her father's evil, for she visited the dungeons and a Manticore, who was near death, told her what had happened. And that night, when the Tower was very quiet, the Princess snuck into her father's secret cabinet, stole the Heart from where he kept it, and fitted it into the Manticore's chest to help her live. She released the Manticore and freed magic back into the world where it belongs. She fled with the Manticore and a guard who had fallen in love with her, but eventually her father caught her and marched her off to the Creeping Waste to her death.

"And that, my dears," Granny said, looking around, "is why we must be ever-vigilant and protect the Manticore at all costs. For the Empress is doing this very thing again, I guarantee it. That's why all the Elementals have been disappearing and why the Creeping Waste keeps growing. She'll make sure there will be no one to aid us this time. We must stay here and ensure that magic survives. Protect the Manticore and protect us all."

There were murmurs of assent that soon fell into whispers and snatches of swaddlesongs. Granny kept the stove open a long time, smoking and staring into the flames.

"But *Nainai*, what happened to Tianlong?" Syrus asked.

Granny looked at him, and it was almost as though her face was wreathed in fire. "Tianlong still sleeps by the river, and there is a hole where his Heart should be. The Manticore is all that stands between us and the Waste."

Syrus fell asleep thinking about Granny's story. It took a long while to drift off. Not only did his thoughts chase around like foxes in a rabbit pen, but the new baby was fussy. He'd grown used to such things, but tonight the baby was as loud as his thoughts.

Nainai often read his face and said he would "change the world." But Syrus wondered how. Certainly, his people thought him special for his gifts. But how could these gifts be used to protect the Manticore and his people? Maybe the Architect he'd met today would open the way. He patted his breast pocket before his thoughts drained away into warm darkness.

The last thing he saw was Granny's outline in front of the stove, smoke drifting from her pipe. He didn't feel the little fingers that slipped down toward his chest, nor did he hear the hushed giggle as his cousin Amalthea worked the stone from his secret pocket and tiptoed back to her place.

Three hours later, when the doors splintered inward and the Raven Guard stormed in, Syrus's searching fingers met with nothing but string, lint, and the jade toad he had stolen from the girl in the carriage.

The Guard had been in the Imperial service since the first Emperor, John Vaunt, had created them. No one knew how the Emperor had made them—no one dared question—but they were obviously the work of some dark, twisted magic. Though the Guard spoke and moved as humans did in their rusting suits of armor, they had the heads of Ravens and, it was rumored, communicated secretly with their winged cousins that patrolled the skies around the Empress's Tower. The Guard were killing machines, powerful and quick and utterly devoid of emotion.

The armored creatures moved through the train car, shaking people out of their quilts. They either shoved the Tinkers toward their compatriots at one end of the car or skewered them. It was only when the blood started to flow that the screaming began. Syrus watched in horror as his cousin Amalthea was pierced and tossed aside while her mother wailed.

Wicked dancing shadows lit the broken panes and dark stains that spread among the quilts on the floor. Granny Reed stood and thrust a rolled blanket into the stove. She lunged toward the nearest Guard, trying to set his feathered head afire, but he turned his long pike on her before she reached him, slitting a dark line from chest to navel. He shoved her body aside, then stamped out the flaming quilt with an armored foot.

"Nainai," Syrus breathed. He was too shocked to yell. He patted his chest all over again for the summoning stone, but the toad mocked him.

"More will die, unless those eligible for Refinery work come quietly with us," one of the Guards said in his spiritless voice.

Someone spat. Otherwise, all Syrus heard was labored breathing and hushed weeping.

"Syrus," his Uncle Gen whispered. "Get out of here before they take you or kill you—do you understand?"

Syrus was about to protest, but then saw the glint of a curved dagger under his uncle's sleeve. Most Tinkers slept with their weapons outside their doors; it was too dangerous to have weapons among a nest of children and babies and grandmothers. But when Syrus thought of how easily the Guard had entered and slain so many before they'd even had a chance to wake, he wished with all his might he'd kept his dagger and dart pipe.

His uncle shook his wrist gently. "Do you understand?" he repeated.

Syrus nodded.

"Out that window there," Uncle Gen said, tilting his head toward it. "And go warn the others if they've not already been captured. There hasn't been a Cull like this since your parents were taken. We've gotten soft."

"But—" Syrus started to say.

The Raven Guard waded toward them.

"Now!" his uncle hissed.

Syrus slithered toward the wall. Hoping none of the Guard would notice, he tugged at the end of a leather flap that had been loosely nailed over a broken window.

His hopes were quickly dashed when a blast of energy sizzled right next to his hand. The only fortunate thing about it was that it blew the leather clean off the window.

"Go now!" Uncle Gen shouted. Syrus saw his uncle throw his dagger, even as a blast of energy took him down. Syrus dove through the window, rolling on the hard, cold ground. As he crouched by a rusting wheel, he realized the Guard had used their pikes merely for effect. Their real weapons were the thunderbusses.

He ran to the next train car and the next, thankful each time that they were empty. The others must have heard and slunk off to the Forest. He was glad they'd escaped, but he was angry, too. Angry that no one had come to help his family, that Granny Reed and Uncle Gen, aunts and tiny cousins had been murdered in their beds. He gritted his teeth against sobs.

Truffler shuffled along behind him, making frightened noises. He turned to the hob as he headed toward the Forest. "Hide," he hissed. "You don't want them to find you and collect you, do you?"

It was then he heard the clanking footsteps behind him. He deeply regretted again that he had hung up his dart pipe in the entryway to the passenger car like everyone else. He wondered what must have happened to the summoning stone the Architect had given him—most likely one of his cousins had managed to steal it. All he was left with was the toad, the toad that Granny Reed had said would bring down trouble. He had to wonder if something he'd done—stealing the toad, helping the Architects—had brought this Cull down on his clan. Best not think on that now.

The Raven Guard was just behind him—Syrus sensed the scrape of metal through the tossing trees, the vague scent of guano and rust over the forest loam as the wind changed direction. The Guard didn't call or taunt; his threat was in his steadiness of purpose, a purpose given by the Empress in her Tower. Syrus knew the Guard would find him and destroy him or bundle him off to the Refinery with the rest of his clan.

Syrus found the low mound by memory rather than sight. It rose like a giant, bracken-covered turtle shell through the trees. He knew he'd arrived by the smell—the odor of carrion and cat piss was strong. He thought he heard the Guard slow, as if he too had caught the scent and had suddenly become unsure. Faint ticking issued from the mouth of the mound.

Syrus swung up into a tree, climbing as fast as he could before the Guard fully entered the clearing. Two swift, sharp sounds—*tink, tank*—and the Guard was on his knees. Spines in his feathered neck and the shoulder joint of his armor glinted with their own deadly light.

Then, the great maned head emerged and before the Guard could shriek, he disappeared into the Manticore's maw.

Syrus clutched the tree, gasping. A sharp breeze rattled the dry leaves. He looked down, and a face peered up at him through the trees—a wide, razor-toothed face that was all the more horrible for its very human grin.

And all along there was that ticking, as of a muffled clock. Or a faintly beating heart.

Thank you, the Manticore said. *I was quite hungry*. Her voice was liquid silver, exquisite as the Harpy's.

"You're . . . you're welcome," Syrus stuttered.

You may come down now, boy, the Manticore said. Fierce red energy pulsed around her. Her power scorched his feet and he wondered that the tree didn't shrivel into ashes.

He clutched the trunk tight and said, "You . . . uh . . . sure you're full? 'Cause there's plenty more where that one came from in the trainyard, and I wouldn't mind you having your fill of them."

The Manticore chuckled. *I will not eat you, if that is what you fear.*

"Well, let's just say I want to make certain you don't change your mind. I'm sure I'm a mite more tasty than one of them old Guards."

That is most likely true, the Manticore conceded. The creature sat on her haunches, the shadow of her barbed tail curving around her paws. *Still, you are far less edible because you are much more interesting.*

"Eh?"

I take it there has been a Cull, the Manticore said.

Syrus nodded, then realized the Manticore mightn't be able to see him. "Yes," he said. He began his descent, picking and choosing until he came to the last branch just a few feet from the Manticore's smiling jaws.

"All my family were taken or killed," Syrus said.

The Manticore's eyes were like two small moons as she looked up at him. *All my family have been taken or killed, too.*

Syrus remembered another old tale Granny used to tell—about Lord Virulen killing the Manticore's child long ago on a Hunt. Anger flared like white-hot lightning. "Then why don't you do something about it?" he shouted. The rational part of him realized he had just sassed the Manticore and that she could kill him with a well-placed barb from her tail if she chose. He shrank against the trunk again.

Instead, she laughed, as if she read his mind. *You may as well come down.*

He considered, figured there was nothing left to lose, and

slithered down to land square on his bum in front of her giant paws.

He had never been this close to her before; he had only seen her at a rare distance whenever the clans made their offerings at the edge of her clearing. He looked up at her in awe. Red light pulsed around her heart. But it was no ordinary heart. Cross-hatched with wires and hoses and gears, it sang out its rhythm like a clock. Something was scrawled on it in the old language that Granny had taught him; the characters read: ENDURANCE.

I have done nothing because I thought there was nothing I could do, the Manticore said. *But perhaps you have shown me the beginnings of a way.*

"I have?" Syrus said.

Bring me the young witch from the City, the Manticore said. *And then we shall see what might be.*

"A witch?" Syrus scratched his head. "But aren't all the witches dead?"

Everyone knew all the witches had been killed right around the time the Emperor had executed his daughter for openly declaring herself a witch. He had sent hundreds to die on the fatal sands of the Creeping Waste. Only the Architects had escaped, and they were all men. Every Emperor since had sponsored periodic purges from time to time; the Empress had enforced the most recent perhaps fifty years ago. All the witches, as far as Syrus knew, were gone.

Would I ask you to bring me someone who does not exist? Do as I say, boy, the Manticore said. He heard the steel in her grin. *Find the witch and together we will free our families.*

"But how?" Syrus asked. He thought about what his Granny had said—that the Manticore must be protected at all costs to keep the Waste at bay. In the old tales, it was a witch who had stolen the

Heart in the first place. What would the Manticore want with her? Wouldn't she be dangerous? He wished again that his talent was great enough to be of use.

Bring her to me and you will see.

Chapter 7 ⭤

Father hasn't said anything to me about the unfortunate incident of yesterday, in which I nearly destroyed all of New London (and Pedant Simian's collection) single-handedly. Nor have I said anything to Father about the Waste, for fear of reminding him of my part in the near-misadventure. I want to ask him about Pedant Lumin's odd behavior, but I remain silent.

Truth be told, I don't want to say anything about that because it implicates me just as much as it implicates him. But the thought nags at me that I should report him because he's obviously a heretic. Fraternizing with sylphids! Feeding them jam cake! It should give me shudders, but mostly it just makes me jealous that I can't keep a sylphid in my own pocket.

And then there was also the ridiculous notion that the young Pedant might kiss me. . . .

I shake my head and keep my eyes down. Aunt Minta watches me with the attentiveness of a cat sizing up a mouse. She asked me about the scrape on my nose the other night. I told her I did it on a door. I don't think she believes me.

When Father is ready to depart for the trolley, I stand with him.

He looks askance at me. "I think you had better stay here with Aunt Minta today, Vee," he says.

I look at him in shock. I've been afraid that one day he wouldn't take me to the Museum, that he'd force me to stay here. I've always felt sure I would die on that day. There's nothing I love more than the Museum. Father knows it.

Aunt Minta's eyes glimmer, but she wisely says nothing. I'm a constant disappointment to her. She wants to make me into a proper lady and has only lately, I think, finally given up. I've been able to stave her off this long because, as I said, I'm very good at what I do. Father has always said that someday it would all have to end, but I never quite wanted to believe him. Now Aunt Minta may finally get her chance.

I can't let that happen, not yet.

I follow Father out into the hall, where our copy of *The Chastening of Athena* painting hangs. Up until now, I've thought Athena had a look of dreadful repentance, but now I'm thinking she looks quite defiant, despite the scarlet *W* embroidered on her execution gown.

"Father," I say, plucking at his sleeve. "Please. I will do anything, anything. Just . . . don't make me stop coming with you to the Museum."

"Vee," he says. He cradles my head, though the pins in my hair prevent him from tousling it as he once did.

I meet his eyes and hate the sadness I see there.

"You know this must end soon. It's just not proper, your working at the Museum. There's already talk—"

"The loss of those sylphids—that wasn't entirely my fault! And I promise never to barge into your office again, Father!"

Despite my recurring curiosity, I still don't mention the Waste. I must pretend I didn't see what I saw or that I give it not a second thought, if I ever want to know more about it. And yet, it's nearly all I can think of. Why would Father experiment on something as dangerous and unpredictable as the Waste? It swallows everything in its path. The Wall around New London was built by Refiners and Pedants working together to keep our city safe. Why bring such danger right into the heart of New London after all the attempts to keep it out?

"Neither of those things are the problem," he says, after a long, thoughtful pause. "It's just . . . you must start thinking about your future."

"I know what I want my future to be. I want to stay and work at the Museum with you."

"I know," he says softly. "But that is not the way of the world." His eyes flick to the painting.

I tighten my grip on his sleeve. "I know what you're thinking. You're thinking I'll end up like her." I jerk my head toward Athena.

He opens his mouth to refute me, but I say in a rush, "I won't. I swear I won't. Please don't make me leave the Museum just yet. Please." I'm embarrassed by the tears that clench my throat and burn my eyes. It isn't very logical to get worked up like this; it probably only proves his point.

But Father has no son, no one to follow in his profession. I am the only person in the household he can talk to about science and unnatural affairs. Neither of us want to lose that, and yet he's saying that we must.

Aunt Minta lingers at the dining room door.

"All right," he relents with a sad smile.

I start to speak my gratitude, but he stops me.

"But only for a little while. Your aunt is right. You are a young lady and your thoughts must turn eventually to making a good match. Today I think you should stay here and consider that."

Now I open my mouth to protest, but he stops me again.

"Listen, Vee. We're not too badly off, but we're certainly not wealthy and I'm quite old. It may be difficult for me to support our family in the coming years, my dear. Your duty is to see that we're all cared for and I know you can. When the New Year comes, you must put these childish dreams aside, and work with your aunt on finding the perfect match. You're a good girl, and I know you'll do what is right for your family."

He sighs. I know he hates making these pronouncements and he seldom sticks to them. But I have a feeling that he'll stick to this one like no other. I am saddened into complete silence.

I nod.

I glance at Aunt Minta. She's smiling. It's not an unkind smile, but she's never understood my obsession with unnatural things. A little part of me knows deep down that she and Father are right. I hate that most of all.

I follow Father to the foyer where our maid Lorna stands ready with his coat and hat. We are too poor to afford a wardrobe wight. Father puts on the Sheep of Learning, his robes, and beret. Aunt Minta still hasn't said a word. I guess she knows she's won, and now she can gloat over it all day in the parlor as I prick my fingers doing embroidery or some equally dull task. Except that Aunt Minta really is too kind a soul to gloat.

We say our good-byes. I step out on the porch to watch Father go and I nearly trip over the deliveryman who stacks bricks of bound *myth* for our furnace. The City Refinery in Lowtown processes raw *myth* from the *myth*mines in the north and then distributes each family's allotment. I've heard some families in Lowtown receive nothing because they can't pay, or are reduced to buying wood gathered by the Tinkers. It's said the Tinkers refuse to use *myth*—something about it bringing bad dreams or bad luck. And no one exactly knows what happens in the Imperial Refinery attached to the Empress's Tower, beyond supplying the Empress's household with an endless quantity of *myth*.

The deliveryman nods to me as he finishes his chore and hurries to his cart and the next house. I shove my hands in my pockets and find the embroidered handkerchief, a red secret as deadly as the letters stitched on Athena's execution gown. Will Pedant Lumin notice I'm absent today? I don't really care so much except that I wonder what he would think about the boy who stole my toad, about the Waste locked in the box in Father's office. What should I say about his rescue of Piskel the sylphid? The fact that he is an Architect? Or that he thinks I'm a witch?

I stare at the steep street filled with people going about their business and long for a life as uncomplicated as theirs.

Aunt Minta's arm steals around my waist as her chin presses softly into my shoulder. I grit my teeth, imagining what she would say if she knew what I'm clutching in my fist.

"Come inside, darling," she says. The compassion in her voice is almost more than I can bear; she melts my resistance.

"I should be with him," I say, nodding toward Father's retreating figure.

"I know it seems that way," she says. "But your father is right; it's getting time for you to lay childhood aside and think about your future."

She ushers me back through the door and into the hallway with its glowing everlanterns. Even during the day, the lanterns are needed to dispel the eternal gloom of the Refineries. They say every city isn't like this. Scientia is brilliant with light because of the prevailing winds off the Winedark Sea. Euclidea, which was halfway between New London and Scientia, was once green and rich with hanging gardens before the Waste swallowed it whole.

Aunt Minta draws me from such gloomy thoughts into the parlor where the radiators hiss with *myth*-made steam. She's had a fire laid on too, for she knows how much I love the crackle-dance of true flame. I've heard that my mother loved such things too—Father told me so once when I was little and stared too long at the flames. I think again of the lost toad, the only thing I had from her, with a morose sigh. Aunt Minta pats the settee beside her and takes out her tatting as I sit. I watch, trying not to twist my hands in my lap.

"I'm making this for your trousseau," Aunt Minta says, smiling. "It'll make a beautiful collar on a dressing gown."

"Aunt Minta . . ." I begin.

She looks at me sharp as the needle she's holding in her hand.

"You heard your father, darling. We need to start thinking about these things."

"Did my mother think about them?"

Aunt Minta's lips crimp ever so slightly. She doesn't like talking about my mother. No one does, actually. I learned that when I was very small.

"Well, of course she did, dear. She married your father, didn't she?"

I can hardly imagine my own dear father bestirring himself from his laboratory or experiments long enough to notice anyone. "And she was a proper lady?"

The fire snaps through the long silence.

"But of course, dear," Aunt Minta finally says. "Your father was quite enchanted with her."

It's a rather odd thing to say, considering the position of the Church on enchantments. "Yes," I ask, "but did your family approve of her? I mean, were they happy with the marriage?"

Another knot, another loop pulled tight. "It was approved by the Imperial Matchmaker and done with all the proper forms," she says at last.

"That wasn't what I asked."

She looks up at me with that same sharpness. "Why are you asking these questions? Have you someone in mind already? Someone you fear is unsuitable?"

"I . . . just wanted to know about Mother," I say softly.

"She found her place. As will you," my aunt says. She reaches into her tatting basket and hands me an extra shuttle and thread. She pats my shoulder as my fingers fumble, trying to remember the patterns of knots I'd mercifully forgotten since the last time I resisted her teaching. "Don't worry so much about it all, dear. We'll help you. Once we finally get you out into Society, I know the perfect match will appear."

"But what if he doesn't?" I ask. "Or what if it's someone Father disapproves of?" *Or someone I disapprove of?* No one really seems to care about that.

She nods toward the shuttle. "First things first. Learn to be a lady. The rest will take care of itself."

CHAPTER 8

Syrus waited until the next night to return to the trainyard. If this was truly a Cull, the Guard wouldn't have waited around very long. They would have hurried their catch as quickly as possible to the Lowtown Refinery. But he also knew that a Guard had been lost following him, and while they surely wouldn't waste time trying to find him, they might at the very least have spies posted around the trainyard just in case he should be foolish enough to return.

And, foolish though it might have been, he went back, because he knew his extended clan would expect it of him. Nothing would be done with the Reed clan's passenger car until it was determined without a shadow of a doubt that all had been killed or taken. It was his duty as the remaining free member of the clan to dispose properly of the bodies.

He came when the cookfires leaped around the rusting wheels. There was no music and no laughter, and there wouldn't be for a while. Uncle Gen had been right about it being a long time since the last Cull. Everyone had begun to think perhaps the Cityfolk no longer needed new bodies for their Refineries, that perhaps the clans could finally live in as much peace as they could expect.

Suddenly, Syrus hated them all for being so naive.

At the edge of the trainyard, he heard muted voices inside one of the passenger cars. The Thornishes were a new family, still without a clan, who lived on the edge of Tinkerville; no one knew them very well. A stewpot bubbled over an unattended fire; he guessed perhaps they'd gone inside to find salt or bowls or somesuch. He took none of the stew, but he did steal a shawl and old bloomers from their laundry line. He draped the shawl around his head and neck, then wrapped a branch with the bloomers. He set them alight in the fire and walked off before the Thornishes could find him.

He left whispering silence in his wake as he passed through the trainyard with the burning branch. No one spoke to him or tried to stop him. They all knew why he was here.

Syrus's heart thundered, sure at any minute he'd be accosted by a Guard. He glanced toward the caved-in roofs of passenger cars and iron engines, searching for ravens, but there were none that he could see. When he came to his family's former home, he saw Truffler sobbing by the steps.

The hob's great nose was even larger then usual—swollen and red with his crying. Syrus ignored him and his clutching hands and went up the steps.

The smell was the first thing that hit him. That and the sound of buzzing flies. He held the torch as close to himself as he dared, so that he could only smell the scents of burning cloth and wood, only hear the crackle of fire eating linen.

He stayed longer than he needed in the entryway, looking at all the things still hanging there—the weapons, coats, and other implements left undisturbed by the Guard in their passing. Standing in this entryway, seeing everyone's things and noting who was in and who wasn't had always been how he'd known he was home. And yet this would never be his home again.

He took a deep breath, wrapping the shawl tightly around his nose and mouth. Then he stepped in.

A macabre landscape of twisted blankets and bodies spread before him—a foot here, a dead eye gleaming there. Syrus wanted to retch, but his body was entirely empty. He could think of nothing to say, nothing to do that would somehow honor the fallen. He thought of Granny Reed's stories of roaming, vengeful spirits, and he felt sure that these spirits would haunt him forever. Unless he somehow managed to free those who had been taken to the Lowtown Refinery.

But to do that, he would need help. And to get help from the Manticore, he would need a witch.

Something glittered nearby in the torchlight as he swung it around, something that was neither an eye nor the mirrors some of his uncles had sewed onto their hunting jackets. He stooped and saw the thing clutched in a small, pale hand. The hand of his cousin Amalthea.

He pried the Architect's summoning stone free from her palm.

And then he yelled curses such as no thirteen-year-old boy should know. He blamed the Refiners and the Empress and her demonic Raven Guard. He blamed the damnable Architects and their magic that had brought this Cull to pass. But most of all he blamed himself.

Syrus backed away from his cousin's body and stood in the entryway again. He scanned the items that hung there, taking only the few things that he might need—fairy darts, a skinning knife, a hardened gourd canteen.

Then he threw the torch through the door.

He stood with Truffler at a safe distance, watching the train car burn. Other people came to stand nearby. He saw some people wetting the ground or their own cars so that the sparks wouldn't catch. And then the low mourning chant began. Its call and response sang far above the roaring flames—a testament to the Reed clan, to all its members lost or taken, to the lone boy who remained.

When at last the fire died and his former home was nothing more than a hulk of twisted metal on smoking wheels, Syrus turned his face toward New London. The dark Tower menaced him from its broken hill while the Refineries belched their ugly, green-tinged smoke. But still that secret Heart pulled at him, the promise of the great Dragon resting along the river—Tianlong of the old stories his grandmother would never tell again.

He looked aside at Truffler, who stood wringing his hairy hands next to him.

"You shouldn't go with me," Syrus said. "Stay here and work for another family who needs you."

He started toward the City road, but Truffler was at his heels, grabbing his trousers. "Bad place. Bad," he said.

"I know," Syrus said. He squatted down next to the hob. "But the Manticore said I must find her a witch in the City."

Truffler sighed. He touched his nose. "I smell for you."

Syrus put his hand on Truffler's shoulder. "I know you would, my friend. And maybe if it comes to that, I'll call on you. But the Refiners would light on you in a heartbeat if they could. I'd rather you stay put where you could escape to the Forest, if need be."

Truffler sighed. He stepped back, tears running in rivulets down his big nose. "Be brave," he said.

Syrus nodded.

He walked away from the smoking ruin and the little hob beside it, his spine stiff as iron.

CHAPTER 9 —

The next day, Father takes pity on me, much to Aunt Minta's disappointment. Perhaps it's the asymmetrical bit of lace I present him with over our porridge or the mournful expression that accompanies it, but he relents, saying I may go with him to the Museum every other day so long as I will attend to Aunt Minta's lessons on the off-days without complaint. Aunt Minta makes the best of the compromise.

Father doesn't speak as we hurry down the steep streets of Midtown, nor does he say anything as we board the trolley to Chimera Park. I try to keep my expression as neutral as possible, though sometimes I put my face out in the glowing drizzle and grin like a fool.

We wind down Industrial Way, past the entrance to the Night Emporium which spans the length of the Vaunting Bridge over the River. Little humps of land rise here and there like the back of an old sea serpent. Houses climb up and down them and the Empress's Tower sits like a ragged crown on the tallest one.

It's said that when Saint Tesla's Grand Experiment in the London Of Which We Do Not Speak (Old London for short) tore a hole in the Universe, buildings from every era were miraculously

transferred here to New London. That, I suppose, accounts for all
the different architectural styles and various states of disrepair from
the Night Emporium to the Imperial Tower. It's a bleeding mess, if
you ask me.

Some people whisper the Old Londoners called this place
Fairyland or Arcadia or Elysium, that Saint Tesla drew our ancestors all through a door that should never have been opened. They
say we don't belong here. But people say lots of things. And whatever is true, it's a fact that we're here now and have been for nearly
six hundred years. And it's also a fact that if Old London isn't just
a tale, we can never go back to it. It's been tried many times and
many men have died in the trying.

Still, I do love the swirling colors of the onion domes, and looking up at the ravens wheeling around the Empress's Tower always
gives me a creeping thrill.

We alight at the last stop and make our way around the square
to the University grounds. I smile when we pass under the great
archway with its ever-watchful statues of Saint Bacon and Saint
Newton. A scroll stretched between their stone hands bears our
motto in Old Scientific: *In Scientia Veritas*. In Science there is Truth.

We pass into the domed atrium and I'm surrounded by my own
handiwork, all the glimmering wings, the glass-eyed faces, the
milkweed-tuft hair. I think of the little sylphid Piskel glaring at me
from Pedant Lumin's pocket, and for the first time shame wars with
pride as I look upon my displays.

Father stops by one case and something about his manner keeps
me silent. We both stare through the glass. I'm wishing for the key
to this display so I can straighten one of the placards near a desert
sylphid, when Father says, "I allowed you to come for a reason

today, Vee. I've an errand that I cannot trust to anyone lightly, and I unfortunately can't spare Charles."

I brighten at the thought that Father once again has important work for me to do. Perhaps if I do this well, I can regain his trust and all these silly notions of ladylike behavior and making a good match and so on will be forgotten.

"I'm happy to do it, Father," I say.

He nods and pulls a thin envelope from the breast pocket of his robes. The neverseal tingles as it passes into my palm. Only the recipient of this letter may open it or else the letter will dissolve in hissing green flames. Yet another necessary, if alarming, invention of the Refineries.

I look at the address. *Arthur Rackham's Antiquities, Rookery Square, Lowtown.*

Father is sending me alone to Lowtown? Excitement battles with dread. Though I love adventure, Lowtown is dangerous, especially for an unescorted young lady.

"Don't tell anyone. Your Aunt would have my head, but there's no one I trust more than you, Vee."

He embraces me, resting his chin on the top of my head, while I curl against him. Father is so tall and gangly, it's like being hugged by a tree. When he releases me, I secure the letter in my pocket. This is a way for me to redeem myself for the failings of the other day, even though Father has never accused me of anything openly. Just how I shall get there and back is another thing entirely.

"Send word of your return, eh?"

"Yes, Father," I say.

He pats me on the shoulder and hurries off toward his office.

I look back into the case at the sylphids among the dried mosses and stones. There's a little one I'm particularly proud of that I managed to pose light as a leaf on a branch, but Piskel again has me wondering if I should be proud at all. I push those thoughts out of my mind with trying to think of the best way to Lowtown, as most drivers from this section of Midtown would simply refuse to take a young lady there. The notion of walking down there is even less appealing. Perhaps I should disguise myself as a Scholar. . . .

A shadow slides across the glass. I stiffen, thinking of that mysterious push the other day that sent me through the paralytic field.

Pedant Lumin's face appears behind mine. I can see in my reflection that the damp breeze on the trolley has sent my curls springing everywhere, but I refuse to tidy them. At least my gown is still neat and my bootlaces are tied this time!

His eyes meet mine. I see his face clearly, and the shock of his handsomeness initially takes my breath. I had not thought him handsome before; somehow his features have been difficult to discern. But in this moment, it's as though the sun has come from behind a cloud. I manage to plaster a frown on my face before I turn.

"Miss Nyx," he says bowing. I peer at him; he's plain and unobtrusive again, his features indistinct. I recall the Church instructing us in detecting glamours should we ever fall into the clutches of a rogue Architect. But the Church always said that glamours were used to make the warlock exceedingly handsome so that he could seduce young women. Not the other way round. Part of me wants to shout his true identity aloud and have him carted away for heresy. And yet, another part of me is thrilled to know his dangerous secret and even more thrilled to be included. My frown deepens.

"Pedant Lumin."

Pedant Lumin clears his throat and says, "I couldn't help over-hearing your conversation with your father as I was passing. If there is some important errand, I would be happy to escort you, as my lecture isn't until this afternoon."

"To Lowtown?" I say, hoping my raised brow looks ironic rather than silly. "Thank you, but I think I can manage, Pedant."

His expression darkens. "You shouldn't go alone there, Miss Nyx. It could be quite dangerous for one such as you."

"One such as me?"

Pedant Lumin nods. "I can protect you as no one else can. Did I not do so the other day?"

I glance toward the Grand Exhibit Hall. The edge of the field that holds the Sphinx captive pulses a vivid blue. I remember the ticking of her claws, how he stood boldly between her and me. If events had transpired in a logical way, I should be dead now. I look back at Pedant Lumin, unsure. His gaze holds mine and, for just a moment, it feels as if the atrium inhales around us, as if some secret breeze stirs the still wings of the sylphids into life. I can imagine them, floating around us in a shimmering column. . . .

A patron tries to squeeze between me and the display case, jolt-ing me back to the now. "Very well," I say. "I'll trust you just this once, Pedant Lumin. Let us hope you show yourself equal to the task."

Pedant Lumin bows again, his expression carefully neutral. "Thank you, miss. You will not have cause to regret it, I assure you." He looks up at me and grins. For just one moment, I consider run-ning away to my laboratory and locking myself inside, but the nev-ered letter pulses its slim warning in my pocket.

"Shall we, then?" he asks.

I nod and together we pass through the doors out into New London's glimmering gloom.

The hansom we hire is cramped, its cushions dusty and threadbare. I find myself picking at the seams, trying to ignore the fact that Pedant Lumin's knees are nearly touching mine, so close is our confinement.

The curtains are drawn and so his face is mercifully hidden from me. That is, until a tiny, glowing head pops up from his waistcoat pocket.

Piskel floats toward me, lighting the entire hansom cab like a little sun.

"Don't make any sudden movements," Pedant Lumin says. "Just let him have a look at you."

"He won't bite me again, will he?" I ask, barely breathing.

The sylphid makes a face at me. Then he darts back into Pedant Lumin's pocket, where he shakes a shining fist before crossing his arms and glaring at me.

"Did he understand what I just said?"

Pedant Lumin laughs. He fishes around in another pocket for more bits of cake, which he feeds to Piskel with soft words. Then he looks up at me. "What do you think?"

In the fey light, his eyes are again so brilliant I'm almost blinded.

"Why do you keep changing?" I ask.

He frowns and I realize it's the first time I've really seen him do so. "I suppose I should have expected that you would see through my attempts at disguise."

"Why?"

"Because of what you are," he says. His gaze is mesmerizing, but

I can't tell if that's because he's using forbidden magic on me or if it's something else entirely.

"A witch?" I raise my chin.

"Not so loudly," he says. "You can still be heard, even in here." Piskel shakes a finger at me. "But yes. You see through illusion, among other things."

This time when Pedant Lumin smiles, I see it fully for the first time. It burns me so completely my face reddens. "Other things? What else can witches do?"

He leans forward. "Anything they desire," he says. The low pulse of his voice makes me clutch the cushion.

He's close enough to kiss. I'm trying to figure out if I should, if he will, trying not to think about the wrongness of this, when a squeak of protest startles us both. Pedant Lumin sits back so as not to crush Piskel. "Sorry, little man."

Piskel grumbles and burrows down into his pocket, taking his light with him.

The darkness is a relief. When I speak, I try my best to maintain an even, businesslike tone. "Pedant Lumin, I could have you reported. I should. You are a heretic Architect. The Church and the Empress would reward my family handsomely for one such as you."

He's entirely nonplussed by my threats. "But you won't," he says.

"What do you mean I won't?"

"You won't report me because I'm the only one who can help you."

"Help me do what?"

"Survive."

I'm so angry I can feel sparks flying off my fingertips even if I can't see them. I clench my fists over my knees. "Pedant Lumin, if you're suggesting—"

He reaches forward, slipping his fingers close enough to touch my fists. Close enough but not quite. Without touching me, somehow he draws off the anger, shapes it, lights it with a single breath. "Hal," he says softly, holding the energy he's transformed from me as though it's a paper lantern. "The name is Hal."

The rush of emotions is too much. I can't speak.

"Tell me this," he says. "How long have you known you were different? Has anyone else ever noticed?"

I'm about to answer but his gaze encourages me to examine his questions. It's there at the root of me—the inner wisdom he's seeking. I always knew I wasn't meant for the Seminary. I thought it was just because I wanted knowledge they didn't possess. It was that, but . . . there's more.

A dim memory surfaces of looking with Father at a display of sylphids. Remarkably, they'd been kept alive. We walked through a tunnel engineered to allow us into their enclosure, my small hand clasped in Father's. But something happened when we reached the middle of the tunnel. The protective field dropped. Suddenly, the sylphids were all around me and I laughed and let them play in my hair and sing to me, even though I couldn't understand their words. Father didn't laugh. Refiners came and turned the sylphids into glittering dust. And I wept because I knew they would never have harmed me. And then there was the kobold who bowed to me before he left Miss Marmalade's . . .

Could it really be true? Everything I've been taught, everything I've hoped for goes against it. If anyone finds out . . .

"It can't be," I whisper. My words are harsh with rising tears. "It just can't."

"Why not?" he says gently.

"Because . . ." My voice cracks. *Because if I am, there is no future. If I am, then even the dream I dare not speak is lost to me. If I am, then I am a heretic and damned to an eternity of sand.* . . . It is all I can do not to break down sobbing.

"Miss Nyx . . ." His hand brushes mine. "It is not so horrible as you might imagine. Your fate is still your own if you have the courage to see beyond your fear."

That straightens my spine a bit. I find voice enough to ask: "But how did it happen? And what do I do?"

"You act as if being a witch is completely unnatural. Nothing could be further from the truth. Wielding magic is normal. What is not normal is how the Empress hoards all of the magic herself, turning it to her own evil designs and persecuting anyone who tries to use it for good. What you do about it is up to you. You can try to hide or you can fight, as we Architects have chosen to do."

I digest this in silence. Then I freeze.

He senses the change in my demeanor. "What?"

"I think someone pushed me through the field the other day. I think they wanted to see what would happen to me." I think again of Charles's horrid smirk and shudder.

"Someone was trying to test you."

"But why would it matter? What could they gain? And how could they have done it when no one but a fussy woman was standing next to me?"

"The answer to all those questions is simply this: magic. And if you are still unschooled, as I'm quite sure you are, you're vulnerable. Your power is therefore accessible to any warlock or witch unscrupulous enough to seize it."

I shrink against the seat. Accessible? Unscrupulous? "But I thought—"

"What? That we are all dead or exiled beyond the walls of this fair City? That only Architects are heretics, as you call us?" A bitter smile thins his lips. "I think you can see that is not the case. Forbidden as it may be, there are still some few of us who practice. And even fewer still who practice for the greater good."

There's an edge to his voice, a hidden dagger behind his words. Something wounds him. I can't help it. "Who are you, really?" I ask.

There's a breath, a tightening of his expression. How many glamours can one warlock possess?

"Who you see before you," he says carefully.

"Pedant Lumin."

He scowls. "Who I am does not matter. What you are, though— that is everything."

"Why?" I whisper. Why should I matter so much? I am no one. My father is important, perhaps, to Men of Science. I think about my desire to be the first successful female Pedant and nearly laugh out loud. That especially will now be denied me.

"Because you are the catalyst. With your power, all kinds of things are possible. That frightens people, makes them greedy, all sorts of things."

"But I don't know how to use it. I don't know what it *means*."

He smiles. "We shall have to remedy that, Miss Nyx."

I chew my lip, looking at the fading magenta lantern in his hand. I make my decision. "Vespa," I say.

"Vespa." He says my name as if it's a spell or a holy charm, something blessed. The lantern dissolves into magenta butterflies which float lazily around the carriage until they disappear.

Saint Darwin and all his apes! What am I doing? I must not let this happen!

Just then, the carriage lurches to a halt and the driver cries out that we've arrived.

Hal opens the door onto the choking stench of Lowtown. It stinks of sewage and tanneries and the ever-present odor of burning bone from the nearby Refinery. He climbs out first, making sure the stairs are stable. Then he gives me his hand. "Miss," he bows, and that rakish grin tricks a smile from me, no matter how much I'd just sworn myself against it.

Arthur Rackham's is just along the alley, thank the Ineffable Watchmaker. Bells announce us when I open the door. A thin, bewhiskered man sits at the counter, a jeweler's monocle over one eye. His mouth is pursed like a prune as he wipes blue grease over the guts of a tarnished, compasslike object.

"Whassis?" he says. He swings to look at us, his eye hideously magnified by his monocle. Next to him on the counter squats a small jar with a lid that looks a bit like a grinning mouth. I suppress a shiver of disgust.

"A missive for you, from Pedant Malcolm Nyx, Head of the Museum of Unnatural History and my father," I say. I'm pleased at how steadily I manage to say it. Hal wanders over to a wall of shelves.

Arthur Rackham nods, grumbling. He puts down the thing he's working on and fingers a greasy rag before taking the letter. The neverseal sighs as he breaks it open. He unrolls the letter and reads it so slowly that I join Hal.

"Do you see?" he whispers.

I notice that the wall is blurry, rather like his glamour has been at times.

"Look beyond," he says.

The usual sorts of permissible antiquities are here—soap dishes, soup tureens, tarnished spoons, chamber pots, and moldering portraits. I look beyond them, *behind* them. The wall of shelves shimmers like silk. Through it, I see vials of things with labels so dusty I can barely read them. I glance at Rackham, but he's still poring over the letter, sounding out every word in hisses and whispers through his broken teeth.

I reach through the illusion (for so it must be) and smudge one vial with a fingertip. *Philtre d'Amour*. Thick tomes murmur to themselves. *Hexogony. Curses and Charms of the First Order.* I touch the spine of the last one, about to pull it off the shelf. A little dark spark jumps from the cover, colder even than the nevered strongbox.

"Careful." Hal looks as though he wants to grab my hand, but he doesn't.

"This is a hexshop, isn't it?"

He nods slightly.

I've heard rumors of such places, shops where heretics and the desperate go to obtain forbidden magics. Naturally, I've never been to such a place before and I can't imagine why my father would send me here now. What does my father, a Rational Man of Science, want in a place like this?

Rackham clears his throat and we return to the counter. The strange silver object near Rackham's hand trembles. One of its delicate arms sweeps toward me, pointing like a compass finding its true north.

The old man stares at the quivering needle and then up at me.

His eyes narrow and an ugly grin splits his face. He looks rather like the jacklanterns people still carve for the Carnival of Saints.

"You tell your ole dad that what he's looking for is right in front of him. If you make it that far."

"I beg your pardon?" I say.

The letter begins to unravel in a hiss of spitting green sparks between us and I can't help but jump.

When I look up, Rackham is staring at me. I feel as though I've once again opened Father's office door and the Waste is stirring, stirring in the strongbox on the desk, sand spilled from an hourglass waiting to spell doom.

He reaches forward and grips my wrist. I'd almost swear the dark jar chuckles at me. "You know very well what I mean, witch!" He spits the last word as though it's a curse.

"Here now," Hal says. "Unhand her this instant!"

I struggle against the man's greasy grip. All I can think is that I want to be free, that this man is hurting me and therefore deserves harm himself. Before I realize what's happening, heat crackles in my wrist. An invisible tentacle of energy snaps and Rackham yelps and releases me.

I cover my surprise with a smirk and we make our way out, only to be confronted by a group of ruffians firmly intent on subduing us. Their faces are hard; their eyes gleaming. I don't know if they've been summoned or simply take us for easy marks. Hal brushes my elbow with his fingertips as they approach. Even through coat and sleeve, his touch is like a divining rod striking a deeply imbedded river far beneath my skin.

I'm in trouble, both from within and without.

CHAPTER 10

Syrus may have been a Gatherer, but finding a witch in a city that forbade magic was quite a bit different than finding midnight morels. He had searched for many days, not sure how to identify the witch he sought. He chewed at a toothpick he'd swiped from a gin palace, swaggering down an alley toward a hexshop he knew. It would never do to look out of place or afraid here. He hoped Rackham would have some information that might lead him in the proper direction in exchange for the cursed toad. Perhaps there'd be enough coin for a pork pie, to boot.

Dark figures clotted the alley ahead not far from the hexshop door. It looked as though some rookery thugs had gotten the notion of a payday off some Uptowners. Syrus crept closer. Crates stacked by a permanently sealed door afforded cover and vantage. He spat out his toothpick and climbed them as quietly as he could, but his foot slipped on a broken slat. He peeped out from under a line of sad, gray laundry, heart crowding his throat. But all attention was focused on the two beleagured Uptowners—no one heard.

He started so hard then that he nearly fell off the box. For the girl in the ring was none other than the one whose stolen toad he kept in his patched coat pocket. A Pedant stood beside her, bristling, his gaze defiant. What were they doing in Lowtown, at a hexshop of all places? Any Uptowner with any sense would never come here, even in what passed for daylight in this place. Syrus withdrew his pipe and loaded it.

The leader of the rookery said something Syrus couldn't quite catch before he tried to seize the girl. Syrus aimed and blew. His dart caught the ruffian right in the web between thumb and forefinger. The leader howled, plucking at the barbed dart once before he slid to the slimy stones. The others moved in. Syrus considered using the Architect's summoning stone that nestled close to the toad, but he had no idea whether the man would come.

Then the Pedant lifted his hands and Syrus saw the stone was unnecessary. Syrus's eyes widened as the Pedant shaped a rapier from the shadows, a long blade of darkness that dissected the very air as the Pedant swiped at his foes. Though shadow may have produced it, the cuts it made drew real blood. Around the Pedant blazed a tiny light—a wee will-o'-the-wisp, by the looks of it—who bit and threw curses at his foes with gusto. The Pedant was an Architect, perhaps the very one he had encountered earlier, though he couldn't be sure.

The girl cast about, as though she sought either a weapon or victim. Syrus blew another dart at a ruffian who was losing his resolve with the leader down and thus moved too slowly. The dart sent him to the stones with others who moaned of their injuries. The last two decided to flee. The girl looked up and her eyes met Syrus's over the edge of the tall crate.

"You!" she shouted.

The Pedant looked in his direction, his eyes flashing blue lightning. Syrus cringed.

"Come," the Architect said. "With this much magic discharged, I'm surprised the Raven Guard isn't on us already. And those ruffians and Rackham, presumably"—he glanced at the still-closed door nearby—"will report us for certain. Best we thank our young benefactor there and get out of here."

"But he stole my toad!"

Syrus was surprised she didn't stamp her foot when she said it. What a prat.

"I'm sure if he had it, he'd return it," the Architect said, looking meaningfully toward Syrus. Syrus had the grace to blush, but then his mouth firmed. He wouldn't return anything to a girl so stuck up, so obviously ungrateful. He and his people had saved her once and he'd helped save her again. Now all his people were dead and he alone remained. And she was still worried about a silly toad?

"We must hurry," the Architect implored. The will o' the wisp floated about them, making frantic gestures of escape.

"But, Hal . . ."

He placed his hand on her arm and she went silent. "There's no time," he said.

With one last glower over her shoulder at Syrus, the girl let the Architect usher her from the alley.

Syrus climbed down off the crates once the alley was completely still again. Rackham had never once come out of his shop during the entire affair. Which meant either he was behind the ordeal or too cowardly to get involved. Syrus sighed. He took the toad out of his inner chest pocket. What little light was in the dim alley gathered in its carnelian eyes. *Nainai* had said there was a curse on it. When Syrus flipped it over, he could see the faint characters carved in the bottom. He recognized the character for magic and another character that had to do with stopping or subduing. Why had a girl like that one carried this toad? And why had she been in a hexshop in Lowtown, a place where no girl of good breeding would go?

Only one way to find out.

Rackham was at the far end of his shop, arranging books and other curiosities when Syrus entered. He came real quick-like when he saw Syrus's patched coat. Hexshop owners like this were all the same—they wanted whatever a Tinker brought in, but didn't want Tinkers lingering too long with their light fingers. It was a false prejudice for the most part; Tinker grannies always told cautionary tales of what happened when you stole an item without knowing its workings. Syrus guessed he was a victim of one of those tales even now.

"May I help you, young sir?" Rackham asked, dusting his hands on a dirty rag. Beside him, an ugly jar gaped and gurgled. Rackham put an uneasy hand on it to quiet it.

Another thing these hexshop owners knew—it paid to be polite, at least on the surface.

Rackham slid behind his counter, and Syrus faced him across it. Syrus hadn't been here in a while; all his family's trade had been honest trade the last few years—whatever they'd found in their Gathering, mechanical bits they fixed for those who liked such curiosities. That fact made Syrus all the angrier about the Cull. Used to be the Raven Guard would come and Cull a family who were known dealers in hexes and magic, but his family had been clean for many a year.

"May I help you?" Rackham said more forcefully.

Syrus blinked.

He brought out the three-legged toad and sat it on the counter. Its carnelian eyes glowed.

"What do you think of this?"

Rackham arranged a tattler across from him. The device whirred, its arched gears spinning until the needle pointed to the upper end of the magical potency register. The dealer looked up at Syrus as he screwed his monocle into place.

"Where did you get this?" he asked.

"Does it matter?" Syrus asked. The tattler confirmed what he'd already known. This thing had enough forbidden magic in it to draw a goodly sum, at the very least. And it certainly should be good enough for the information he sought. Now it just came down to the bargaining. Luckily, his granny had taught him that, too.

Rackham's left eye was gigantic as he looked at Syrus. He shrugged. "Suppose not."

Rackham bent to inspect it, but Syrus snatched it off the countertop.

"Eh?" Rackham asked, looking up at him. The careful expression on his face melted into something darker, more harrowed.

"I'm interested in coin," Syrus said, "but a fair trade for this toad also involves information."

Rackham frowned. He sat back from the counter, trying to feign nonchalance. But his brow was sweating, and he mopped at it, mussing the wispy hairs across his pate into disarray. He reminded Syrus a little of Truffler, and the boy frowned at the memory.

"What kind of information?" Rackham asked.

Just then, the shop bells chimed, and a bearded man entered. He seemed young, though beards were not generally fashionable among the younger set. He wore plain fine clothes, but the way he carried himself meant that he must come at least from Midtown, possibly Uptown. There was something about his eyes that looked familiar, something decidedly unpleasant that Syrus couldn't place. Syrus glared at him. What was with all the Uptowners invading Lowtown today?

The young man smiled with the same look one might give a growling bear cub and drifted to the back of the shop.

Syrus leaned closer to Rackham.

"A girl. A girl was just in here with a Pedant. I want to know who she was and what she wanted."

Rackham's eyes went opaque, almost black. He seemed about to change his mind regarding the toad.

"You know how rare this is," Syrus said. "Even I know, and I don't know nearly as much about it as you do. The more you tell me, the less coin I'll ask. I'm giving you a fortune and you know it."

"But . . . I maintain a respectable relationship with all my clients and correspondents. I couldn't possibly . . ."

Syrus suppressed a laugh. He swept one hand around the shop. "You call this respectable? A hexshop in Lowtown?"

Rackham's chin wobbled. His glance flitted to the other customer.

Syrus drew back, shoving the toad into his pocket. He half-turned toward the door. The bearded man was just at the edge of his vision, perusing a wall of antiques. It was probably an illusion; Rackham had to be hiding his contraband behind one somewhere.

"I suppose I'll just have to take my business elsewhere, then," he said. He went to the door, his hand faintly stirring the bells on the latch.

The young gentleman looked at him. The bemused smile was plastered on his face, but his eyes were sharp.

"Wait," Rackham said. "Wait."

Syrus turned, careful not to smile. The fish wasn't quite reeled in yet.

"Let me see it again."

Syrus nodded and put the toad on the counter again. The tattler needle stood at attention.

Rackham bent over it, careful not to touch the toad for fear Syrus would snatch it away again.

"Vespa Nyx," Rackham whispered. He said her name casually, as though he was speaking of something else—the weather or something he'd found at market. "Daughter of Malcolm Nyx, Head of the Museum of Unnatural History. He was seeking"—he lowered his voice so that Syrus strained to hear—"a Manticore lure."

Syrus frowned. "A lure?"

"Yes, something to trap the Manticore. To take the Heart of All Matter, presumably," Rackham said.

Syrus knew what he was talking about, but he wanted to be sure. "What is that?"

Rackham gazed at him sidelong, his giant eye making Syrus want to shrink from the counter.

"I'd think you'd already know, you being a Tinker who lives by the Manticore's grace."

Syrus stared at him.

Rackham's fingers drifted toward the toad. "Surely you've heard the story of what the Manticore stole?" he whispered. "Old Man Nyx needs the Heart for one of his experiments. But before that he needs . . . a witch. That's the only lure that will draw the Manticore from her lair." He looked around as if a Raven Guard might step from the shadows and arrest him at any moment.

Syrus thought of the Manticore's strange Heart with all its wires and hoses, its pulsing red light as she'd swallowed the Raven Guard whole.

"Why?" Syrus asked.

"Because she's the only one that can get close enough to the Manticore to draw it out of its den and make it give over the Heart."

Syrus knew the first bit to be false. Hadn't the Manticore come out for him?

"This girl, this Vespa Nyx—is she a witch?"

Rackham's lips wavered around his stained teeth. "Most assuredly. Funny that what Nyx wants has been in front of him all along. Reckon he wouldn't want to have to sacrifice his own daughter, though." He flung a few coins across the counter.

Syrus nodded, pocketing his payment. He headed toward the door, aware of the bearded man's strange gaze on his back. He regretted that he'd had to cut a deal with Rackham with the stranger nearby; surely he had heard some of their conversation, despite their attempts to muffle it.

"Careful, boy," Rackham said, before Syrus slid out of the door. "You may be stepping into things far beyond your ken."

That he certainly knew to be true. He nodded swiftly again, and the little bells ushered him out.

As the door closed behind him, the young man walked to the counter.

"I'll have that toad," he said in a husky voice.

The tattler vibrated so hard it broke.

"And this," he said, cradling the jar with a pale hand. "I'll have this, too."

He lifted his hand and a white mist rose around Rackham's head, swirling much like the mist that had brought the Architects to the aid of the Harpy. The young man opened the jar and the mist hastened inside.

Rackham's eyes went white. His mouth and shoulders slackened; but his fingers crept restlessly over the counter.

"There is no further use for you," the bearded man said.

Without a word, Rackham pulled an antique dagger from below the counter and stabbed himself through the heart.

Before he left, the bearded man spoke a quiet word.

The room burst into flames.

CHAPTER 11 ━

I've spent the past few days feigning illness and hiding in my room. Father has again come and said his good-byes to my door—I say I won't see him for fear of contagion. Only my maid and Aunt Minta are allowed entry.

I wasn't frightened the day Hal called me a witch, the day I nearly let the Waste loose on the entire city. But something about the encounter with Rackham and the thugs outside his shop has made this witch business all too real. It's not that I can't accept it. I'm still not entirely sure what it means, despite Hal's words in the carriage. (Oh, those magenta-shadowed words!) Whether I can survive it, though, that's the question. All I can see in my mind is the blank desert of the Waste spreading before me. Perhaps it's no more than I deserve, heretic that I'm becoming.

And Hal . . . Nothing more was said after the incident at Rackham's. We returned to the Museum in silence and he left me at the atrium without a backward glance. I struggle with what he must think and feel, what *I* feel. Princess Athena loved a guard in her father's house, one who became the founder of the Architects. He was hunted all his days and it's said that he met a dark and deeply unnatural end. I am no princess and Hal is no guard, but I have no doubt we would also be hunted—the Empress is as intolerant as her ancestors. Perhaps I'm getting ahead of myself. Perhaps I'm only imagining that something lies between us, something more than the vast expanse of the Waste.

And I'm still a little angry with Hal for letting that boy who stole my toad get away, even if he did help us.

So, when Aunt Minta proposes that we go shopping in the Night Emporium, I'm filled with trepidation. Are Raven Guards out looking for me this very instant? Have Rackham or his thugs set a price on my head? Maybe that Tinker boy Syrus will change his mind and join in the hunt, take me down like an Unnatural with one of his darts.

"You can't stay in there forever," Aunt Minta says at the door of my room. "I've never seen you like this, Vee. I'd almost swear you were pining over someone if I didn't know better."

That settles it. I'm not some missish creature, overwhelmed by fate or sentimentality.

I bounce off of my bed and open the door.

Aunt Minta's look of surprise vanishes into a smile when I say, "All right, then."

If I'm to die soon, at least perhaps I should try just once to look fetching beforehand. And perhaps the next time I run into Hal, he'll see an entirely new me.

We're at the great crossroads of Chimera Park when the carriage halts abruptly.

"Sweet saints!" the driver exclaims above the hue and cry of traffic.

I throw open the curtain and look out, against Aunt Minta's

protests. At first I can't make sense of what's happening. Before us lies the great intersection of Industrial Way and several other boulevards. The old observatory dome of the Museum and the roofs of the University halls poke through the green fog.

Then, I see him. A man wending his way through traffic, stumbling, shuffling . . . Is he drunk? Wherever he passes, carriage animals rear and scream, trying to get away from him. Drivers and handlers struggle to maintain control. But then he passes a carriage drawn by *myth*work unicorns, a conveyance only to be used by House Virulen, the third most powerful house in the realm.

What happens next I have never seen before and hope never to see again.

Steel sides heaving and joints steaming, the unicorns rear and plunge. Like the Refineries, they are also powered by *myth*. And like that power, they are supposed to be completely dependable.

But they aren't now.

A trolley flies down the hill; its brakes are out. The conductor screams as the *myth*work unicorns head straight for it. The crazy, stumbling man will be crushed between them if someone doesn't stop the collision.

I leap out of my hansom. Aunt Minta's shout is lost in the scream and press of traffic.

My lungs want to implode, but I push myself through the pain. The patrol officer shrieks at me with his whistle. The trolley flies down the hill toward the Museum entrance, the conductor waving his arms frantically. From the other side of the track, Hal races toward the nearest unicorn's bridle.

I have no idea where he's come from—perhaps on his way to afternoon classes after some errand of the Architects—but he sees me at the same moment I see him. *Help me*, he says, and it's as though he's right next to me, whispering in my ear. Then he leaps at the bridle. His hands glow with pale, familiar light. I move toward the trolley and the man bent on putting himself in its path. I don't know how Hal thinks I can help him exactly, but I remember how I escaped Rackham's grasp. I set my thoughts on the trolley and imagine it braking to an impossible halt before it reaches the intersection. I imagine the man safe. A barely perceptible glow builds around the trolley's front wheels.

The man raises his head and howls—the scalding scream of unoiled gears. His eyes, white and milky as flint, meet mine. My concentration breaks. In that moment, I'd swear the man throws himself directly in the trolley's path.

I look away, shuddering, as the trolley squeals into the intersection, grinding the blind man beneath its wheels.

All is still. I can't hear anything for a long while except the man's scream answered by the trolley's brakes. I can't help but feel I've failed in some crucial way, and I'm so overcome that I stand there in the eternal drizzle of glowing soot and steam, watching my tears darken the backs of my kid gloves.

"Vespa!" I hear my name from across the tracks. I start toward Hal, my legs weak as porridge. But when I see the condition of the *myth*work carriage, I run again.

Though Hal must have stopped the unicorns just in time, the carriage didn't fare quite as well. The traces have twisted and the wheels collapsed under the enormous strain of stopping too quickly. The carriage lies on its side. The driving wight is a twitching wreck. Together, Hal and I clear away the shattered stairs and pull at the door. Someone pushes to get out.

"That was good work," Hal says under his breath. "You almost stopped the trolley."

"Thank you."

Hal's knowing gaze makes me blush. "Where have you been these many days?" he says so steady and low.

Thankfully, I don't have to stammer my excuses because we finally pull the door open.

A young lady stands in the wreckage of her carriage. She's the vision of beauty—snapping dark eyes and tumbling black curls—with not a hair out of place.

"Mistress Virulen," Hal says, his voice suddenly gone formal and stiff. "Allow us to assist you." There's a strangeness in his voice I can't place.

A crowd gathers around us, whispering in awe.

"This is the most unfortunate circumstance for a meeting," the young lady says, as we help her out of the wreckage. Her voice is gracious and musical; she seems not the least bit troubled to emerge to a throng of gawking admirers.

"To whom do I owe my rescue?" she asks. A smile plays about her lips, and I can imagine how the newspapers will eat this up. MISTRESS VIRULEN PULLED SMILING FROM THE WRECKAGE OF HER CARRIAGE, and so on.

We introduce ourselves. Mistress Virulen's eyes hold mine for a beat longer than they do Hal's, but she keeps hold of Hal's hand long after she releases mine.

"Is there somewhere we can escort you, my lady, until a safe conveyance can be hired for you?" he asks. "I suppose your father will send dray oxen to fetch his carriage." I watch the tender way he releases her. Jealousy snaps at me with green jaws.

Her perfume is both heavenly and heavy—bergamot, damask rose, spice. She waves her free hand as if there's nothing to trouble over. "I'll hire a hansom to take me home." She looks around at the expectant crowd, smiling. "Surely one of these noble people will kindly return me to my father's estate."

Several affirmative shouts answer her.

"But first, let us see the cause of all this hullabaloo." She pulls us toward the front of the trolley.

"My lady, I don't think—" Hal begins, but one look from her silences him.

We move forward.

I don't want to look, but Mistress Virulen's grip is too strong to resist. She pulls me toward the still-smoking front wheels. Another crowd has gathered there—officers, a barrister or two, and a few Pedants. Father is among them, crumbs still dotting his cravat. He must have been taking his lunch in his favorite pub, the Surly Wench, up the street.

When he sees me, he blanches whiter than the Sheep of Learning.

"Vee!" he says. He comes to me as if he wants to embrace me, but Mistress Virulen's hold on my hand stops him.

"Mistress," he says, bowing toward her.

She inclines her head.

A light drizzle begins. Mistress Virulen releases me so I can pull my hood up over my hair. Some thoughtful person brings her hat, miraculously undamaged, from the wreckage of her carriage and she affixes it over her gorgeous black curls. I resist the urge to fiddle with my hair. Why can my curls not be so tidy? They rebel against order, which is why I most often wind them up in braids or chignon, despite the unfashionableness of such styles.

She grabs my hand again and pulls me onward, as if we've been fast friends forever. I don't know her at all, except what little gossip I hear in the Museum halls and at the dinner table. I recall Aunt Minta saying once that Mistress Virulen was on the hunt for the perfect match, that the Virulen Estate isn't as prosperous as it once was. But if her gown and hat are any indication, her family is prospering quite well.

I sigh in relief to find that the body is already covered with a white sheet, though blood slicks the cobbles, the front of the wheels. I can see from the depressions in the quickly staining sheet that the body has been cleaved in two, and I'm torn between fascination and horror.

Mistress Virulen has a strangely fervid expression. I'd almost say she finds this exciting, but it would be wrong for a lady of quality to be anything but grieved by death.

"Ladies," Father says, "perhaps you should step over to the café there, out of view of this tragedy. We shall join you momentarily."

A swift look passes between Hal and me, but Father picks up on it. He glares at Hal.

Mistress Virulen reluctantly allows me to draw her to the café across the road. Room is made among the crowding patrons for us to have a seat by the window, and I am glad to be surrounded by the smell of coffee grown deep in the Eastern wildlands rather than the death and smoke outside.

Mistress Virulen is restless, staring out the window. She smiles at me when our coffee comes, her full attention finally bent on me.

"Miss Nyx," she says, "I have a proposition that may interest you." She looks at me over her teacup. Her teeth are whiter than the bone china.

"Oh?" I say. I take a long sip.

"How would you like to be my Companion?"

I splutter and then do my best to recover my dignity by hiding behind my napkin. When I've swallowed my incredulity along with the scalding coffee, I say, "Come again, my lady?"

She laughs. "You silly bird! You know what I said!"

"But, my lady, I'm hardly qualified for such an honor. And you barely know me."

"That is precisely why I would rather have you!" she says. "Any girl who is brave enough to try to stop a trolley to save me certainly deserves a reward."

It's as if the cold outside seeps into my veins instead of the warmth I seek from my coffee. I gulp it hurriedly, trying to steel myself, and nearly sear my tongue off in the process.

"I've no idea what you mean," I manage to say.

She laughs at me again. "Oh, don't be coy. Of course you do! I saw you through my carriage window before everything turned upside down. You were practically glowing with"—she leans closer, the feathers on her hat nodding toward me—"*magic.*"

My face is hotter than the dregs of coffee in my cup. If she saw, then everyone must have seen. And with the incident at the Museum with the Sphinx, it's a wonder newspapermen aren't beating down our townhouse doors to get answers. Or that the Raven Guard haven't come to lock me away. I wonder if she saw Hal, too, and if she will try to blackmail him. Perhaps he's better at hiding it than I am. He must be, if he hasn't been caught yet.

"We could be of much use to each other, you and I," she says.

"And what if I'd rather not?" I try to sound arch, but I come off more like a petulant child.

"I suspect you'd find your life a deal more uncomfortable than you already do." She leans even closer, so that the topmost feather on her hat almost tickles my nose. "You should understand, Miss Nyx, that I always get my way."

I force a smile, but it is more truthfully a grimace.

Father and Hal wade through the crowd. Aunt Minta comes behind them.

"We've a hansom for you, Mistress Virulen," Father says. His eyes wander between us. "That is . . . if the two of you are finished?"

She stands, her skirts hissing against the table. I stand with her. "I believe we are, Pedant Nyx," she says, holding my gaze. That wicked smile curves her lips again.

She takes my hand. "I shall send the formal invitation to you as soon as I return home. I'll look forward to your acceptance."

I nod. Under better circumstances, Father's quizzical gaze would make me laugh. Hal looks between us, his expression completely unreadable.

Mistress Virulen is off in a whisper of exotic perfume and puff of nodding feathers.

"Invitation?" Father asks.

"She wants me to be her Companion," I say.

Realization dawns on his face just before he embraces me. He knows what this means—that I will be exposed to more connections in higher places than he and Aunt Minta could ever reach. Such a position almost guarantees me a match far beyond his wildest dreams.

As long as I don't botch it up. And as long as Mistress Virulen keeps her knowledge to herself. Therein lies the bargain.

I rest my cheek against his robes, breathing in the damp, scholarly smell and loving it more fiercely than ever. My eyes meet Hal's over Father's shoulder. I think he knows what this means too. No more Museum for me. And perhaps no more magic, if I am to survive. His gaze is hard, his eyes almost too brilliant to bear.

"I'm so proud of you, Vee! Today has truly been a red-letter day," Aunt Minta says, as she arrives. The news apparently is already being whispered about; my indiscretion in racing from the carriage is already forgotten.

I think of the scarlet letter on Athena's robes at her execution and can only agree.

Chapter 12 ━

After his visit to Rackham's, Syrus had watched the witch for many days. He wished he could write her a letter, but he didn't know how to write in the Cityfolk language. And he didn't have the coin to pay someone to take dictation, even if he had thought it wise to put such information in a letter, which it wasn't. And how did he expect her to respond? "Your father plots against you and the Manticore needs you." He doubted if he was a City girl and someone told him such a thing that he'd respond favorably. When he added the fact that he'd stolen something precious to her . . . well, he didn't expect she'd welcome any contact from him, really.

But it had to be done.

Things were very busy about the Nyx household. There was much to-ing and fro-ing. The witch often went out with her aunt on long shopping excursions in Midtown or to Uptown for the Manticore knew what. Syrus couldn't follow her very easily into Uptown; only respectable sorts were allowed there, so he was forced to climb wicked-looking fences and skulk around flower urns, hoping no one would drag him by the ears out of the gates.

He asked a servant what all the fuss was about and the old man smiled. "Our young miss is to be Companion to Mistress Virulen.

She's preparing to move to the Virulen Estate after Carnival."

Syrus nodded, feeling the urgency of his mission press even more closely. He needed to speak to her before she went to Virulen. She'd be closer to the Manticore then but much harder to reach. And who knew what would happen to her beforehand?

No matter how he tried, though, he couldn't get close enough to her at a moment when she was alone. Unless he just happened to hide in the right dressing room at the Night Emporium, he didn't see himself managing it. And the mere thought of that gave him the willies.

Still . . . He eyed the townhouse. There was one place and one time when she'd be alone, when he could be certain no one would disturb her or interrupt him. Her bedroom at night. This thought didn't make him much more comfortable than the idea of catching her in the dressing room, but it still might be a better alternative, unless she screamed or triggered the banshee alarm. He rolled his eyes. Surely, she was more sensible than the average City female. She had seemed very practical and quite brave when she had stepped in to keep the highwayman from taking the strongbox in her carriage. She'd been brave during the fight at Rackham's too, even if she'd still wanted to come after him for the accursed toad.

Surely, she'd see reason if he could make her understand the urgency of the matter. He had, in fact, tried to return to Rackham's to steal the toad back, but was astonished to discover that Rackham's was now a burnt-out husk. The rest of the block had barely escaped going up in flames, and no one knew what had happened or where Rackham had got to. Some said it was the Raven Guard belatedly getting around to torching a hexshop. But if so, why hadn't Rackham's arrest and execution date been made public? The

Guard generally made a big show. This quiet bit of arson wasn't their style. Had the Architect come back later for revenge?

Syrus sighed as he slipped down the alley alongside the witch's townhouse. Whatever the circumstances, the toad was gone. She would just have to accept his apology and believe that he was telling the truth.

He wasn't sure which was her bedroom, but from the flower-printed curtains he could just see above him, he'd guess this was the one. He wished for a moment that Truffler was with him; his friend would have been able to sniff her out just as well as he did any rare mushroom. Not that she'd like being compared to a fungus, Syrus imagined.

He waited until night fell completely to climb up the drainpipe and onto what he hoped was her window ledge. He listened for a while. As far as he could tell, everyone was still downstairs. Dinner was surely over and perhaps they were in the parlor, reading or— The sound of a pianoforte tinkled up the stairs. Syrus tested the window. It was closed but not locked. It only took a little force from his file and wedge to lever it up enough for him to slide through.

He closed it quietly. An everlantern cast a dim glow over the room, and the *myth* radiator plinked and hissed near the window. A fire had been laid on the hearth against the chill; Syrus was thankful he wouldn't have to worry over frightening a maid. He turned, taking in the flounced petticoats draped over a chair, the carelessly piled books everywhere. Definitely her room.

Although he was more than used to picking pockets, he'd never quite graduated to outright thievery like many of the lads in Low-town. It was uncomfortable standing here surrounded by all the witch's things, knowing he could easily take more of her valuables, except for the fact that he was here to persuade rather than rob.

The room itself was discomfiting to him just by its very existence. The bed looked warm and deep; he couldn't help but press down on it with his palm—cloud-soft goose down. He had always slept cocooned in thin quilts with his family in the leaky passenger car, hearing Granny Reed get up in the night to feed the old potbelly stove, wondering if he would ever know what it was like to be warm all over all at once. This sort of luxury he'd never imagined, though he knew that by Cityfolk lights, the Nyxes were not rich. Still, there were paintings and other art on the walls, dried flowers in a vase, an embroidered dressing screen.

Syrus felt terribly out of place. He looked for somewhere he could hide until the appropriate moment. He settled in a corner between the hulking wardrobe and a bookshelf. He didn't want to hide in anything and unduly frighten her, much as the idea of springing out of a wardrobe amused him.

He crouched down and stared at the spines of all the books with their indecipherable letters. He hoped he would never have to learn to read the Cityfolk's language. The thought of their deadly dull thoughts pressing in on him made him dizzy.

He stiffened and hunched as close to the wall as he could when the door opened.

"Good night, Aunt," he heard the witch say. With a swish of skirts, she and her maid disappeared behind her dressing screen. He tried to think of something else, so as not to hear her undressing. He had kissed a girl behind the train car before, but that was as far as things had gone. The thought of what a witch would do if she caught him peeping at her was quite unpleasant.

The maid banked the fire and left. Syrus waited until he was sure the witch had climbed into bed and pulled the covers up around her. Then, he slipped out from behind the wardrobe.

He coughed slightly. "Miss Nyx," he said, "I must speak with you."

She sat bolt upright. It was hard for him not to laugh at her in her nightcap with the covers pulled up around her and possibly the most indignant look on her face he'd ever seen on any female. She narrowed her eyes.

"You!" she said.

"Listen, Miss Nyx, I . . ." he began. Such formal language coming out of his mouth was odd, but he didn't want to offend her either. He knew the forms for dealing with Elementals, but a witch? He wasn't quite sure what was proper.

"Give me one reason why I should not sound the banshee alarm at once," she said.

"Because I've come to tell you . . . that is . . . we have reason to believe that you are. . ."

She let the covers fall and crossed her arms over her chest, much as she'd done when the clan surrounded her carriage.

"What?" she said.

"In danger," Syrus said.

The expression on her face was indescribable. It was as though a mirror cracked, revealing something under the surface that was powerful but also very afraid. It was hard to tell in the dim room, but he thought her skin turned several shades of red until it was almost purple. The dimmed everlantern made obvious what day did not readily disclose—her features were very Tinker-like—high cheekbones, round face, somewhat tilted eyes. He'd never noticed before; perhaps it was her pale coloring or the way she wore her hair.

Syrus wished he could move toward the window and flee, but his feet were rooted to the carpet. This was not going well at all.

"You broke into my room in the middle of the night to tell me something I already know?" she said.

"The window was mostly open," Syrus protested. "And it's not the middle of the night."

She glared. "The boy who stole my toad and won't return it feels compelled to break into my room to tell me I'm in danger? That's rich, indeed."

He sighed. "Look, I'm sorry now that I took it. You don't know how sorry. I've tried to get it back, but the place where I sold it . . . well, it's been burned to the ground."

Narrowed eyes again. The distinct and uncomfortable possibility occurred to him that she could shoot flames from her eyeballs and burn him to a crisp. This time, his feet managed to move a little. He shuffled toward the window.

"You have ten seconds to hand over the toad or I'm sounding the alarm."

"I don't have it!"

"One-one thousand, two-one thousand . . ."

"I really don't!" He turned out his coat pockets.

"Three one-thousand . . ."

He unbuttoned the frog buttons of his coat and showed her the inner pockets. *"I don't have it!"*

"Vespa," a voice called from the landing, "who are you talking to in there?"

"Five one-thousand, six one-thousand . . ."

"Look, I know you don't believe me. I know you think I'm a no-good Tinker thief. Your father is planning to use you as bait to lure the Manticore. He wants her Heart for some dreadful purpose. She needs your help. If you'd just be reasonable . . ."

"Nine one-thousand. Ten." She smirked.

Syrus dove for the window as she reached for the lever over her bed. He shimmied down the drainpipe as fast as he could. Just as he touched ground, the banshee alarm atop the house began its ear-shattering scream. It was soon taken up by other alarms along his route as he dodged between shadow and everlantern down through Midtown.

CHAPTER 13

Talk at every meal for the last several days has been nothing but building castles in the air. It's almost as though the break-in with the Tinker thief never happened. Aunt Minta rambles on about the fine clothes and jewelry I'll have, the engagements with Lady Whatsit and Viscount So-and-so. I talk with her of these things because it feels too dangerous to speak of anything else. I keep hearing the Tinker boy's words in my head. *Your father is planning to use you to lure the Manticore.* I can't begin to imagine what he means by that. And I've still heard nothing from Hal.

Discussing dresses and shoes is a relief, but there's no greater relief than being allowed to enter the Museum at Father's side. I have so much work to catch up on. It's wonderful to pretend that life is as it has always been—no Tinker thieves or dangerous Architects, no witchcraft in my blood. I can even imagine that Lucy Virulen will forget about me. Somehow, I doubt I'll be so lucky.

I try to distract myself as we walk up the steps to the Museum's arched entrance by asking Father what he thought of the strange, white-eyed man who leaped in front of the trolley. I haven't asked at home because Aunt Minta wouldn't find it fitting conversation for a lady.

Father frowns. "White-eyed man?"

"Yes, the one who caused the accident. What was wrong with him, do you reckon?"

"I don't know what you mean about white eyes." He sounds irritated. *Why?* "But," he continues, "I'd guess he was just a vagrant. No one to concern yourself with. You have much greater things to worry over now." His smile is weak as he pushes open the heavy wooden door.

He's lying. He remembers just as well as I do. But why would he pretend that he doesn't? As far as I know, Father has never lied to me. Why would he start now over such a trivial thing?

Unless it's not trivial at all.

Might it have something to do with his Experiment?

A chill slithers up my spine.

We pass through the atrium with all my display cases filled with glittering wings and false eyes. I think again of Piskel stuffing his cheeks with jam cake, and I feel like a butcher rather than a skilled unnaturalist.

There's a commotion when we enter the Main Hall. I look toward the Sphinx, ready to engage in our customary morning battle of wills, pretending to forget that day when it nearly became a battle of life and death, but her plinth is empty.

The Sphinx is gone.

Father and I look around wildly, all conversation regarding the white-eyed man forgotten. Everything else is in order—the Wyvern, the Dragon hatchling exhibit, and the Griffin are all still in their places. There are no signs of struggle. Several Pedants and Scholars are examining the plinth and the nearby field box.

"What happened?" Father asks.

"She's just gone," old Pedant Tycho says.

"Are you certain?" Father says. "You've checked all the Halls and places where she might hide?"

Pedant Tycho nods. "'Twould be very hard to hide a Sphinx. And we've already seen how she might react were she set loose." His eyes slide toward me. "Looks like an inside job," he says. Despite his intimation, everyone can see that this is not my fault. I haven't been here for several days.

"Like the Grue," someone else mutters.

"Have the Architects infiltrated us?" another asks.

I can't help but look around for Hal at that, but he's nowhere to be seen. I don't want to believe he would be behind such a thing, but then again, he's the only Architect I know. The Architects steal or release Unnaturals from time to time, saints only know why. Father has always been certain that's what happened to the Grue when it disappeared last year shortly after Charles came. I think about the breathing I heard in the dark downstairs and shiver.

Dim greenish light filters down onto the empty exhibit. It tricks out the scales of the Wyvern in the adjacent alcove. If the Architects are stealing specimens, what are they doing with them? And what will become of the Museum? I'm suddenly angry at Hal. If he is behind this, more than just his precious Unnaturals could be affected. I look at Father, who's rubbing his chin with a gnarled hand. Ultimately, the responsibility for all of this rests on Father's shoulders. I know there were repercussions from the loss of the Grue, though Father never speaks of it. I cannot imagine how he will fare with the loss of a prime exhibit like the Sphinx.

Father shakes my elbow to make me pay attention. "I must go to my office now, Vee," he says. "This security issue is very serious.

Stay in the Cataloguing Chamber today, do you hear?" He mops sweat from under the Sheep of Learning with his handkerchief.

I nod. His black robes swish down the corridor and off toward the old observatory.

He's not going to his office.

Hm.

I follow him, far enough behind that I can see the edge of his robe as he turns corners. He vanishes through the observatory doors just as I peep into the corridor.

I follow, walking as softly as I can, but there's no need. There's a deep hum and rumble from within that obscures all sound. One of the doors is still ajar. I slip inside.

I've always loved the old observatory and was sad when it was mostly dismantled. The Pedants of the Astronomy Division said the ambient light from the Refineries made it hard to see the stars, so they moved the telescope to one of the mountains outside Scientia. But the old orrery is still here; the planets on its skeletal arms are connected by long cobwebs. Near it rises the sleek dome of a hellish-looking machine I've never seen before. Hoses snake out from its center like tentacles toward laboratory benches. A glass container sits under the mouth of the machine, and in it stirs the restless black sand of the Waste.

Father is over on the other side of the array. And there's someone with him. Two someones.

I creep a little closer, hoping I'm well-hidden in the shadows of the entryway. I know I should be writing my letter of apology to Pedant Simian about the loss of his collection or perhaps helping the Scholars search for the missing Sphinx (if they would allow me), but I want to know what Father's doing. He used to tell me everything; I don't understand why he won't now.

Charles leads a girl to the table, a girl with a checkered headband and long, dark hair. A Tinker? What is Charles doing with a Tinker girl?

"Don't you have other things to do besides skulking around your father's laboratory?" someone whispers behind me. All the hairs on my neck shiver.

Hal.

I do my best to turn slowly and keep my expression icy-calm.

"Don't you have better things to do than sneaking up on people?" I retort.

"Vespa, if you have any sense at all, which I begin to doubt, you will come with me now before we are discovered and all my work is in vain."

He's so close to me now that I can smell him—crushed roses, ink, a whiff of jam cake. Piskel looks up at me from his pocket, nodding fiercely.

I turn and walk out of the observatory and down the corridor back toward the Main Hall. Reaction makes my knees hot and wobbly. If the Sphinx leaped at me from some corner right now, I don't think I could run fast enough to get away from her. Hal catches up to me in silence.

"What do you want, Pedant?" I say, finally.

He slides a cream-colored, neversealed envelope into view. "This was delivered to your Father's office. The clerk asked me to give it to you when he passed me a bit ago; he couldn't find you," he says.

The invitation from Lucy Virulen. It's sealed with a tiny Manticore.

"Just in time, it appears," he says, looking back toward the corridor where he found me.

My hands shake. I touch the seal and it dissolves. The letter unfolds like a living creature and rests lightly in my palm.

"Yes," I say. Words with all their arabesques and illuminations swim before my eyes.

"What were you doing back there?" he asks. His voice is stiff.

"Why are you angry? Because I was about to discover information you haven't dared to find out for yourself?"

Hal looks around at the flood of Pedants and Scholars moving through the Main Hall on their way to morning lecture or laboratories. A search party is still wandering through the halls, but I'm guessing they'll call in the Raven Guard when they get desperate enough. Or else just forget about it and hope nothing untoward happens, as they did with the Grue.

"Not here," he says. He takes my elbow. A little shock zips past my sleeve and beneath my skin. Before I can protest, we're on the stairs toward the storage basement.

I clutch the letter like a limp bird in my hand as we descend. Fear slips through me—why should I trust Hal? He is an Architect and a heretic. He's had every chance to use my own powers (about which I know nothing) against me. And yet he has risked his life for me more than once. He has kept my secret. Whatever else there may or may not be between us, he's the only person in the world who could possibly understand me, perhaps even help me. Why, then, is he so angry with me now?

We go to a storage room beyond the iron gate. I peer down the narrow stair as we pass. That elusive breathing haunts me with thoughts of the lost Unnaturals.

A single everlight wanders an endless circuit around the room Hal chooses. Skeletons, collection boxes, and specimen jars cast strange shadows, but the musty smell of ancient things is infinitely comforting. I would like to hide here for quite a long while.

Hal releases me. "Do you have any idea what's at stake here? Do you have any idea how much you risk if we are exposed?" His anger flashes cerulean in the gloom.

I raise my chin and arch my brow in the way the Instructor of Refinement once taught us at Seminary. "We?"

"Yes, damn it," he says. "You are part of this now, whether you like it or not."

"Why? And I don't particularly appreciate your cursing at me, Pedant Lumin." I would almost swear the boggle fetus in its jar trembles at the frost in my words.

Hal closes his eyes and pinches the bridge of his nose with a long sigh of frustration. Piskel peeks out of Hal's waistcoat pocket. He glares at me and shakes his fist, as if reminding me that he'll bite me again if I don't cooperate, even though I'm not exactly sure what I'm to cooperate with. He slips out of Hal's pocket and floats over to examine the specimens on the shelves.

"Well?" I ask.

"I am trying with all my might, little as it is, to shield you and keep you safe. And yet you are continually putting yourself in harm's way."

"It seems I'm putting myself in harm's way no matter what I do. But I don't see what that has to do with anything. Are you just jealous because I'm on the verge of discovering things you aren't? Is that it?"

"Vespa, don't you see? You're at the center of a vast web of darkness that is about to close in on you. The Empress sits at the center like a spider, waiting for one such as you to be delivered into her clutches. And your father is just the one to do it."

The everlight slowly travels the perimeter of the storage room. Things leap from the shadows—goblin spines, kelpie eggs preserved in spirits. Piskel floats between them, humming sadly.

I hear the Tinker thief's words in my head again. "That's what the Tinker thief said, that he meant to use me as bait. . . ." I choke on the words, unable to finish them aloud.

"The Tinker thief? What?"

I tell him of the boy Syrus breaking into my room, the things he said that I don't want to believe.

He closes his eyes for a moment. When he opens them, he says, "It is worse, so much worse than we thought."

"I don't understand." My voice squeaks inelegantly on the last syllable.

"First, did you tell your father what Rackham said to you that day?"

I shake my head.

His shoulders relax somewhat under his Pedant robes. "Good. Then perhaps he is not yet fully cognizant of your role."

"Of what?"

"Do you know of the Heart of All Matter?"

It's a non sequitur, meaning "a thing that doesn't quite follow" in the Old Scientific language, but it's firmer ground than the present subject matter. I swallow the scratchiness in my throat. "It's said that the Manticore bewitched Athena into giving the Heart to her. That Athena ran off with the Manticore and the guard who seduced her to live in the Forest until her father, the Emperor, rescued her.

And that Athena would not bend to her father's insistence that she restore the Heart to him. He could not protect her any longer from her own witchery, and thus she was sent to die on the black sands." I can still hear the rector telling the tale to us every Chastening Day, his eyes agleam with the zeal of Logic and Reason.

"That is a falsehood," Hal says, a dangerous edge to his voice.

"How? The Church teaches—"

He retorts, "Everything it teaches is meant to ensure our compliance with Imperial mandate. The Empress needs us to believe in her religion. Otherwise, like Athena, we might discover the truth."

Now *I* am angry. How dare he? I almost expect Saint Darwin to send his apes to carry this heretic away to the Infinitesimal Void right now! "And just what is that truth, if you are so sure you know it?"

"This world is alive, Vespa. And it is founded on magic." He paces away from me, gesturing at the racks. "All these beings you see here—they are part of a great Circle of Being. They are sentient nations unto themselves, just as we are. But unlike us, this world needs them to survive. The more Elementals there are, the more this world thrives. When they are destroyed or taken from their native places, those places become a desert of null energy, what we call the Creeping Waste. Elementals continue to disappear and the Waste keeps growing. Our very lives may depend on the existence of things we are so thoughtlessly destroying. That is the true science."

Piskel floats toward us, nodding and making chirruping noises of agreement.

"But if that's true . . ." I fall silent, looking between Piskel and the jars of preserved things. I've always secretly thought there was more to the Unnaturals than meets the eye, but that they are intelligent beings, that our lives depend on them, that we are willfully destroying them for no reason—it goes against everything I've ever been taught.

"The problem is we can't figure out what's happening to them," Hal continues. "That's part of why I was sent here, to discover what the Refineries do with them after their capture. We think we know, but it's all still conjecture at this point."

"Part of why you were sent?"

A strange expression crosses Hal's face. "I was also sent to investigate . . ." He pauses and shakes his head. "It's delicate. All I will say is that I suspect your father's assistant may be other than he seems. Have a care around him."

I nod. I've always been careful of The Wad. I don't really see how I could do more.

"What I didn't expect to find is that your father is also involved in some kind of dangerous experiment, something involving the Waste. I never expected to find that he is trying to procure the Heart of All Matter from the Manticore as part of his experiment. Why would he need something so powerful? Surely, the Waste will overwhelm the City, if he attempts to use it as our theories suggest. I didn't expect to find Nyx's daughter a witch into the bargain, a witch it appears he will try to use for his own ends."

"But it can't be true, can it? My own *father* . . ."

Memory threatens to crush me utterly. All our tea times in his office, long walks by Chimera Park, Father's approving smile whenever I showed him a particularly good sketch or mount, that day long ago when the sylphids crowded around me and he had them destroyed . . . I stare down at my shoelaces, noting absently that one is untied again before everything dissolves in runnels of silver and darkness.

"Vespa," Hal says in that same low tone he used to keep me from looking at the Sphinx. I look into his eyes. His sad smile nearly takes my breath.

"I will teach you all I can. You will learn to protect yourself with your magic. No one will harm you."

I can't say anything. I find myself absorbed in the curve of Hal's mouth, the edge of his cheek, the blue ocean of his eyes so very close to me. I don't think about it. I lean forward and kiss him, just like we used to do in Seminary when we practiced on the backs of our own hands.

But this is so different from kissing one's own hand.

For a moment, his lips yield to mine. The magic between us— for that's what it must be—stings with gentle heat. Our thoughts merge, like that day in the laboratory, only more softly. We are together in a golden field with the sun pouring down all around us. I have never been so warm, so awash in light. Sylphids dance through the air in a sparkling cloud around us, playing in our hair, whispering their sibilant love charms. Other Elementals come to the edge of the light; I see their shapes before I'm entirely blinded. I sigh his name against his lips in wonder.

He breaks the kiss almost roughly, standing back and adjusting his robes with trembling hands. The darkness of the moldy storage room eats holes through the golden world until it's gone. Piskel drifts near, shaking a finger at us. Then he sees what's between us, and his little face darkens in confusion.

"Hal?"

Hal shakes his head, almost like a dog coming out from under a waterfall. "We mustn't. I mustn't. I don't want—" He stops.

"What?" I feel cold outside his embrace, though my lips still burn with his kiss. I cross my arms over my chest. "You don't want what? To dally with a witch?"

He glowers. "It's not that. You know it's not. It's just . . . It's not safe. . . ."

We hear the footsteps simultaneously. Piskel dives between jars, dousing his light under a werehound skull.

I am not sure what to do. In perhaps the most useless gesture of all time, I gather some dusty charts into my arms, trying to pretend that I'm fetching them as the Pedant's assistant.

Two black-coated gentlemen enter. They are very well-dressed. Both of them wear a Wyvern brooch pinned on their cravats. They certainly carry themselves as if they hail from Uptown. They dip their heads and sweep their tricorns from their white wigs almost in unison.

"If you will come with us, sir," one of them says.

Hal's gaze moves from me to the two gentlemen as if he's contemplating some insane magical feat.

Then his shoulders slump. He walks toward the gentlemen like a condemned man, letting them take his arms.

"Hal?" I whisper. "What—"

They usher him past me with sidelong glances of scorn. Hal looks back at me over his shoulder. "Be safe. Be wise. Be vigilant."

And in my mind, I hear a whisper, *I will come to you when I can.*

He turns and allows them to escort him from the door without another glance. I hear their feet on the steps as the charts slide from my arms onto the floor.

Chapter 14

Syrus hadn't bothered looking up at the ghastly, shrieking things tethered to the roofs. He put his hands over his ears and ran as fast as he could, their cries following his progress until they died away at the gates of Midtown. A regiment of sentry wights tried to seal off the Midtown gate and called mechanically after him as he ducked through them. One persistent wight chased him all the way across the Night Emporium Bridge and almost to the Dials before it was reined in by its own warding field and returned to its proper post. Human sentries picked up where they left off, chasing him through Lowtown.

In the end, Syrus lost them only by cutting through the maze of alleys that led to the Lowtown Refinery. Just before dawn, he found himself alone, staring up at the glowing smokestacks, the scent of burned bone filling his aching lungs.

Stupid witch, he thought, gulping at the foul air. Why couldn't she see reason? He'd never get into Midtown again after that episode. And how was he to get her to understand if he couldn't speak to her again? What did the Manticore need her for, anyway? He realized that he didn't even know. He was just acting on orders, unsure of whether anything he hoped would come to pass as a result.

He clutched at the iron-spiked fence to hold himself up. The nevered bars stung and he pulled away. Somehow, when he did so, the bar slid off its base, leaving a gap in the fence wide enough for him to slip through. He stared. Someone had obviously been filing away at the fence in secret, trying to escape. The gap was wide enough that he might be able to slip his family through it if he could just get them out. But was the fence armed with banshee alarms like the houses in Midtown?

He looked around. No one was about. He slid his hand through the gap in the bars. No werehounds came, no alarms sounded. All he heard was the steady chugging of machinery deep within the Refinery.

He was through the fence almost before he'd decided what to do. The nevered bars stung his skin until he stood completely within the fence's perimeter. If the witch wouldn't help and if the Manticore couldn't help without her, then maybe it was time to help himself.

He had heard horrendous things about the Refineries and how the Refiners kept their secrets to themselves. Werehound guards were one thing, but the illusion mines were another. It was said that if you stepped on one, a beautiful illusion sprang up all around you that held you in thrall until guards came or the mine itself blew. And in the green-glowing darkness, one edge of tile could just as well be a trip plate as another. He'd had three cousins who'd tried to break into this Refinery on a lark once. (No one ever tried to break into the Imperial Refinery near the Tower. That would have been suicide). Only one of them had come back to tell the tale, and he hadn't made it inside before the werehounds chased him off. He was the only reason Syrus knew about the mines, but also the reason why no one had tried breaking into this Refinery again.

Still. Syrus had come through the fence. He wasn't going to allow something to catch him while he stood here like a complete ninnyhammer, as *Nainai* used to say.

There was a long, paved courtyard, and then what looked like another fence. He swallowed a raw burning in his throat. Surely if someone had managed to file this fence down, they'd done so on the inner fence too?

He knelt and picked up some gravel at the edge of the tiled courtyard, enough to help him get across to the other fence, he hoped.

He skidded the stone across the tiles. Nothing. He followed the pebble's path as best he could, wishing that he had the witch's unused powers so he could float above the ground. He gritted his teeth against the thought that he wouldn't be in this mess if she'd only see reason. He forced himself to concentrate on following the pebble instead.

Syrus was very nearly across, his muscles clenching, his mouth cotton-dry, when the stone he threw triggered a mine. A gout of green flame sprung up around it and the pebble popped as it shattered into dust.

Trembling, Syrus heaved another pebble and inched forward.

He was almost to the fence when he heard the howling.

It was worse than the banshee alarms because he knew exactly what it meant if he was caught. He scrabbled over the last of the tiles, forgetting entirely about testing them, hoping only that he would find the gap in the fence in time and that more werehounds would not be waiting on the other side.

He was oblivious to the pain of the nevered bars as he desperately rattled them, trying to find the loose one. He cursed under his breath. He could hear the hounds now, their claws clicking across the tiles as they picked their way toward him. The Refiners had made them specifically to guard their precious Refineries. No one knew how they'd done it, and no one dared breathe that it had to do with magic. The Cityfolk said such things were heresy.

Syrus didn't really know what heresy was, but he did know that at least the werehounds were behind instead of in front of him. That would have been a good thing, except that there were no loose bars in this fence. They bayed as he pulled himself up the bars. He bit his lip against the numbing pain, refusing to look behind him.

But before he could pull himself higher, teeth sank into his heel. For one swift moment, he was sure the pressure had broken his ankle. He kicked at the werehound's nose with his other foot as hard as he could. It winced, and its teeth slid out of his foot, but it still had a firm grasp on his boot heel. He dug the toe of his undamaged boot down into the other and pushed it off. Then, he pulled with all his strength, leaving the werehound with a mouthful of worn leather. He came down hard on the other side, falling to his knees in agony. He couldn't see his foot very well, except that it was slick with blood. Whether he could stand and walk on it, he had no idea.

He looked up and saw the white werehounds fighting over the scraps of his bloody boot until nothing remained. He wouldn't get out that way. And he'd have to move fast if he wanted to keep his freedom.

But how would he keep guards or hounds from following his blood trail? He tore a broad strip off the bottom of his cotton shirt beneath his coat. As best he could in the green-tinged gloom, he bound his foot and tried to stand on it.

A little voice inside warned him that now might be a damn good time to use the Architect's summoning stone. But just a little farther and he might at least be able to figure out a way to free his family and any other Tinkers enslaved by the Refiners.

He hobbled toward the door and found it locked, but then he heard rattling on the other side. He slunk back against the wall. A guard emerged, wedging the door open with a bit of wood. He investigated the hounds along the fence, shouting at them when they continued to fight.

Syrus didn't waste the opportunity. He slipped through the shadows and into the open door.

The chill was the first thing that hit him. It was face-numbingly, bone-achingly cold inside. Syrus had expected something entirely different. And the smell was strange; the chill masked it to some extent, but he could still get a whiff of something dead. Or dying.

He hurried up the stairs and along a corridor, his heel aching with the pain. Luckily, the cold floor was slowing the blood flow, but he didn't know how long he could stump along on it before he was forced to hop on one foot. He was quite sure he couldn't run very far. He palmed the summoning stone. Would an Architect really come to him if he summoned one here? Or had it all just been talk?

Another door led him to a catwalk, and he was now at the core of the freezing building. He edged along, watching carefully for guards or workers until he found a spot along the catwalk where he could sink down and take stock.

Beneath his feet, the giant Refinery boiler boomed and pulsed, steam belching occasionally out of its joints. The noise was so loud that his heart struggled against it, slipping back and forth between his own rhythm and that of the machine. Phosphorescent icicles coated the rusting pipes. Figures moved in the steam-shrouded gloom—Tinkers, he was quite certain, though he wasn't close enough to tell whether any of them were from his lost clan.

A metal door wrenched open. Refiners in their black coats and goggles pulled something through the door. Something that shone with its own light, much like the Harpy had.

He remembered how they had been waiting on the Harpy when her carriage arrived at the outer walls. He remembered what Granny Reed had said about what happened to the Elementals when they passed through that door.

He hadn't really wanted to believe her. After all, who had been inside a Refinery and escaped to tell the true tale of what went on there? It had all been rumors and hearsay and the ever-present worry about whose clan might be next.

Until now.

The thing below waved wild tentacles of light. Syrus couldn't tell what it was, except that it rolled and gasped and stared up at him with its great watery eye as if it saw him crouching there.

Some kind of water spirit, Syrus thought.

He had only a second to wonder what the Refiners were doing with it before the purpose became all too clear. He heard a metallic clang as the door to the boiler was thrown open.

Whatever the thing was—Kraken or Undine—began to wail. Its wailing was the purest, saddest music Syrus had ever heard. It sang of rivers melting toward the sea, of the great uncharted oceans and all their kingdoms. It sang of water as the blood of the world, the deep, pulsing tide without which life would cease. And it pleaded, as the Harpy had, for its own desperate release.

Syrus clenched his fists around the bars of the catwalk, waiting for someone to do something. The Refiners tugged and shouted, using thunderbusses that stunned but didn't kill it. They certainly couldn't silence the beauty or volume of its song.

Syrus was sure at least some of the Tinkers working around the perimeter would come to the beast's aid, and he was momentarily gratified when some of them moved closer until he realized that they were doing so to help the Refiners.

Together, the Tinkers and Refiners shoved and pulled the creature toward the open door. It struggled, using some of its tentacles to hold itself at the threshold.

But the Refiners kept jabbing at it with their sticks, stuffing its billowy body into the sickly-green mouth of the boiler.

Sudden understanding was as painful and sharp as the were-hound's bite. *Nainai* had been absolutely, utterly right. There were no *myth*mines to the north. This was why the Elementals were disappearing and the Culls had resumed. The Manticore was in terrible danger; her request for help was perhaps more pressing even than his own need to free his people.

As the last tentacle slipped into the boiler, Syrus couldn't bear it any longer.

"STOP!" he screamed.

A gasp of light and a surge of cold sound almost knocked his heart completely out of rhythm. Jets of steam spurted from the merrily rocking engine. Everything went still, except for bits of frozen ash that glimmered green in the gloom. The Elemental's song ceased.

All eyes turned to him. Syrus gasped, not just because of his own foolishness, but because the eyes of the Tinkers were as white and cloudy as flint. And yet they moved like those who could see, because they were running toward the catwalk stairs to catch him.

Syrus started running, but was soon reduced to hobbling by the pain in his foot. He pulled at the door he'd come through, but it was locked from the other side. And there was no going below. He glimpsed a tiny door high on the dome. If he could get there maybe he could crawl out and eventually find a way down. He swallowed and limped for it as fast as he could.

The Tinkers gained on him as he plunged up the metal stairs, but he noticed that their gait was odd. His people had a native grace, developed first from learning the forest and then often enough from learning the stealth required to survive in New London. But those who chased him stumbled along awkwardly, as if they'd forgotten how to move. Their white eyes gleamed.

Tongues of energy licked up along the metal walkways from below. The Refiners tried their best to take him down too, with their thunderbusses, though he saw that none of them were willing to climb the many flights of stairs. As he lifted himself up yet another flight toward the beckoning little door, he heard the telltale howling. They were sending werehounds after him, too.

A hand clutched at him and then another. He turned and kicked one person in the shins with his good foot, and they went down together in a tangle of limbs because his bitten foot couldn't support his weight anymore. He crawled free, punching and scratching, trying to save his little dagger as a last resort. When he'd crawled up to another landing, he loaded his dart pipe with trembling hands and blew two darts into the closest white-eyed Tinkers. At least they'd only be asleep for a little while, rather than permanently hurt.

The darts bought him some time, but not enough. The first of the werehounds was soon upon him, grabbing him by the back of the coat and shaking him away from the door. He twisted, drawing the little knife. He stabbed as he could, the werehound dancing and leaping and trying to drag him down the stairs. The last blow slid between the ribs, puncturing a lung.

The werehound loosened its grip, slumping against the rail, wheezing and whistling. It gazed up at him with a look so human that Syrus felt queasy. He watched as it shimmered and slowly shifted into the form of his cousin Raine, the one who had proudly declared she would use his earnings as her dowry. Now, she clutched her side, desperately trying to draw air into her collapsed lung.

He stared. The Refiners had taken his people and turned them into dogs. And he had killed his cousin.

He reached for her, but she gestured him away. "Go," she breathed. He could barely hear her over the howls of her kin, the throbbing of the boilers far below. She nodded toward the door.

He went, closing it just as more jaws sought the hem of his coat. He looked desperately for something to wedge the door shut, and found a bit of rusting railing to wedge through the door handle. But with enough time and strength, they'd surely break through.

A small widow's walk circled the smokestack that belched glowing smog above him. Syrus's eyes and nose streamed; the burning bone smell seared like acid now. He couldn't stay up here much longer, but as he looked over the edge, he had absolutely no idea how he would get down.

He crouched against the smokestack, out of sight of the door. The white-eyed Tinkers banged against it; the werehounds howled for his blood.

Syrus put his head in his hands. He wanted to cry. His foot throbbed with pain; his lungs hurt from trying to breathe the acrid air. But more than that, his heart hurt that his world was even crueler than Granny Reed had once said. Everyone with any sense knew that this world belonged to the Elementals and their kind. Humans were just visitors in this land. But now, all indications were that the New Londoners were much worse than he'd ever dreamed. They were not only destroying Elementals to power their infernal machines, but turning his people into monsters. How much further would they go? All he knew for sure was that he couldn't stop them by himself. And yet, something had to be done.

Thunk, ka-thunk, thunk.

His people would soon have that door open, and then what?

He pressed the heels of his hands against his eyes to stop the seeping tears. He went to the railing and looked down over the edge of the dome. The ground was lost in pre-dawn mist.

He could just make out the rusting rungs of what looked like a ladder built into the side of the dome, but he would have to free-climb for several hundred yards before he made it. He could probably do it on any average day. But with a bum foot and werehounds possibly waiting for him below . . .

He withdrew the stone from his pocket. Couldn't hurt to give it a try.

"*Et in Arcadia ego,*" he whispered.

Light shivered next to him and spat out a handsome man in a dressing gown, who stared at him disapprovingly and said, "Athena's Girdle, boy! Could you pick a less decent hour to summon a chap?"

Syrus stared. This was the same Architect who had been with the witch outside Rackham's, the one the witch had called Hal.

The Architect looked around. "I doubt there's any less decent place, either. How did you . . . ?"

He saw Syrus's injury and heard the banging at the door simultaneously. He made a sound of disgust.

"Never mind. Come here and take hold of my sleeve," he said.

Syrus hesitated. It occurred to him that he could be jumping from the kettle into the fire, as *Nainai* would say.

"Oh, dash it all, boy!" the Architect said. "I am not leading you to certain doom! Take hold of my sleeve or stay here and suffer your fate. I'm under house arrest. If my valet finds I'm gone, there'll be more than a pack of angry Refiners waiting, I promise you."

Syrus took hold of the Architect's sleeve just as the Tinkers burst through the door. Their white eyes dissolved into the green haze of the New London dawn.

Chapter 15 ━

I've never been particularly enraptured with girlish things. Give me a sylphid net, a capture box, and a sketchbook and I'm the closest to Scientific Paradise one can rationally get. Now I feel guilty for my enjoyment of those things, with Piskel riding comfortably in my pocket by day and sleeping in a little nest I've made for him in my wardrobe by night. I had to coax him out from under the werehound's skull with the mere promise of jam cake after Hal was escorted away. It wasn't easy.

Hal. I have no idea what's become of him. I tried to ask Father, but he very quickly set aside my queries. "Pedant Lumin was dismissed," he said, not looking me in the eye, when I asked one evening. "He will soon be replaced, have no fear. You should turn your mind to other matters. You have much to learn before taking up your place in the Virulen household." And with a snap of his newspaper, he'd ended the discussion. There has been no letter, no magic whisper, nothing since. Even when I ask Piskel about Hal, the sylphid only shakes his head and sighs.

So, I was actually relieved when Mistress Virulen's request came for me to join her at the Night Emporium this afternoon. We're to begin shopping for our Carnival gowns and she has promised to take me to high tea at The Menagerie, an exclusive Uptown ladies' club, afterward.

Aunt Minta won't allow me to take the trolley to the Emporium unaccompanied. "Let's hire a carriage instead. There's been trouble at the Lowtown Refinery and more predicted throughout the City," she says, as she pulls on her kid gloves. "They suspect the Architects are involved."

I try not to show any emotion at the mention of them. I have left Piskel behind in his wardrobe nest today, as his presence might be too dangerous for both of us. He must not be seen. He would be mounted for a Museum display and I would be sent to the decontamination asylum for certain if the sylphid were to be found on my person.

We wait in the foyer until the carriage is announced and then step out into another gray New London afternoon. The air is sharp with the promise of an autumn storm; green-edged gusts skirl down the cobbled street, catching our skirts and tangling them about our legs. I hold my new bonnet tight against my head as we hurry to the carriage; the driving wight blinks at us as we nearly trip over him in our haste to get inside.

"The Night Emporium," Aunt Minta calls through the speaking tube, and we're off, rocking down through the blustery streets.

We don't speak much until we're almost at my destination, and then Aunt Minta puts her hand over mine. "Now, my dear," she says, "remember what we've been working toward. Discretion and decorum—these will be of utmost value to your new mistress."

I nod. We've been through so many things over the last few days that I can scarcely remember more than pacing up and down in the parlor balancing a book on my head while Aunt Minta corrected every flaw in my posture with an old cane. "Shoulders back, bosom *out*—we want them to appreciate your attributes, my dear, not wonder whether you're even female. . . ."

And the blushing, the hideous blushing, as my corsets were laced tighter, my gowns cut lower, a bustle added to make sure "back there" was as well-proportioned as "up front." I have never thought of any of it before and now it seems it's all I can think of, because I can't bear to think about anything else.

Aunt Minta squeezes my hand, bringing me out of my gloom. The carriage has stopped at the entrance to the Night Emporium. Aunt Minta peeps out the door. "Ah, there they are." She points out the guards near the gate. A Manticore rears red on their livery. "They'll take you to Mistress Virulen." She smiles and kisses me briskly on both cheeks. "Out you go. And remember—discretion and decorum, my dear!"

I embrace Aunt Minta, inhaling one last comforting whiff of her verbena and orange blossom perfume. Then I step out with the driving wight's help, buffeted by the gusts that have chased us all the way down from High Street in Midtown. His grip is odd—one moment insubstantial, another firm as death. The Imperial Refinery just alongside the Tower makes and programs the wights to customer specifications, but the process of their making is a great trade secret. It's said only the Empress knows how the wights are truly made. I've always thought of wights as mindless automata, but knowing the truth about the Elementals has made me question everything. The driver's expressionless face flickers and then he drifts back toward the carriage as Aunt Minta calls to be returned to High Street. I'm left standing with no real answers.

The Night Emporium's violet-swirled domes bloom over me,

spanning half of the bridge that vaults the River Vaunting and joins Lowtown on the other side. Closer to Lowtown, there are gambling houses and other dens of iniquity, but on this side of the great bridge, we're still firmly in Midtown. The arched gates are lit by twinkling everlights that flash like Piskel when he's excited or happy. Various shop wights circulate through the crowd, offering samples of candied apples or eversilk ribbons. It seems a bit odd to me that a lady of such stature as Mistress Virulen would come here to seek Carnival gear, but perhaps she is bored of the Uptown boutiques and looking for a bit more local color.

I exhale a long, slow breath, approach the liveried guards, and hand them my invitation as instructed. Their appraising looks make me want to shrink back into myself, but I haven't spent the past several days walking with a book on my head for nothing. I throw my shoulders back and say, "Take me to Mistress Virulen, please," as if I'm giving a Scholar directions for finding a lecture in the labyrinthine Museum.

They turn in unison and begin shouting for the way to be cleared.

We pass through the arched gates with their fanciful lights and glimmering faces. People look askance and whisper behind their hands as I follow the guards. I wave away several wights before we enter Hooke & Smee's, a ladies' costume shop. The shop is empty of all but Mistress Virulen and a few of her retainers. She glances up from the fabric the seamstress wights have spread before her and rushes toward me across the honey-golden boards.

"Vespa," she says, taking both my hands in hers. "I may call you that, mayn't I?"

"Of course, my lady . . ." My voice doesn't even sound like my own.

"Oh, stuff and nonsense, do call me Lucy. When we're in intimate circumstances like this, of course."

I nod, then blush when I realize I've forgotten to remove my bonnet.

Her eyes travel to it just as I reach for the gray ribbons. She clucks at me. "Wherever did you find *that*?" She touches it briefly, as if it might bite her.

"I . . . that is to say . . . my aunt . . ." I stammer, as she swiftly unties it, lifts it off my head, and passes it to one of her attendants.

"We shall do much better for you by far." She turns to her attendant and says, "Get rid of that dowdy thing, will you?"

The attendant bows and hurries off to do her bidding.

Lucy turns back to me, her dark eyes intent on my face, lifting her small, porcelain-perfect hand to brush at my temperamental curls. "Yes, I can see it. You will be quite the catch when I'm done with you." She leans forward so only I can hear. "And so shall I when you're done with me, eh?" she whispers, winking.

I swallow my stammering and simply nod. I try not to follow the progress of the brand-new bonnet out to the wastebin with my eyes. Both Aunt Minta and I had thought it the height of fashion when we bought it last week. Somehow, I know better than to say that to Lucy Virulen.

"Now, come," she says, taking my arm and leading me down the long aisles toward where the seamstress wights still spread fabrics across the boards. "Let's decide our Carnival theme."

And so it begins. Eversilk, organza, batiste, yards of lace, gilt thread, and feathers of every kind and description. Lucy's eyes light up at a pile of feathers so brilliant, I'm certain they must have once belonged to a Phoenix. I turn the cerulean pinions, watch them change to fiery gold under the shop lights. Definitely Phoenix. Sickness clenches at my gut, especially when Lucy practically leaps at the feathers, crying, "Yes! These will be just the thing!"

"They're Phoenix feathers." My voice is stiff with unspoken things.

She tickles my nose with one. It smells of embers and sorrow. "Of course I know that, dear. That's why I want them. I shall attend the ball tricked out as a magnificent Phoenix before her ascent in flame. But we have been thinking too much about me. What would you like to be, Vespa?"

My gaze wanders helplessly across the sheen of fabrics and glittering thread. "Whatever you want me to be, Mistress."

"Such a cautious creature!" She smiles, running her hands along the fabrics on the table. The seamstress wight blinks, caught between holding out a swatch of peacock-blue silk and some golden braid.

"With that hair and those eyes," Lucy continues, "we must be careful. But that doesn't mean we can't still be dramatic."

I nod. Aunt Minta often says that I'm not easy to dress because of my coloring. Therefore, I mostly keep myself to shades of gray, when I worry about it at all.

Lucy wanders down the table to where dark silk sparkles with silver threads, a swatch of night sky plucked from the clean air beyond the City walls. There's a half-finished owl mask here; a few downy white feathers grace the edges of its hooked beak. I pray to the saints that no rare owl lost its feathers for this.

As if the saints would care. I'm beginning to suspect they don't care about anything.

Lucy pounces on the mask and holds it up to my face.

"Bewitching!" She smiles that infectious smile and I can't help but return it. "How would you feel about going as the Strix, my dear?"

The Strix is a flesh-eating, owl-like creature, rumored to haunt the great rivers and caverns of the East. I've seen a stuffed one in the dustier vaults of the Museum, her feathers moth-eaten, her glass eyes vacant. But I imagine that if she had been preserved alive like the Sphinx or the Grue, she would have been very fearsome indeed.

"I've always found the Strix interesting," I say carefully. I consider saying more about the one in the vault at the Museum or the Eastern expedition to capture her decades ago, but Aunt Minta has cautioned me not to speak too much of my work with Unnaturals.

"Very well, then," Lucy says. "You'll be the Strix and I shall be the Phoenix. What a glamorous pair we'll make for Carnival!"

One of the shop proprietors—Mr. Hooke, I believe—sweeps up to us, bowing and making grand flourishes with his scarlet sleeves. With little more than a pause for breath, Lucy launches into detailed instructions which Mr. Hooke copies onto a gilt-edged pad with an elaborate quill, somehow managing not to stain his lacy cuffs with everink as he writes.

Before I know it, seamstress wights are pushing me off toward the dressing rooms, where they whisk off my gown and under-garments, leaving me in little more than my stockings and a cold breeze. They take my measurements, their fingers appearing and disappearing as if I'm looking at them through running water. They pin a swath of the starry silk here and there, hold up the owl mask, nearly blinding me with the feather tips. There's a low murmuring between them not unlike language, but still unintelligible.

While I'm still blinking with shock, the measuring tapes, pins, and fabric swatches are swept away, my clothes restored to me, and I'm returned to where Lucy chats with Mr. Hooke near the coveted pile of Phoenix feathers.

I would very much like to ask Mr. Hooke how he came by them, though I fear he would be coy. Phoenixes are terribly rare, far too rare to be found in some Midtown shop. And yet, I know without a doubt that these feathers are the genuine article.

Lucy takes my arm before I can open my mouth. "Mr. Hooke, we must be off, but I trust you will produce gowns that will make us the envy of Carnival!"

"Indeed, my lady!" He bows to us with yet another flourish. "Of that you may be certain!"

Lucy turns us and I nearly stumble. "Grace, my dear," she whispers, "grace even before these rabble."

I look back at Mr. Hooke whose nose is still nearly sweeping the floorboards in his aristocratic bow.

"Rabble?"

"My darling, everyone is rabble save for me and thee," she says, patting my arm. "And you must start acting like it, lest people take advantage. I may dress you up, but you must learn to play the part."

"The part?" I repeat, like some mindless parrot.

"Well, how else will you bag a handsome duke or baron for a husband unless you act like one of us?"

Hm. Such thoughts have never occurred to me, even as I realize that these are just the sort of thoughts Father and Aunt Minta expect me to have. I think of Hal and for one moment allow myself to imagine being swept along on his arm the way Lucy is sweeping me now.

We climb into the Virulen carriage that awaits us by the gates.

The *myth*work unicorns look newly polished and the old carriage has been replaced. I remember how Hal and I helped Lucy out of the wreckage. Memories of him are everywhere, thick as the glimmering New London fog. My gut twists so hard with sadness and frustration that it's all I can do not to cry out. Perhaps Lucy's right. Perhaps it will be better if I marry some duke or baron I don't love.

"Why, my dear, you look positively wretched!" Lucy says, as she settles herself and looks over at me. Unlike the public carriages, this one is well-lit with an interior everlantern, so she can easily see my distress. I run my palm along the silver brocade walls. A tiny red Manticore rears against my fingertips. I remember how the Tinker boy was so desperate for me to find the Manticore. Somehow, that night I pulled the alarm on him seems like ages ago rather than a few weeks.

Lucy opens a compartment next to her and pulls out a bottle filled with carnelian liquid. "Perhaps you'd like a bit of cordial as a restorative before our tea?"

Two crystal tumblers clink gently together on the seat.

Her kindness undoes me.

"Yes," I sigh. "Yes, indeed."

She pours the blood-bright liquid and hands me a glass.

"To new endeavors and new friends!" she says, clinking her glass with mine.

"To new endeavors and new friends," I say, trying to sound more enthusiastic than I feel. The cordial slides down my throat smooth as a dream.

"I believe we're going to get along just smashingly," Lucy says with her wicked little smile.

I can only hope she's right.

Lucy chatters at me all the way to The Menagerie. I listen to her with one ear, but with the other I'm listening to the clatter and press of Midtown give way to the seething tranquility of Uptown. The cordial that's made her overflow with gossip has calmed me and made me interested again in my surroundings. It's said that the lords and wealthy merchants pay handsomely to have their district of New London clean and wholesome with everscrubbers and doubled security wights. I believe it. The quiet here is almost alarming; the manicured lawns of the townhouses and estates are immaculately green.

We stop where a building stands literally at the corner of several perfectly cobbled streets, its rounded cornices guarded by a grinning two-headed Amphisbaena. THE MENAGERIE is written below it in letters shaped like gilded Unnaturals, which turn to preen, swat at one another, or glare at passersby, never once forsaking the form of the word they spell.

"Come on, darling," Lucy says. "You're gawking." She draws me inside.

The club seems much bigger somehow on the inside than out. We follow faint music and laughter down a colonnade, past alcoves of women murmuring at one another behind fans or plucking plump strawberries from platters carried by drifting serving wights.

The colonnade gives way to a forest. That's the only way I can think to describe this vaulted room with its white, tree-shaped columns, the deep, mossy carpets, and the laughing stream that burbles and trips through the room. Unnaturals move here and there through sprays of flowers and curling vines, their wings trailing the ground as they bear trays of food or steaming cups of coffee.

Others pose above or peep around the columns, their eyes following the movement of the patrons as they come and go.

"What is this?" It escapes my mouth before I can keep silent.

"Why, The Menagerie, of course." Lucy spreads her hands to encompass it all and laughs. She leads me across a bridge to a little dell by the stream. We sit on mushroom ottomans before a table made from a single slice of a giant tree trunk. It's then I realize the Unnaturals are either *myth*work automata or servants done up in elaborate costume. It unnerves me deeply—the casual acceptance of this simulated reality. Here, people may pretend they are among the danger and mystery of the Unnatural world without harm or fear. Here, these Uptown ladies may even bend that unknown world to their will, forcing it to serve them cakes and tea. I shift on my mushroom, trying to ignore the *myth*work Phoenix that dips its head toward me every so often. I don't want to think about that pile of feathers that will soon grace Lucy's skirts.

Lucy's lips thin. "Do you find this disagreeable, my dear?"

"No," I try to say, but my voice comes hoarsely. I clear my throat and force a smile. "Not at all. It's just a bit of a shock."

Lucy tilts her head. Her dark eyes sparkle with unspoken questions.

"I just never imagined that ladies of such standing would prefer this kind of venue."

"And what did you think we might prefer instead?"

My gaze follows the brook. A *myth*work naiad lifts her head above the water and grins at me, then slowly retreats back into the water again. Her mechanical grin looks more like a grimace. "Well, something more in keeping with Logic and Rationality," I say carefully. "Something less . . . fanciful."

"Pish tosh." Lucy waves her hand. "It's all merely for amusement. Just wait until you see Carnival! This will seem like nothing in comparison."

At the wave of her hand, one of the servants comes over the bridge to us. She's dressed as a sylphid, with giant, luminous wings that whisper along the path behind her. Lucy orders high tea—cakes, scones, sandwiches, teas, and other assorted tidbits. The servant bows and disappears back across the bridge. Lucy digs through her purple velvet reticule until she pulls out several books, which, at first glance, would seem too large to fit in any proper reticule.

Then, I understand. Her reticule is evered to contain whatever she likes. Within reason, of course. It isn't as if she could stuff a pony in there. But she can store a number of items that wouldn't otherwise fit into such a tiny contraption, which is why generally only the gentry are allowed to possess such items. If a thief got hold of such a thing, one could only imagine the disaster!

Lucy places the books on the table and slides them gently toward me, along with another reticule, this one a claret color.

"When you look at these later in the privacy and comfort of your own rooms"—she looks at me significantly—"you'll understand why I gave them to you and what they're to be used for. I expect you to study them well. I need you well-prepared for Carnival. I'm hoping these will serve."

I slide my fingers over the covers. Tiny little shocks of magic slide under my fingernails. Unlike the dark curse manuals at Rackham's, these books tickle all the way up my arms. I restrain myself from opening them, though their delightful magic is nearly irresistible. "Where did you get them?"

Lucy half-smiles. "That hardly matters, does it? The point is that they have what I—that is to say *we*—need."

"And what is that?"

Lucy's eyes hold mine. "A love charm, my dear. Possibly several. The Heir to Grimgorn will be at Carnival and rumor has it he's seeking a wife. Or his parents are seeking one for him, at any rate. I want him to want only me, do you understand? My family needs this alliance desperately; Grimgorn is second only to the Empress in wealth and stature. They practically rule Scientia! Imagine what could be achieved there!"

I shudder to think. I slip the books into the claret reticule, thinking again of Athena's scarlet-lettered execution gown. "This is the price for saving your life?" I ask.

"For not being wise enough to hide your powers from a sharp-eyed girl." She smiles. "Would you believe I have secretly wanted to be one such as you all my life? But though I can see and feel it, the magic does not let me wield it."

"Perhaps you could be taught."

"Perhaps," she says. "But for now, you will serve, I think." She eyes me and the scarlet circle under my hand. "Won't you?"

Have I any choice in the matter? I want to ask. But I already know her answer.

"I will." I wish those two little words didn't feel like a binding spell.

Chapter 16

Syrus perched on the gold damask settee in the Architect's sitting room. The room was paneled in gilt and white, with long gold curtains that shut out New London's eternal gloom. There was a great fireplace at one end of the room, held up by kneeling marble nymphs. Above the mantel hung an ancient tapestry of a blue Wyvern in a golden field embroidered with white lilies. Syrus sensed a great weight of tradition in that tapestry, but what it meant or what it might have to do with the Architect, he was uncertain.

A book was open on the Tinker boy's lap and he glanced down at it, flipping its thick pages to and fro, though he couldn't read the City words. He was nervous as a caged hob. Though the Architect had taken good care of him since his rescue—seeing to his wounds, bringing him meals, keeping a fire going with his own hands—Syrus knew something was amiss. He was locked in the room and had been strictly warned not to even try escaping.

"Everything depends on your cooperation," the Architect had said that first morning. "If you allow curiosity to overwhelm your judgment, everything will suffer for your foolishness."

That had naturally made Syrus think of the Cull. He was sure the Guard had come because he'd helped the Harpy. And while he didn't repent of saving her, he knew he must act with the utmost care, especially after his latest misadventure at the Refinery. But that had been weeks ago. Syrus was now mostly healed of his wounds and the need to bring the witch to the Manticore was stronger than ever. He was beginning to think he might have to break free after all, despite the Architect's admonitions.

Voices rose in the next room.

Syrus crept closer, pleased that he barely limped now. He supposed if he was Cityfolk, he'd be leaving offerings at Saint Pasteur's chapel.

A man's voice—not the Architect, someone much older—was saying, "Bayne, you will do your duty or suffer the consequences."

Bayne? Syrus thought. Hadn't the witch called him Hal after the rumble in Lowtown? Who was he?

"You have another son."

A woman's high-pitched, incredulous laughter. "But he is not the eldest. You are our heir—"

"But you have another son!" The Architect's shout made him sound like he wasn't much older than Syrus. He was so much younger than the Tinker had thought when they'd first met. How could an Architect be so young? He must have worn a glamour that night they'd saved the Harpy.

And now here he was arguing with his parents like some spoiled lordling. Which in fact was exactly what it sounded like he must be. What did they want him to do? Syrus wished he could send Truffler through the door so he could listen and report back, even if his words were halting.

The voices rose and fell and then the man spoke a final declaration. "Enough. The offers are in my study. You will select the two best candidates, or you will leave this house forever. You have put us in bad enough straits with your behavior as it is, Bayne. Someone of your station masquerading as a Pedant! It's despicable and childish. Why in the name of Saint Newton would you do such a thing?"

The Architect grumbled something Syrus couldn't catch.

"You owe us this much," his mother said. "I know you will do your duty."

Silence stretched. Syrus leaned in as far as he could, trying to hear.

He nearly fell into the floor when the door was pulled open. "S-s-s-sorry, my lord," Syrus stammered.

The Architect shook his head. "If you must call me anything, call me Bayne."

"But I thought—"

"Hal Lumin was my identity at the Museum while I investigated certain matters of interest to my brethren. But Bayne is my true name. I entrust this to you now that you may know I am worthy of trust."

And because I've already heard it anyway, Syrus thought. The boy nodded.

"I suppose you heard every word."

"Well . . ."

The Architect raised a brow.

Syrus peeked out into the bedchamber beyond. He glimpsed vaulting ceilings, a monstrous carved bed with a sugar-mountain of white coverlets and pillows before Bayne snapped the door shut.

"Whatever you may have heard, you can't imagine the full truth of it," the Architect said.

"Let me guess. Spoiled lordling gets bored and decides to slum it, but his parents catch him at it and try to force him into marriage, dashing all his low-class fun. That about the long and short of it?" Syrus asked.

Bayne scowled. "Only part of it."

"Which part?"

"The last bit. Minus the low-class fun," Bayne said.

"So, who's the lucky girl?" Syrus asked.

The Architect paced over to the window, twitching back the curtain and looking out. "I don't know yet."

"Why not shack up with the witch? You being two birds of a feather and all."

"You can't possibly understand what you're suggesting," Bayne said. "It would be too dangerous for her and me, especially now that my parents have discovered at least part of my secret."

"But—"

"Enough. It cannot be. They would not look favorably upon her, especially since I met her at the Museum where I was . . . slumming, as you put it. The only way to preserve my involvement with the Architects is to do what my parents say. The secret of my magic must remain hidden at all costs."

He locked eyes with the boy. Syrus nodded in agreement, hoping that would lessen the intensity of the Architect's regard.

The tension passed as Bayne's gaze dropped to Syrus's foot. "How is your wound?"

"It'll do," Syrus said. "I won't be dancing any jigs at the gin palace tonight, but it'll do."

Bayne chuckled. "Is that something you normally do?"

"Oh, every now and then."

Bayne gestured to the settee nearest the fire. "Let me see."

The boy obeyed. Curious as he was, he didn't want to rouse the man's ire any further. He'd seen what Bayne had done to that Refiner back when they freed the Harpy.

Despite the tautness in his shoulders, Bayne unwrapped Syrus's bindings gently enough. "I'm no physick, but I believe you're healed, boy. Have you noticed anything else odd?"

Syrus cocked his head.

"Any odd sensations? Or . . . ?"

"Am I wanting to bay at the moon and gnaw on babies' leg-bones, you mean?"

Bayne frowned. He rewrapped the bandage in silence.

"No," Syrus said. "I'm really fine. No need to take me out behind the train and make me a head shorter." He tried not to think of his cousin as she'd slumped against the iron railing in the Refinery, trying to breathe with her punctured lung. But her image hung there behind his eyes. It might be there forever.

"I wasn't suggesting . . ." the Architect began.

Syrus forced himself to smile. A small smile tugged at Bayne's lips when he realized Syrus was joking.

Bayne sat back on his heels, the buckles on his shoes shining in the firelight. The air was close and still, except for the fire's murmur. "I've been thinking on what you saw. And I believe that we should alert my brethren regarding it."

Syrus nodded. He hoped that Bayne and the Architects would help him break into the Lowtown Refinery again and free his people. Maybe they'd even convince the witch to help before they took her to the Manticore.

"And what about the witch?"

Bayne froze. For a moment, naked despair clouded his eyes until he closed them. "She will soon be at Virulen," he said, standing and putting his back to Syrus. "We can find her there and persuade her to go to the Manticore after we meet with the Architects."

There seemed to be no brooking his argument. He was resolute.

"All right," Syrus said, despite a gnawing sense of misgiving. The Manticore had said he must bring a witch to free both the Elementals and his own people. But he had grown tired of waiting and hoping that the witch would comply.

Bayne must have seen his unease, for he returned from the fire and laid a hand on Syrus's shoulder. "I understand your impatience. We'll go tonight. It'll be dangerous and difficult because of . . . certain matters, but never you mind. I'll sort all that out. Just rest and be ready."

"All right," Syrus said. He would give the Architect this one chance, but if all went awry, Bayne's key would be in his pocket before dawn.

Syrus had fallen asleep waiting, but when the door clicked he was wide awake. The fire had burned into embers and the book Syrus had been idling through for days—maps of Old London—had slid to the floor.

Bayne slipped into the room, holding a candle rather than the everlantern most Cityfolk would have used. "Come," he whispered.

Syrus followed past the hulking bed and a massive wardrobe that threatened to trip him in the dark.

"They've nevered the door against my leaving, but not against a skilled lockpick." Bayne's smile was ghoulish in the flickering candlelight. He handed Syrus the tools of his trade.

The boy rolled his eyes and bent to the task, hoping it wouldn't be like the Harpy's cage. His wrists still smarted just thinking of those little iron hands grasping them.

As the tumblers turned, there was a spark and a fizz. One jolt whizzed into Syrus's thumb. He shook his hand, cursing.

Bayne watched him expectantly. "Once the lock is sprung, I can disable the rest." Syrus sighed and turned back to the work.

At last, the door opened. Bayne whispered something and Syrus saw a faint web stretched between the doorposts dissolve into glimmering nothingness.

The house was vast and echoing; Syrus felt swallowed by it. They crept through everlit halls hung with dour portraits and mounts of things both Elemental and not. Down a curving, creaking staircase, back along another hall, through the silent kitchen with its spit-boy snoring by the hearth, and to yet another door Syrus was forced to pick open. Then along a cobbled corridor, through a garden and a courtyard to an iron side gate that sizzled with warding magic.

"A moment," Bayne said. He stretched his palms toward the gate. Then he paused, looking over at Syrus. "Can you run if required?" he asked, glancing down at Syrus's foot.

Syrus nodded, grinning.

The next thing he knew, Bayne seized him by the sleeve and *pulled* him. One moment, they were on one side of the fence, the next they were on the other, running madly through the deserted Uptown street while a banshee alarm wailed behind them. The Empress's Tower reared so very close on its hill that Syrus thought he could almost see faces looking out at him from the windows. The Imperial Refinery coughed green smoke just beyond it.

"Couldn't avoid that one, I'm afraid!" Bayne shouted. He grabbed the boy's sleeve again and yanked him through space and darkness and wailing alarms to stand before the maw of a cave on the River Vaunting.

Syrus put his hands to his head to stop everything from spinning. "Think you could warn me first?" he gasped.

Bayne chuckled. "That was a bit rough. The danger and suddenness and all that. Didn't have much time to prepare."

"Why couldn't we have just done that from your room to here like we did the other night?" Syrus asked. His temples throbbed.

"A little more difficult getting out than getting in. And the summoning stones . . . well . . . their magic is older and more refined than what little we've managed to learn in these dark days. The stone draws me to it; I can't help but go to it. But on my own, without a witch. . . *Pffffft.*" He gestured lamely and half-smiled.

"Without a witch? She makes you stronger?" Syrus asked.

"Indeed," Bayne said. "Which is why we've been hoping one would arise for so very long. Without her, we're rather like a hive of drones without a queen bee. Everything depends on her."

Syrus nodded, though he wasn't exactly sure about all this talk of drones and bees and whatnot. Sounded like something *Nainai* would've understood much better than he did.

"But don't tell her I said so," Bayne added suddenly. "Wouldn't want her to get a swelled head."

"I think you're too late to prevent that," Syrus said.

Bayne chuckled. "She's a saucy thing, is she not?"

"Minxish is more what I'd say," Syrus muttered. He glanced at the Architect. Shadows hid most of his face, but the City lights from far above tricked out a glimmer of something that chased the amusement from his expression. That hardness, whatever it was, wherever it came from, returned.

Bayne looked up at the wavering everlights of the Night Emporium and the phantasmagoric smoke of the Refineries. "We'd best get moving," he said. "Getting back into my family's house won't be easy."

The stench of the river mud and City offal slimed the back of Syrus's throat. He coughed as they climbed over detritus and battered rock. He had been down on the shores of Lowtown, where the mudlarks scavenged the refuse caught in the river bend. But he'd never been this far—never had he imagined anything like this existed within the walls of New London. Crumbling columns and pediments carved with weathered faces loomed over them. Even higher, armless dancers, faceless gods, and curving tails of Elementals wormed through the cliff face.

"What is this place?" Syrus whispered.

"It was a city once, a temple of learning where men came in peace to treat with the Elementals. Now it's a ruin. It's also a convenient hiding place. No one comes here for fear of what may lurk, even though the Museum up above is built on the old city's bones," Bayne said.

The Architect opened his palm and a light sprang into it, a pure, living flame, so very different than the sickly green everlanterns all the Cityfolk used. Syrus followed him under the shattered eaves and through the labyrinth of fallen ceilings and vanished doors, while the river's muttering echoed in the cavern ceiling overhead. Things looked at him out of the shadows—little nyxes or water sprites or other things he couldn't guess in the darkness. Syrus missed Truffler fiercely and wondered if he would ever see the hob again.

Bayne didn't seem to notice the Elementals, but was concentrating on a path only he could discern. At the center of a soaring cavern, a great stair spiraled down from the roof. Old rusting pipes crisscrossed here and there from other tunnels and up along the staircase. There was a sound far below—a whooshing noise that reminded Syrus of the Refinery bellows breathing in and out, fueling the furnace into which the Refiners had thrust the poor Elemental.

"What's down there?" he asked.

Bayne looked back at him. "Down there? The Lowtown Refinery pipes join up with the Museum fittings in the roof. Just steam, most likely. Come on."

Syrus followed him around the pit; there was a landing where the sound was particularly loud. A tunnel carved roughly in the living rock plunged off to the left, gated by rusting bars that rattled with the noise.

Syrus stopped and listened. There was a hitch and then a drawn-out snore. No *myth*-powered machine made a noise like that.

"It sounds like a sleeping animal," Syrus said.

Bayne listened. "Maybe all those stories about the Beast in the Well are true," he chuckled.

"The Beast in the Well?"

"It's said that when Tesla's Grand Experiment landed our ancestors here on the river bank, they encountered a temple enclosing a deep well. And that if you looked into it, it would look back at you. Some people think the Well ended up underneath the Museum, but no one really knows. I imagine everyone was surprised enough to be here, much less to have buildings showing up at random for several days afterward."

"I suppose," Syrus said. He remembered Granny Reed's story about Tianlong the night she'd died. Could that be the same thing? The Beast whose Heart had been stolen and given to the New Londoner's Saint Tesla? He didn't know much about how the New Londoners had gotten here. His people had already been coming here off and on for as long as their tales told. Granny Reed had said that when the Cityfolk showed up, they'd somehow shut the gate behind them so no one could enter or leave again. And that was why everything was in such a terrible mess.

He wished there was some way to open the gate up again and shove all of New London through it.

"Or," Bayne said, "it could be the Grue that got loose a couple years ago. I heard no one ever found him, either."

Bayne half-grinned, but Syrus blanched. A Grue loose in the Museum? He'd heard tales of them from some of his kin who used to wander in the southlands. There were legends of the Grue that were deeply unpleasant. He shivered and drew the collar of his jacket up a bit more around his neck.

Bayne led Syrus at last to another rusting gate set into the living rock. The gate swung loosely on its hinges and its grating whine subsumed the well's sighs. Beyond the gate, a hall tunneled back into the rock. The hairs stood up along Syrus's arms. Everything about this corridor warned him away.

Bayne frowned. "Something is wrong."

Syrus nodded. It didn't take an Architect to figure that out.

"Stay close," Bayne said. Syrus patted his pockets and realized all his weapons had been removed. Bayne drew a familiar knife and handed it to him. "I would guess this is what you're missing. Just don't stab me in the back, eh?"

"Not until you get me out of here, at least," Syrus said. The Architect looked back at him with a raised brow. Then, he blew the flame from his hand. It danced off into the air, moving before them like a will-o'-the-wisp.

They followed it down the corridor into a silence so deep Syrus's ears buzzed with it. They came to a battered door. Bayne passed his hand over it, as if to remove an illusion, but there was no magic. The door remained as it was.

"No," he whispered.

He pushed past the shattered wood, the flame bursting into a great ball of light in a cavernous room. The Architect stood there for long, silent moments. His shoulders slumped and he put his face in his hands.

Syrus came to stand beside him, and it took every ounce of his will not to scream.

The Architects were dead.

They sprawled obscenely around a long, scarred table. Syrus walked toward it, but he wasn't seeing this room. He was walking again into the train car with its empty hands and unseeing eyes.

"They're all dead. All of them. I'm the only one left in all the Empire," Bayne whispered.

Then Bayne saw the white eyes of one of the Architects. "They're all like the man who leaped in front of the trolley."

"The trolley?"

As Bayne wandered around the table, gently closing his fellow Architects' eyes, he related the story of how the man had run out into the square and been crushed, how he and Vespa had narrowly managed to save Lucy Virulen in the process. "There is foul magic at work here," Bayne said. "Magic such as I've never seen before."

"And just how much have you seen?" Syrus asked, trying and failing to look away from what Bayne was doing. He was still incredulous of the man's youth. And now that he had some inkling of his high birth, he was even more so.

"These men were my teachers. They taught me everything they could, everything we knew from these Archives. They asked me to come here to investigate one of our order who had gone renegade and was working at the Museum. I never thought it would end like this," Bayne said, gesturing around the expansive room.

The movement of his fingers unfettered Syrus's gaze. The room was a shambles—broken glass and fixtures, slashed chairs, books and magical items pulled from their cases and dashed on the floor. Even books from shelves high overhead had been scattered; their pages drifted here and there like spiritless wings.

"He must have come while they were at Council and taken them by surprise. All that knowledge, all our efforts and plans—gone," he whispered. His voice shook so hard Syrus feared he was on the verge of tears.

"Who did it?" Syrus asked.

Bayne shook his head, unable to speak as he went from body to body, gently closing their eyes.

Syrus moved away. He would cry himself if he looked at those old men a moment longer. They reminded him far too much of his poor dear *Nainai*.

"Well, whoever he was, he definitely was looking for something," Syrus said, at last, noting all the scattered books. "But how would you ever know if anything was missing?"

Bayne finished his ministrations to the dead and began helping Syrus look around the room.

"There's just so much destruction, I can't tell," Bayne said. "It might take days to sort this out, and we don't have that."

Then they saw it—a book on the table, large and flat-stitched across the spine. Its cover was slashed and pages had been torn out of it. It was filled with schematics, all written in the old language of Syrus's people. Syrus read a few entries about immortality elixirs and opening of heavenly gates before he said, "This . . . this must be what he's trying to do."

Bayne bent over his shoulder. "What? You can read that scribbling?"

Syrus frowned at him. "It's not scribbling. It's the sacred language of my people. See here . . . these words mean 'eternal life.' And this one is about a heavenly gate. . . ."

Bayne's gaze followed Syrus's fingers along the characters beside the torn schematic.

"A machine to return to the World Before," Bayne said softly. "Is that what Malcolm Nyx and Charles Waddingly are building?"

"Malcolm Nyx and Charles Waddingly?" Syrus asked, frowning. He recognized the first man's surname as belonging to the witch, but couldn't place the other.

"Vespa's father and his assistant, Charles. I was shadowing Charles on the suspicion that he may have been the rogue warlock who left our order several months ago. But he was so different from what he had been and his magic so slippery that his true identity has been nearly impossible to uncover. This Machine must be part of the reason for his defection, if he is indeed the one I seek."

"Well, he must be very frustrated that he can't quite understand how to make it," Syrus said.

Bayne said, "That must be why Nyx and Charles collected the Waste. He's using it as a power source. But why would he want to risk destroying everything? He knows how deadly the Waste is, especially if he's one of us!" He looked back at the schematic. "It looks like he needs a catalyst, too. Could that be why he's seeking the Heart?"

A hollow clapping sound echoed through the dome. Syrus and Bayne both turned as a young man stepped from a shadowed alcove. Under an old-fashioned cloak, the man wore a motley doublet and hose, like an actor just come from playing the Fool on stage, or someone preemptively dressed for Carnival.

Syrus recognized the young man then—the bearded fellow who had been in Rackham's hexshop the day Syrus had sold the toad for information.

"Congratulations," he said. "You've gotten it all wrong once again."

"Bennon," Bayne said. "Or should I call you Charles?"

Bennon's visage sloughed off. A tall, thin young man with weasel-brown eyes regarded him. "Ha. A shame you never paid better attention. You always did underestimate me, Bayne."

"How could I underestimate what apparently wasn't even worth my regard?" Bayne said.

Syrus didn't recognize him at first, but then he remembered. Charles had been the young man in the carriage with Vespa and her father, the one Syrus had darted at the outset of the clan raid. He didn't seem quite human—something about the way he moved, the way his eyes flitted here and there. There were many Elementals who could take human shape, and Syrus had been taught the signs of such shapeshifting, but none of them were present here.

Still, Syrus sensed that things were not at all right with this Waddingly fellow.

Charles laughed.

"Enough!" Bayne said. "What do you want? Why did you kill all our brethren?"

Charles withdrew something from under his cloak—the ugly dark jar Syrus had seen on Rackham's counter. "It was all merely an experiment. As everything is, really. I wanted to test whether this little soul jar worked. One always needs to test the merchandise, yes?"

"Bayne . . ." Syrus said. He started to back away, but Bayne put a reassuring hand on his shoulder.

"Have no fear," Bayne said.

"Wrong again!" Charles laughed. "Do you know why?"

"I feel sure you'll tell me," Bayne said.

"Because," Charles said, as he walked closer, "I'm going to take your souls now. And once the witch gets me the Heart, then I'll have everything I need to power a second Etheric Engine to rival Tesla's—one that will open the gates which have been closed for far too long."

"So, that's it, then?" Bayne said. "You're just doing this to take a jaunt to historic Old London? I just want to be sure I know whom to blame when this Grand Experiment fails and we all die miserably!"

"It can't fail!" Charles said, spitting in fury. Some of his spittle hit the table and pitted the surface. "It will open the Gate!"

Definitely not human.

"Bayne, I really think we should—" Syrus said again.

But Bayne pressed onward. "You do understand that the Waste is not to be trifled with? Even the most skilled Architect, even a group of us with a full-fledged witch at our head, would never be able to handle it! We discovered that at Euclidea when we tried to build a gate back to the Old World the first time! Nyx should know better. And so should you."

"Such a weak-minded fool!" Charles said. "Your lack of imagination truly dazzles me. Though I must admit that your going undercover as a lowly Pedant to find me did rather surprise me. I didn't think a lord would stoop to such a thing!"

"I did stoop, much good has it done me. And them," Bayne gestured toward the fallen Architects.

Charles laughed. "Yes, well. I suppose there are those with imaginations less clever than yours. Or were, I should say. And I suppose those who lack imagination have their uses. Nyx, for example. He thinks he's building a new Engine to power the Refineries; he has no idea what's going on. He does as I bid. As for me, I don't care what happens with the Waste after I'm gone. It can swallow this world whole for all I care. And good riddance!"

"But this world is the seat of your power! How can you possibly—"

"I've no time to debate Magical Philosophy!" Charles snarled. "That Well of Power theory is just that—a theory. No one knows if it's true. Now into the jar you go! I have a witch to catch. And she is a wily one, isn't she?" The renegade warlock smirked.

"If you so much as lay a finger on her . . ." Bayne growled.

"*Bayne,*" Syrus pleaded. He began backing away.

"What?" Bayne said. He turned toward Syrus in a feint, raising his other hand. The glowing ball of light that had been hovering in the ceiling streaked toward Charles like a comet.

Charles barely lifted a finger. The ball dissipated in hisses and sparks that arced around him like the coils of Saint Tesla's fabled Engine.

"By Athena," Bayne breathed.

Syrus cursed.

"Surely that's not the extent of your power, my lord," Charles purred. He set the jar on the table as he moved toward them. His hands shone with ghastly light.

"Run, Syrus!" Bayne said. He raised his hands.

"But—"

"Run, I said!" the Architect shouted.

Lightning coruscated throughout the chamber. Syrus dove between the legs of dead Architects and under the scarred table as blazing tentacles of light threatened to choke him. He skidded out from under the table and ran, cursing that he was without darts, that Bayne was such a noble fool, that this Charles—whatever he was—would most likely kill everyone.

He skirted the pit in the darkness with only the glimmer of phosphorescent moss and the occasional terrible lashing of light to guide him. He had no idea what he would do. There was no one to help him, no one to whom he could appeal. There was only himself and the stones at his feet. He bent to pick up a few, surprised by tears of rage. This helplessness had preyed upon him in the train car and again in the Refinery. He'd believed that with Bayne's help, he'd never be powerless again. He'd been wrong.

He knew one thing, though. He couldn't just leave. He had to help however he could. This monster could not be allowed to unleash the Waste or destroy the Manticore to do it. As he stood, stones clicking in his pocket, he realized that not all of the glow above him came from moss. Dozens of eyes watched him from various crevices—the little Elementals he'd seen here and there when they'd first entered the old temple.

He whispered words of friendship in the sacred language. *"Wode pengyo. Heping."* My friends. Peace.

Some of them crept closer. They were listening.

"I beg you, please give us aid," Syrus said.

The nearest pair of eyes materialized into a cave sprite. He hung upside down by his toes like a bat, his glowing eyes nearly level with Syrus's.

"And what will you give in return, child of the Guest People?" the sprite asked.

"Whatever you ask, if you will only help us dispose of this treacherous warlock."

A shout presaged another ball of light blasting down the tunnel.

Another sprite crawled closer to perch near his fellow. "Whatever we ask, eh?"

Then a third voice came, from behind a shattered cornice near Syrus's leg. "But the Law says we must not harm our kin. We cannot interfere."

A debate began in a language of clicks and trills that Syrus didn't know. Syrus listened for several seconds before he interrupted. "Please! We need your aid. You know what happened here. No matter what this warlock may be, if he goes free, death will come to your people many times over, I promise you. He's planning to unleash the Waste!"

More conferring.

Then, one said, "The Law says that Elemental may not harm Elemental, but it does not say we cannot distract or halt his progess."

"Yes."

"Yes."

"Yes."

Many more agreed, little heads popping up from everywhere, sprites surrounding Syrus with their lantern-eyes. "We will help if you will one day help us in return."

Syrus spoke the ritual words of agreement.

"Well-mannered, that one," the first cave sprite said.

"He'll go far, I'm sure."

"Didn't you see his face? Of course he will!"

Syrus smiled as they bubbled ahead of him down the tunnel. They reminded him strongly of his clan, happily babbling about this and that, but they also made him wonder if Truffler was more articulate than he had ever let on.

The one Syrus had come to identify as the leader crept down the tunnel wall until he was close to Syrus's ear. "You go in first with your stones and then we will do the rest," he whispered. "You can spirit the poor Architect away yourself, yes?"

Syrus nodded.

"Well, then. Remember our bargain."

"Wo shi." I will.

Syrus looked around the broken door. Bayne was crouched under a failing shield he'd made against Charles's incessant magic. More and more etheric energy was leaking through the glowing bubble, causing the Architect to cry out every so often in pain. Charles grinned and pressed harder.

Syrus snuck closer, wishing that he at least had a sling. He could hear Bayne whispering, gasping out the words that would hold his shield until they couldn't.

Syrus aimed. His first pebble hit. Charles started; the eruptions of deadly flame weakened. Syrus pressed his advantage, and hurled several pebbles in rapid succession.

Charles whirled. "You are as much of a fool as this one, I see!" There was a dark ring around his mouth. "Don't think I've forgotten that dart of yours, boy. You will pay for that now."

Faster than lightning could fly from Charles's fingertips, the cave sprites whirled around him, like a tornado of bats. Charles shouted at them, things that Syrus couldn't quite understand. He feared for a moment the sprites wouldn't be able to withstand whatever dark Elemental walked in the warlock's skin. Several of them disappeared with shrieks under the whirlwind; Syrus guessed Charles had caught those and destroyed them, despite the Law. But the rest held firm. They pushed and pulled him toward the door and out into the hall, winding around him like thread on a drop spindle.

Syrus rushed to Bayne, who was still chanting feverishly, his arms trembling, eyes closed.

"Bayne," Syrus said. "Bayne!"

The chanting stopped. Bayne's eyes opened. His arms fell to his sides, but his hands didn't cease shaking. His fingers were black, as if scorched by gunpowder.

"We've got to go! Can you get us out of here? I don't know how long the sprites can hold him!"

"I can't travel through this much rock. Not now. Just . . . get me outside," Bayne whispered.

Syrus helped him rise, though the full weight of the Architect on his slender frame nearly toppled him. Together, they limped out into the hall, skirting the pit. Syrus listened for the sprites, but all he heard was Charles's incoherent shouting from somewhere deep in the pit. Then there was a great rumble, almost like a snort. The entire cavern shook with it.

"Maybe the Beast ate him," Syrus said. He wished it were so, despite what the sprites had said about the Law of their kind.

"We can only hope," Bayne said, trying to hobble faster.

When they finally cleared the temple mouth, Bayne removed his arm from Syrus's shoulders and draped himself inelegantly over a boulder.

Syrus waited for only a moment, looking back toward the dark entrance. He shifted from foot to foot before he finally opened his mouth.

Bayne held up his hand. "Take my sleeve."

Syrus grasped his magic-stained lace cuff.

And then everything—heart, breath, blood, thought—was ripped apart.

Chapter 17

Two days after tea at The Menagerie a package arrives. I tear it open with unladylike zeal, praying to Mother Curie (though I know he wouldn't like it) that it's a gift, a letter, *something* from Hal.

I hide my face from Aunt Minta when I discover two books, two very unmagical books, sent from the Chatelaine of Virulen Manor to "aid in schooling the Mistress's new Companion." Aunt Minta picks up both *The Handbook of Excellent Service* and *A Primer for Ladies' Companions Throughout the Realm and Beyond*, hugging them to her bosom as if they were the most precious of articles.

Then she drops them and embraces me until I'm gasping.

"I know I've said it so many times, my dear, but I'm so proud of you!" she whispers into my ear. I think my face must be turning blue from suffocation.

The carriage comes not long after the books. Aunt Minta is as tearful and fluttery over my departure as if I'm about to be wed. Father went to the Museum before daybreak, trying to beat the Carnival traffic, he'd said. With all the fluttering about, I've not once had a chance to speak to him about the Museum, and I admit after his forbidding air regarding Hal that I was afraid to try. I have a very disheartening feeling that Father wouldn't tell me the truth about him anyway.

"Oh, my darling, have a wonderful time," Aunt Minta keeps saying. "Write to us as soon as you can!"

I nod, sure if I open my mouth, I'll vomit. I stare over Aunt Minta's shoulder at the painting of Athena as my aunt squeezes all my remaining breath out of me in a last embrace. Looking at the princess this time, I see something different. Athena's hand gleams faintly, as mine does when I do magic. I wonder how she learned and what she learned and why she allowed herself to be executed. Why did she not use her power to free herself? Perhaps there was more to it than anyone knows. I'm beginning to believe that of pretty much everything.

Aunt Minta finally releases me and shoos me toward the *myth*-work carriage outside. I climb in, pretending I don't see all the neighbors peering out from behind their curtains or even watching from their covered porches. Our servants stand along the walkway, the maids dabbing their eyes with their aprons and the gardener removing his cap as I pass. I feel chagrined. I'm quite certain I've never paid this much attention to them.

The driving wight takes my carpet bag and helps me into the cavernous carriage. I sit straight against the red damask seats, clutching the reticule (in which Piskel snores among the magic books) and listening as my trunk is fastened behind. The carriage doesn't sink as the driving wight climbs back into the box; wights are evidently weightless. Soon the unicorns march down the cobbled avenue.

For a blinding flash of a moment, I consider leaping out of the carriage and running away. But to where?

I sink back into the cushions. Surely I am the only girl to face these kinds of problems. And then I think of Athena and realize that I am not.

The carriage pulls into the Virulen's Uptown villa just in time to avoid the first of many evening Carnival parades. A jostling, brightly-festooned crowd follows Saint Galileo from his chapel past all the Great Families' houses to Uptown Square where the saints are housed during Carnival Week. Floats depicting the planets and stars are followed by acrobats in gold and silver trailing banners like streaking comets.

I don't have more than a moment to watch, though, because a bevy of servants whisk me away from the carriage and up into the house. They pull me through the foyer and up the stairs before I can do much more than wonder how vast Virulen Manor must be, if this echoing cavern is really just the family's in-town residence. The maids direct me to a chamber where they very efficiently begin stripping my clothes from me against my protests. Soon, I'm stuffed naked and shivering into a bronze tub, scrubbed until I think my skin will fall off, and then oiled until my eyes sting with the scent of orange blossom.

When they get me into chemise and corset and the hair iron is hot, the door bursts open. Mistress Lucy is in an emerald eversilk dressing gown, her hair up in curling papers, her face devoid of cosmetics. It's a bit startling, but her curving smile snaps me out of gaping at her dishabille.

The maids make me face forward again. Lucy dismisses them with a wave of her hand.

"Tonight's the night, my little witch," she says, putting her hands on my shoulders. She grins at me in the mirror.

I nod, because I don't know what else to say.

"Master Grimgorn will be there, and you must ensure his favor." She squeezes my shoulders. Her cold hands feel a bit like claws.

My mind and heart race each other. I'm not even fully laced into my corset and my breath is so short I feel like I might faint. *The Guide* mentioned a charm for increasing affection, but many of the ingredients were impossible to procure, especially with Aunt Minta watching me like a hawk wherever we went. I'll just have to make substitutions and hope for the best. This notion does not please me at all.

There's a large vase of hothouse roses on the dressing table. I pull one free and sift through the petals until I find a perfectly undamaged one.

"What are you doing?" she asks.

"What you just asked me to do." I force a smile at her in the mirror.

I hold up the petal in my palm. "Kiss this," I say, "and this will act as a seal on the charm to win his affections."

The warm velvet of her lips presses my palm. A tiny spark shivers up my wrist. She looks at me quizzically.

"Place this in the palm of your left glove. It'll work. You'll see." I entrust the rose petal to her with far more confidence than I actually feel. I've no idea whether what I'm doing is right or not. What if it doesn't work? Will she have me sent to the Waste on principle?

"It had better," she says.

She flounces back to her own rooms without further comment, and the maids descend again upon my hair. I look into my own eyes and I don't like the haunted look I see there.

Hours later, steamed, plucked, scented, coiffed, and trussed like some sort of high-class chicken, I critique myself in the mirror. The maids fuss here and there over a stray curl or a ribboned sleeve, but I'm as perfect as they can make me. I hardly recognize myself. My hair glitters with everpowder and is so tall I've no idea how I'll get through the door. I feel guilty and repulsed to know that sylphid bones have been dusted all over my hair, but there's not much to be done about it. I hope Piskel will forgive me.

Silver feathers swirl across my silk skirts. The Strix mask we saw in the shop is finished, festooned with onyxes and owl feathers. Part of me feels ridiculous, but another part cannot believe that this person I see is truly me. I hardly recognize myself in this deadly dangerous gown with its beguiling mask. Would anyone else? Would Hal? I lift my chin. He hasn't seen fit to contact me. So much for his reassurance that he would come find me. Perhaps tonight I will meet my future husband.

I don't like the hitch in my heart as I think of that possibility.

The maids leave me at the foot of the staircase, and I'm looking around bemusedly at the gold-framed portraits of Virulens gone by when I hear a flutter at the top of the stairs. Lucy comes down and her Phoenix-feather gown is so blue it nearly blinds me.

"I must say," Lucy says, "you turned out even more handsomely than I hoped."

Unsure what else to do, I curtsy deeply.

"Oh, stop that, you ninny. You do that to the other duchesses, not to me."

"Yes, my lady." I smile.

Lucy wags a gold-gloved finger at me. "Come along then, my dear Strix!"

Lucy takes my arm and draws me toward the waiting carriage.

"Lord Virulen . . ." I say, looking back over her shoulder as if the house will disgorge him at any moment. I've never actually seen him, though I've heard he's quite hideous. He barely survived an attack from the Manticore while hunting in his youth. He killed the Manticore's offspring, but lost his hand and his handsomeness in the process, if rumors are true.

"Is already at the Hall with the other Lords, drunk as a hoot owl, like as not," Lucy says. That wicked smile plays about her lips, the one I both like and dread.

"Ah."

The carriage pushes through the mad crowd. Lucy slides her fan case to the edge of the curtain so she can peer out. "Oh my," she says, covering her mouth with her silk-gloved hand.

"Here, look." She nods toward my end of the curtain, and I pull it away so I can peek out too.

A few Carnival revelers have gotten early into the wine, it seems. Or else they had only imagined putting on their party clothes. They dance down the streets naked, as unconcerned as if no one is watching.

Lucy laughs at my expression.

"I don't suppose you've seen the Uptown version of Carnival before, have you?" she asks. "It can get rather wild."

"Can't say as I have," I say, dropping the curtain. "Nor that I want to, if that's the way it's going to be."

Lucy laughs again and taps my knee with her fan case. "I can see we have much work to do with you."

I'm afraid to know exactly what kind of work she's talking about.

"Is this your first Ball? You almost looked too young to be out in Society that day we met."

"Not quite my first." I don't want to recount last summer's horrid Pre-Debutante Ball. I managed to rip my dress by catching it under a chair leg to my shame and Aunt Minta's everlasting horror.

"This, I'm sure, will be the most interesting one you've attended yet. I'm not sure what Carnival will be like in the Tower; honestly the Imperial Balls tend to be terribly dull. And the clocks that woman has all over the palace! She's insanely obsessed with them."

"Clocks?"

"Yes, it's quite bizarre. Clocks. Everywhere. Usually all telling the wrong time. And the ticking!" Lucy rolls her eyes. She snaps open her fan and her bergamot perfume fills my nose.

"I've never been."

Lucy rolls her eyes again. "Believe me, it will be quite the education! Just pray to the saints that the Empress doesn't decide to hold every function in the Tower from here on out!"

The wild Carnival revelers dance everywhere, making offerings to the saints where their effigies sit in state at the Uptown Square. An audience crowds around a group of performers as they act out the Pageant of Saint Newton and the Apple, but the carriage turns up Tower Hill before I can see the apple actually hit the saint on the head.

The way up is steep and so narrow that only one carriage can pass at a time. The city falls away behind us. Only the Imperial Refinery's yellowish-green plumes of smoke are visible above the dense thorn hedge that chokes the Hill.

Finally, we top the Hill and come under the Tower's great battlements. A contingent of Raven Guards lines the courtyard, watching silently as we disembark and are shown toward the Tower's Grand Entrance. Their cousins, the tower ravens, perch all along the rooftops, watching them with eyes as eerily empty and yet dangerously alert as the Guards'. The stench of moldering guano almost overpowers me; the walls of the inner buildings are streaked white with it.

My lungs compress, as if filled with dark, damp feathers.

"Can you feel them?" Lucy says. "The nullwards?"

I nod and hurry her inside. *Yes.* I will soon faint if I don't stop feeling it. Now that I know I'm a witch, I know why nullwards make me feel so odd.

We join a long line of partygoers being searched by the Guard and security wights for weapons. Although the women aren't searched as thoroughly as the men, even we don't escape scrutiny. When one Guard attempts to lift Lucy's skirts with a stick to see if she's hidden anything under her voluminous blue layers, she fluffs them at him like an offended ostrich and takes my arm in hers.

"Really! Of all the nerve!" she says loudly enough for everyone to hear.

The Raven Guard steps back, expressionless as always. But his head swings to follow us, the white membrane shuttering his flat eyes in a way that makes me shiver.

Lucy is about to say more, but I drag her along past the cloak-room door. "Enough," I murmur, even as I see my first clock.

Then I look down the corridor. She's right. Clocks are *everywhere.* Cuckoo clocks, grandfather clocks, water clocks, clocks so ornate I'm not sure how they work. They fill the hall with a whirring hum that trembles below the rise and fall of conversation. When they all strike the hour, I wonder if anyone's eardrums will survive intact.

Lucy makes a little growling noise under her breath, but lets me lead her into a vast room of arched, marble gables and circular chandeliers that blaze like wheels of light. It looks more like an ancient chapel than a ballroom, and it's filled to bursting with people in Carnival dress. And there are yet more clocks.

My mouth goes dry as the herald announces us, and the room falls momentarily into silence save for the time-ticking hum.

Lucy barely notices. She's seen people she knows and saunters toward them. I follow, glimpsing the empty throne at the end of the hall, flanked by gilded candelabras fitted with antique black candles.

It is the Companion's duty to be her lady's eyes and ears at any public function, the *Companion Primer* had said. *Thus should she hang as gracefully in the background as a spray of flowers, present, beautiful, and yet not calling undue attention to herself.*

Lucy maneuvers through the crowd, while I keep a wary eye on everyone who meets her, half afraid the Guard will haul her away for her earlier impudence out in the hall. There are several young suitors, some more graceful about their intentions than others, but none of them are the Heir to Grimgorn. What if he isn't here?

Apparently all the highest-ranking nobles are missing. After Lucy manages to get rid of the most recent gawker, she says behind her fan, "These are the ones who couldn't get into the smoking rooms with the other Lords. Wait until Father gets here. Then we'll see something, I wager."

"The Heir to Grimgorn, perhaps?"

Lucy snaps her fan shut and taps me hard on the arm with it. "Shhhhh." A miniature version of that wicked smile plays about her lips. "The rumors are already smoldering. No need to set them fully alight!"

I nod.

"And speak of the devils," Lucy says, nodding toward one of the many arched doorways. "Here they come."

The Lords enter in wreaths of drifting cigar smoke and bright frock coats, like a bevy of peacocks shooed before a heavy fog.

The last of them limps along with the help of a wolf-headed cane, and, unoriginally, wears a silver wolf-mask to match it. His clothing is fine, but rather plain for one of the most powerful peers of the Empire—black with a bit of lace trim and silver embroidery here and there.

He halts for a moment before spotting us.

Silver glints between the lace of his cuff and his leather glove. Rumors are true. The hand that grips the cane is not flesh but *myth-work*.

"Father." Lucy curtsies.

I quickly follow suit.

A single steel blue eye rakes me from behind the wolf-mask. The edge of a thick scar snakes above his left temple between the mask and his wig and the left eyehole is completely dark. "And this is the one you hired for your Companion?" he says. His voice is gritty, as though the inside of his throat is also scarred.

"Yes, Father."

"Isn't she a bit young?"

I try not to bristle. I shouldn't expect him to treat me like anything more than a servant; that's what I am to him, after all.

Lucy looks over at me and pulls me as close to her side as her feathered skirts will allow.

"She's a good deal more talented and intelligent than most older women I've met, Father."

He stares at me again. "As long as the forms are met," he says finally.

Whatever other scorn he wants to heap upon my head is interrupted by a blast of the herald's trumpet.

"Her Most Scientific Majesty the Empress Johanna and the Imperial Heir Olivia! *Scientia et Imperatrix Vincit!*"

Everyone stops what they're doing. If they're seated, they stand. If they're already standing, they drop their masks and put their right hands over their hearts.

It's difficult to see much from a curtsy, but my first impression is of a tiny woman swallowed by her black gown, carrying a gnarled staff on which a large white raven sits. Its red eyes sweep the room and lock with mine for a moment. I shiver and bow my head even lower.

When the Empress sits, she signals that we may relax, candlelight winking off her beringed fingers. Her high collar keeps her head stiffly upright; I'm reminded of forbidden pictures of the ancient queen of Old London. Her face is peculiarly mannish; I can't help noticing her uncannily close resemblance to her ancestor, First Emperor John Vaunt.

Next to her throne stands a fair-haired girl perhaps the age of the Tinker thief—Olivia the Imperial Heir. She's an anemic flicker compared to her royal mother's smothering darkness.

And when the candles dance just right . . . I try not to stare too hard, but it looks as if something binds the princess's lips and hands. Dark threads that only I can see. Someone doesn't want her to speak. I can see how I might unravel the end of the thread and free whatever's being held on her tongue. The urge to unbind her is so powerful, I lift my hand before I realize what I'm doing.

Then I see a Guard pass outside the door. And the red eyes of the ghost raven. Right here, right now, it's far too dangerous.

Something about the spell wards people away from her. No suitors come to court her; no courtiers flatter her. She stands quite alone in the hall of clocks and Carnivalgoers as if she belongs to another world and has been momentarily frozen here for display. *Like an Elemental in the Museum.* I feel a terribly sympathy for her. *Is she a witch, too? And who has bespelled her?*

Musicians tentatively begin the first waltz. Lord Virulen murmurs to Lucy and nods to me before replacing his mask and stumping off to where a crowd of other nobles stand. I've not yet seen Master Grimgorn. I must have missed him in the crowd.

As soon as her father leaves, young lordlets rush to find space on Lucy's dance card. Underneath it all, the clocks hum, inevitably ticking toward the symphony of sound that will deafen us at the top of the hour.

"Vespa!" Lucy says, snapping my gaze to her face. She's looking at me with a mixture of annoyance and impatience; clearly, she's tried to get my attention before now.

"The young baron would like to dance with me." A powdered boy simpers behind Lucy's shoulder. "Hold my things, will you?"

"Yes, my lady." I take her fan and reticule.

She takes her companion's arm delicately, though he's a head shorter than she is, and lets him lead her to the dance floor.

I take a seat with the other servants and Companions. None of them speak to me. Lucy whirls from one partner to another, while I search for some sign of Grimgorn, and the Empress and her spell-stitched heir look on.

Then I spot him—a man dressed in inconspicuous black, which

makes him stand out to me like a dark sun. Hal. He's wearing a wig and carries a horned mask listlessly in one hand. He doesn't see me. I'm not sure what he's doing here. Why would the Empress invite a lowly Pedant to her ball? Has he somehow magicked his way into the ball? I wonder.

It's all I can do not to cry out his name. I bite my lip as he slips out into the hall. What is he up to? The Primer echoes in my head: *A Companion may, under severe compulsion, leave her post. But only if it will cause no harm to her mistress or lasting social repercussions for the family.*

"Saint Darwin and all his apes," I mutter to myself. If I don't go after Hal now, I don't know when I might see him again.

As a new quadrille starts, I slide off my chair and weave through the crowd to one of the many arched doors. I look back. Lucy laughs and spins on the dance floor. I don't want her to see me leaving, so I hold my breath and glide as quickly through the door as I can.

Raven Guards flank the entrances. One stares at me with that empty, clicking gaze. He and his fellows wear the Empress's red and white livery over their armor, but they still smell like rusty guano.

"I must find the water closet, please."

"That way," the bird-headed guard says, pointing his pike down the hall. No matter how often I hear them speak, I can't get used to the human voice emitted by that clacking bird-beak.

The dark magic that made him is palpable. I hope he can't feel my magic, even though I'm not using it just yet. What will happen when I speak the love charm? I suppress a shiver.

I hurry down the corridor, my heeled shoes clattering on the marble, dulled only by the sounds of yet more clocks. They're everywhere here, as well—clocks with ornate, gilded frames, with skeletal faces, or bodies like rearing horses. Portraits and tapestries nestle between them as if incidental to the décor.

Floating everlights beckon me down the corridor toward an ornate arch. The edge of a dark coat whispers round the corner. I want to shout at Hal to wait, but I know that would be foolhardy for us both.

I look back down the hall toward the Guard. The arches and columns block all but the tip of his beak and pike. If I keep to this side of the hall and move quietly, he won't hear me. I slip off my clacking heels and creep past the door to the water closet. I just pray no one comes at me. I'll have to throw a shoe at them before I can get my hands free. And even if I can get my hands free, I'm not sure what I could do. The *Novice's Guide* didn't say much about defensive magic, unfortunately.

The marble freezes my toes before I finally slip into the alcove. The heavy mahogany door is open, and I stop to read the words carved over the lintel. CHAMBER OF CURIOSITIES. Around the winged clock face of the Ineffable Watchmaker are carved these words: *"Glory to Him, who endureth forever, and in whose hands are the keys of unlimited Pardon and unending Punishment."*

Unending punishment. That doesn't sound nice at all. The image of the Creeping Waste sifts into my mind, but I banish it firmly. A Chamber of Curiosities. How can I help but be curious?

Besides, Hal disappeared in here just a moment ago. I must talk to him privately, no matter the cost.

I listen at the crack of the door for just a moment, shifting my shoes into one hand. I slide in and try to shut the door without letting it latch completely. I pride myself on being quieter than a mouse.

Then I turn. And nearly scream.

Shoes clatter to the floor as I cringe from the giant white beast looming above me. It's nearly three times my height and with paws easily large enough to crush my head with one blow. Huge, yellowed teeth protrude from its black gums. I brace for the killing blow. Then I notice the dust on its muzzle, the cobwebs strung from head to shoulders. A plate reads *Ursus maritimus* in the Old Scientific tongue.

Light flares above my head, threatening me with brilliant pain. Instinctively, I raise my palms against it and hold it in abeyance. And then I see how to dissolve it. So, I do. Perhaps I'm better at this than I thought.

"Vespa?" Hal whispers, stalking toward me out of the shadows.

"Who else?" I ask. I can't look into his eyes as they scan me from head to toe, so I look aside at the room instead. The light reveals things I've never imagined. Nearest me is a globe of a world I've never seen, maps of countries—Africa? China?—I've never heard of before. I scan city names until a familiar one jars me. London. On the river . . . Thames?

And then I understand. This is a chamber of wonders from Old London, the place we're never to speak of in polite company, the place we all came from but know so little about. There's a handbill for a lecture given by Charles Darwin at the Royal Academy of Sciences. A portrait shows him with a white beard in a plain dark suit. Not at all like the paintings I've seen of him in green robes and halo, surrounded by mythical apes. The sacrilege astounds me.

Hal glares at me. The circulating everlight in the room makes the powder on his hair and face glitter. He looks like an angry sugarplum, but I'm too hurt to laugh.

"Vespa, why in Athena's name are you following me? Do you realize how much trouble you could get us both into if we're discovered?"

I feel small and stupid, but I won't let him see that. I lift my chin. "I needed to speak to you."

"Well, what do you want?" He turns away and I follow him past skeletons and revolvers, lockets and tea cozies, past a case with a book inside it with *Holy Bible* embossed on its cover in gold letters. Why it's not properly named the *Holy Scientific Bible* as all of ours are, I don't know. This place gives me the chills.

"You promised you would come to me. Where have you been?" I know I sound like a peevish child, and it makes me even more cross and agitated than I already am.

The edges of his mouth fall into a frown as he inspects one of the cases nearest us. "There have been many matters that begged my attention. Not the least of which is staying alive to protect you."

"What do you mean?"

I can't see him perfectly in this light, but his hands are burned and there's a scrape on his cheek that didn't come from a valet wight with an unwieldy razor. "What happened?" I reach for him without thinking. I touch his face for only a moment, before he turns his cheek and leans away from me. My fingers slide down into his collar.

"You shouldn't do that," he says. His voice is flat and dangerous, a tone I've never heard from him before.

Before he can protest, I step into him and drag his head down to mine. "Can I do this?" I whisper, brushing my lips against his. I am startled at my own audacity, but I long to enter that golden country we knew before. Magic sparks along my skin.

"No!" he cries. He seizes my shoulders and sets me aside, hard, against a wall. A giant painting looms over me, a portly, sashed queen frowning at me as the frame cuts into my lower back. Then, the painting and the wall on which it hangs vanish. I fall backward.

"Hal!" I clutch at him, my feet sliding over the edge.

His fingers catch in the folds of my skirt, just as my feet find solid ground. I look behind me. The wall has dissolved and I'm in some kind of lift. Elegant mirrors reflect Hal slowly releasing me. There's a gear box with controls; steam hisses and machinery clinks outside the compartment.

Hal steps inside with me.

"What is this?" I ask.

He looks at the controls, touching the polished levers. He ignores what went on just before and I don't know what to say, how to tell him all the words bubbling up inside my chest. The scent of burned bone nearly gags me.

"It smells of the Refinery in here," he says. "I wonder . . ."

He works the levers. The wall slides closed again and we are falling, humming down toward the saints only know what.

"What are you doing?"

"Finding answers, I hope." He stands with his back to me.

I put my hand on his arm. I must make him look at me. I must make him see me.

"Hal, what is happening between us? I thought . . ."

He looks down at me and I realize just how much taller he is than me.

"Is it because of the gown?" I ask. "I know I look different, but I'm still me. . . ."

His eyes are so cold, so distant. I remember thinking I had never seen blue eyes so warm when first we met, and now I can only think how cold they are. He will freeze me to the floor if I look at him much longer.

Behind the glacial chill lurks a shadow, a whisper, something he's not saying. He turns, though, before I can apprehend the unspoken.

"I . . ." He swallows, staring at the wall. "I made a mistake I should not have made. I must do my duty and only train you as a colleague, not. . ." He pauses, weighing words. "It is unfair to you to treat you otherwise."

All my dreams—all the secret wishes I can't even admit to myself—go up in smoke. Perhaps that's why the smell of burning is almost choking. It's my heart smoldering in my chest like burning paper. "Did I misapprehend your intentions?" I don't know how he hears me above the whistling gears.

Hal turns, his face so tight it could shatter, his eyes cavernous with those unspoken things. "I can't be with you in that way. Don't you see that I can't?"

I close my eyes before he can say more and I feel him turn away. I can't tell if the punch to my gut is from the desolation that sweeps me or the lift settling and stopping. Something rises up in me—a stubbornness. I will not let him have the satisfaction of seeing my pain. I square my shoulders and lift the mask to my face, hoping it'll shade the tears glimmering in my eyes.

"Now," he says, staring at the door, "I don't know what will be on the other side. I may need you to help me, if we are to return to the Empress's ballroom in one piece."

I swallow the ugly words I want to say and simply nod. I don't know if he sees me, but it takes all my energy to keep what little composure is left to me.

The door rattles open, and anything I might say is drowned in the howl of machinery and a chilling blast that numbs my fingers. We walk out carefully, and I repress a hiss at the cold on my stockinged feet. I regret dropping my shoes in the Cabinet. The doors slide closed behind us, the lift rumbling down out of sight. I follow Hal to an observation deck. Despite the chill, greenish steam drifts upward like the exhalation of some vast Greater Unnatural.

We stare down at the floor far below us, waiting for a break in the shifting green fog. The smell is so terrible that I cover my masked face with my handkerchief as best I can. Hal looks askance at me.

I remove my handkerchief only long enough to ask, "Where are we?"

"Deep in the bowels of the Imperial Refinery, I believe. The most secret and guarded place in all the Empire. Funny that I rescued Syrus from the roof of the Lowtown Refinery not long ago and now I'm inside an even more dangerous one."

"Syrus? The Tinker thief?"

"You really should trust him, you know. I think his intentions are ultimately good. When you go to Virulen, do what he asks and visit the Manticore with him."

I don't mention the fact that the boy stole my toad and refuses to give it back. That seems trifling now. "Won't the Manticore eat us both for breakfast?"

Hal half-smiles. "I doubt anyone could have the power to eat you against your will. Especially not for breakfast."

He's joking with me now. As if he didn't just say a few moments ago that he simply cannot have feelings for me. I stare down through the mists. The nevered bars of cages glow through the mist, row upon row of cages that disappear under the eaves of the catwalk. And in them are Unnaturals, scads of them, hordes of them. I glimpse the glitter of a Firebird's wings, the curled horns of a morose Minotaur.

I tug Hal's sleeve. "Look!"

Their voices rise up to me now through the scream of machinery—dirges of werehounds, the plaintive songs of mermaids. A cluster of dryads touches the bars with their leafy fingers, wincing and sobbing at the pain. I've never seen a living dryad before, only a single mounted one in the Museum basement. That one looked like little more than a pile of leaves and twigs, but these are beautiful and proud and sad. Somewhere, I know, an entire forest must be dead without its tree women.

And all because of us.

Then I see a line of people being led to a rusting boiler. I can't see them very well, but the checkered headband gives one of them away—Tinkers.

Hal points at the same time I reach to tug his sleeve again.

We watch as the first Tinker enters the boiler. Stooping door wardens slam the boiler shut. There's a screeching exhalation of both steam and pressure; my eardrums nearly burst from it. I tremble with the force of so much magic used at once. A door on the other side of the boiler opens then, and something airy and light is plucked out with a tool that looks much like a pitchfork.

The airy thing turns and flutters in panic like a trapped butterfly. A Refiner approaches in goggles and hood and touches it with a black device. It stills and then I can see it clearly enough to understand.

"A wight!"

"They make wights from Tinkers," Hal says, his voice thick with disgust and remorse. He closes his eyes, leaning forward as if he might be sick.

I am again at a loss, this time from the sheer devastation of such knowledge. One more punch to the gut will leave me utterly hollow. But this is bigger than anything that has happened to me. Whatever anyone else might think, the Tinkers are people. To warp and enslave them in such a hideous way . . . I can't even begin to comprehend the cruelty. And the poor Unnaturals . . . Their mourning songs tear me wide with grief. A little voice within reminds me that it wasn't so long ago I was quite happily mounting sylphids on boards, little dreaming of their sentience. Now I'm taking magic lessons from one and carrying him about in my reticule. I feel him shuddering against my hip in terror.

But I still just don't want to believe it could be true. "How can it be?" I ask. "How are they doing this? The Empress is the Head of the Church of Science and Technology. Magic is forbidden. . . ." I spout every doctrine I can think of, but none of it changes what's beneath us.

"Because, as I told you before, it's all a lie!" Hal shouts above the grinding blast. "The Empress and her Scientists and Refiners want to keep all the wealth and power for themselves. And this is the effect of their madness. Do you finally believe me?"

I nod. I already believed him, even though I had only the proof of the magic itself as evidence. This . . . this is something else entirely. Something incontrovertible. As ineffable as the Watchmaker is rumored to be, though I do not know if I believe in him anymore.

"This is not what magic was meant for," Hal says, passion trembling in his voice. His knuckles are white on the metal railing.

"What are you going to do?"

He bows his head; frustration sets the muscles in his jaw twitching. "What can I do? I am the only Architect left. I—"

"What do you mean—the only one left?"

"Charles killed them all."

"Charles?" I cover my mouth with my hands, feeling the truth sink in like a splinter. Charles has always nurtured a core of hatred, a core I'd brushed against and made fun of and mostly ignored, even though Hal warned me to be careful of him back in the Museum. But I've seen the burns on Hal's hands and the scar on his cheek. I feel all the things he must have felt at seeing his fellow Architects fallen. "You narrowly escaped being killed yourself, didn't you?"

He nods. "He is filled with a fell magic I do not understand. He was once one of us, but he left the Architects months before I came here. We were wrong to let him go, and it was nearly impossible to be sure that he was the one I sought once I did find him, so powerful is his magic. And now he knows about you."

I think about the day I met Hal, the day someone pushed me through the field. "Do you think he pushed me through the field that day?"

Hal looks down again into the glimmering mist, as if it holds the answer. "It's highly possible, if he was either trying to test or get rid of you. I am certain he will now make it his special mission to kill us both, especially since we know what he wants."

"The Heart of All Matter," I whisper.

"Yes. The Heart of All Matter. Which is why, when you're at

Virulen, you must let Syrus take you to the Manticore. Only she can stop Charles and this fell magic he possesses. I've never seen anything like it. Except for this," he says, gesturing at the glimmering steam and darkness below us. "Charles and the Empress are somehow of the same magical ilk, I think. And they will destroy everything, if we do not stop them."

I'm deep in shock at how the web has closed around me. I feel as constricted as Princess Olivia, with her mouth stitched shut by spells.

"Vespa," he says. He grips my upper arms, shaking me a little to make me look at him. "Please say whatever happens, you will do this thing. You will go to the Manticore and help her. You are the only living witch. You have the power to save us."

I swallow. I want to say so many things, but what comes out is a squeak.

Figures loom behind Hal, Refiners with leashed werehounds and soot-grimed boiler wardens with thunderbusses, their boots rattling the catwalk.

"Hal!"

He looks back. "Hold fast to me," he says in my ear.

I have approximately one second to clutch his dark sleeves before his magic utterly dissolves me.

We become ourselves again in the strange Cabinet of Curiosities. Hal is pale and sweating.

"Go," he says. "We mustn't be seen together."

I release him reluctantly, wishing he would say more though I know he won't.

So I nod, slipping my abandoned shoes on at the polar bear's feet. I pass as silently as I can back out into the hall. The clocks mock me, ticking away the precious time left to those imprisoned below. Tears feather my cheeks behind the Strix mask. But I am not crying for just myself now. I am crying for the beautiful things of this world, so perishable and fragile, and the Tinkers who have cleaved to them selflessly. I am crying for their loss and my loss and the loss that most people here cannot fathom. I am crying for what I have only brushed against but never fully known.

I take several deep breaths in the atrium before proceeding back into the ballroom.

Lucy finds me almost as soon as I step into the press of the onlookers and dancers.

"Where have you been? I've been looking for you everywhere!" she says, locking her arm firmly in mine. I'd very nearly forgotten the rose petal hidden in her glove, and the reason for my being here at all. It's time to set the love charm into motion.

I start to apologize but she interrupts before I can do much more than stammer.

"Never mind. You're here now." She leans closer. "I've not yet seen my future fiancé, but I hear he'll be wearing midnight blue. Are you ready?"

I swallow. I try to inhale, but either my lacings or the crowd won't allow it. All I can do is nod.

The crowd parts at one end of the hall, halfway between us and the dais, halfway between a waltz and the musicians tuning their instruments for the next. A young man in a sumptuous midnight velvet frock coat enters, wearing a horned Wyvern mask and trailing an entourage of admirers. The room seems to sigh in his presence. The Heir of Grimgorn. It must be him.

I grit my teeth when I think about what I must do. I have never, so far as I know, bewitched anyone, and the *Guide* didn't make me feel very hopeful about performing a love spell as my first magical act. But a promise is a promise. And Lucy has me fair caught. I have no doubt that if I'd refused my new mistress, sweet as her smile is, she would not hesitate to send me to the Waste. And that would, in turn, ruin what little hope is left to us. Somehow I must get to the Manticore. The one thing I cannot risk above all others is failure. Especially with all I know now.

I pat Lucy gently on the shoulder. "Go on," I whisper. "I'll be watching." *And working the charm.* Though I don't say it aloud.

Somehow she must get his attention. I schooled her in the three levels of connections with people according to *The Guide*—eye, physical, and heart. *Above all, one should strive to make connections of the heart, which are in turn the engines of affection.* She threads her way toward him.

It is not difficult for Lucy to take a cup of punch and edge close to him as he looks on from behind his mask at those trying to court or entertain him. The Wyvern crest of Grimgorn glimmers in the intricate brocade of his waistcoat, and there's a tiny Wyvern embroidered in the folds of his lace cuffs.

Closer and yet closer. She waits for a moment when everyone is laughing at some young gentleman's expense. She glides close enough that he sees her out of the corner of his eye. *The glance.* It's not hard when someone throws her head back, arms akimbo, to give her a gentle push and . . . her glass of punch spills down his arm, down his side, bleeding the blue velvet purple. The cup breaks like bells at Lucy's feet.

A single shocked gasp ripples across the room; the sea of dancers grows still. All eyes are upon her as she apologizes, and the tremble in her voice is real.

"My lord, I am so very, very sorry."

She reaches for his arm with her handkerchief, trying to soak up as much of the stain as she can. *The touch.*

If he reacts with anger, I won't feel too badly about what I'm doing. But if he's kind. . .

He crushes her hand under his. A servant rushes up with linen napkins from the buffet.

The magic is so potent I can hear him almost as if I'm standing right next to him. "I'll forgive you," he says to Lucy, his voice muffled by the mask, "if you'll give me the next dance."

His eyes are shadowed by his mask, but they're oddly familiar, warm and fathomless as the sea as he looks upon her. Perhaps this will go better than either Lucy or I have imagined.

She bows her head and assents. *The heart.*

He removes his stained coat and hands it to a nearby servant. The edge of his cuff is stained, too, but he ignores it. He leads her out to the floor, and the musicians begin as if he is their cue. As he whirls her into the waltz, Lucy's eyes glitter at me from her Phoenix mask. The young Princess with her stitched mouth stares emptily from her mother's dais.

Then it all falls away, and it's just Lucy, Master Grimgorn, and my spell.

He's a very good dancer. It's easy to be distracted by this, because I've never seen anyone dance the way the two of them do. I want so badly to forget the awfulness of what I've just seen, how shattered I am by Hal's rejection. I lose myself in the magic, in making the two of them hopelessly attracted to each other. Lucy's glove glows where the rose petal is hidden. I push the delicate, prickling magic from her hand to his heart. Their joined palms will surely catch fire soon so strong is the charm I weave.

At last, the waltz winds down and he bows. She curtsies.

Apparently inspired by their magical perfection, the dance master calls across the crowd, "Lord Bayne Grimgorn and Lady Lucy Virulen!"

I send this last arrow of thought into his heart as he leans to kiss her charmed glove to uproarious applause: *If you are well and truly bewitched, you will send the marriage proposal tomorrow.*

Master Grimgorn straightens and tears the mask off as Lucy turns toward me. Hal—no, *Bayne*—stares at me in shock, betrayal in every line of his face. He may have changed his wardrobe since I left him in the Cabinet, but there is no denying the look in his eyes.

The clocks all throughout the Tower begin to chime, but his thoughts are louder even than their tolling. *What have you done? Oh, you foolish girl, what have you done?*

CHAPTER 18 —

The fever had seized Syrus almost as soon as he'd gotten out of the City. Bayne had directed him to make his way to Virulen and offer his services at the kitchen; he'd even written a letter of reference. "Go there and watch over Vespa when she arrives," he'd said. "Take her to the Manticore as soon as you can. We must keep her safe from Charles."

But something was in Syrus's blood—a terrible itching. When the strange and beloved Forest greeted him for the first time in weeks, he fell under its spell as one who has finally found his oasis after wandering in the desert. He very nearly forgot who he was when he heard a distant dryad singing a swaddlesong he remembered from his childhood. He burned to find her, to hear her sing those words to him again. He ambled through the mists and dells, wild as any Elemental. Sometimes, he dreamed that he walked on four feet instead of two.

When at last Truffler found him shivering inside a hollow log, it took days of gentle ministration before the hob could bring the boy back to himself.

Then came the morning that Syrus sat bolt upright in the pile of blankets Truffler had dragged in from Tinkerville, nearly knocking his head against the wooden roof of their makeshift infirmary.

Truffler turned from the makeshift brazier. "Quiet," he said, making gestures of peace.

"But I have to . . . I need to . . ." Syrus remembered the rogue warlock's threats and how only the cave sprites' intervention had saved him and Bayne. He thought of the witch, barely come into her power and mostly defenseless—the perfect target. "I need to go to the Big House!" he said.

Truffler eyed him. "Not now. Quiet."

Syrus remembered a time when he'd been small, not long after Truffler had first bonded with him. He'd tried to climb up a sheer cliff by himself when all the older boys had left him behind. Truffler had wrestled him to the ground with his hairy arms and held him there until he'd succumbed. Syrus had no doubt Truffler could still do the same if he wished.

"All right," he said, lying back down. Rain drummed above his head. He wouldn't admit it out loud, but it was the most comforting thing he could think of—outside of hearing his Granny tell her stories, of course—to be safe in the Forest with Truffler caring for him. He only wished it could last forever, instead of just a little while.

Chapter 19 ━

As we approach Virulen Manor at last, I am still trying not to think of the horrendous Ball a few nights ago, still wishing I could erase the terrible betrayal in the eyes of the one who apparently betrayed me, as well. The Heir to the second most powerful House in the Empire masquerading as a Pedant! It felt as though the person I'd known—Hal Lumin—had died there on the Empress's ballroom floor and Bayne, a man I'd never known, had risen to take his place. No wonder now that he resisted all my advances! Any self-respecting man of his station would have nothing to do with someone like me. His words of that night still echo in my head— *What have you done, you foolish girl?*

He was right. I had been a fool, and for more reasons than just him, though that was by far the most humiliating and heartbreaking. The Raven Guard had smelled the magic I'd made and had frightened many people wading through the crowd with their pikes, but with the density of so many people in the room and the sealing of the charm, they'd been unable to pinpoint its source. I had been lucky, I suppose, to escape them. The dark part of me I try hardest to shut away wishes the Sphinx had managed to take my life on that fateful day but a few months ago.

The driving wight takes my carpetbag. I swallow my nausea, thinking of the wight's true origins, as it helps me and Lucy out of the carriage. A line of servants are waiting. I barely see them, caught between my humiliation and my revulsion at the wight.

But I don't want to think about all of that, so I give the house all my attention. I will remember the way Virulen Manor looks for as long as I live.

I've heard tales of the Manor before, even seen lithographs of it, but none of them did it justice. Domes, cupolas, and scrollwork decorate the roofline like sugar pavilions on a wedding cake. Ivy reaches up toward the blue-tiled roofs. Images of the saints peer from between the arrow-shaped leaves. Here and there, the marble is chipped or a blue tile missing. All about are signs of decay. High on the domes, gargoyles perch like sentinel spirits. One of them is missing an eye; the other a wing. But they're turned toward the far-away Tower, as if holding congress with the Empress's ravens. I shiver a little, but the fading majesty of the house remains.

"If you will come this way, Lady, miss," the Chatelaine says. Her belt of keys jingles as she leads us into the house. Servants follow with the few things I've brought from home. The rest is already here.

It's hard for me not to gawk as soon as we enter the Grand Foyer, but I have been to the Tower now, and I know that gawking will mark me more surely than acting aloof will. I lift my chin and stare at the *trompe l'oiel* work of gilded Manticores and vines as if I've seen it all before. In places, the wallpaper is peeling. In some ceiling corners, I see water stains.

Displayed along the walls are the heads of various Unnaturals slain by the previous Lords Virulen. Some of the mounts are better than others. A Unicorn's glass eyes glare at me; that one is particularly awful. But the Dragon . . . I want to touch its scaly cheek. Even dead, its heavy, earthen power can still be felt. I try and fail not to think of all the Unnaturals, trapped in the Refinery prisons back in the City.

Lucy is greeted by her father, who takes her arm and leads her toward another hallway, eager to discuss nuptial strategies, I suppose. She nods at me as they pass and I curtsy low, afraid to meet Lord Virulen's steely eye. The Chatelaine takes me up the Grand Staircase, a double-helix monstrosity designed like staircases in antique books. She guides me along an arched corridor; oil portraits of Virulens past stare at me from the everlit gloom. One particular woman strikes me—tall and thin like Lucy, but without that wicked sparkle in her eye. I wonder if she was Lucy's mother. Thus far, all I've heard is that the Lady Virulen died when Lucy was quite young and no one could stomach marrying her widower father after his near-fatal brush with the Manticore. I've been too shy to ask Lucy for confirmation; it certainly isn't a subject of pleasant conversation.

Then I hear the keys jangle, and the Chatelaine throws open the door to my new room.

Or rooms, I should say.

She shows me into a sitting room with peridot velvet settees and a marble mantel held up by winged Griffins.

"Your bedchamber is through there." She points toward an open door framed in oaken scrollwork. I glimpse old hanging tapestries, more oak, and overflowing trunks as a manservant carries in my carpetbag. He bows, sets down the bag, and makes a hasty retreat.

"My lady will call for you shortly," the Chatelaine says.

Then she leaves me alone, the door scraping shut behind her.

The rooms are larger than anything I've ever slept in. The bed crouches on clawed feet.

I wonder if it will belch when it swallows me. Everything smells like lemon oil with a hint of must underneath. There's a little toilet room off the bedchamber with a brass bath and a flushing water closet, rather like the one at home but more elegant and rudimentary at the same time.

I wander from the wardrobe filled with new clothes around the trunks of shoes, hats, and underthings to the window. The view is of the formal gardens. The house curves around them. To the right extends a decrepit-looking wing that can't be seen from the approach to the Grand Entrance. The broken dome of an old house Refinery is overgrown with ivy. All the Great Houses once had their own, but this one seems to have fallen into disuse. Even from this distance, a neverlock shimmers darkly on its doors.

Already, it seems I have something to explore.

A knock comes at the door. I hurry to open it, nearly tripping over a trunk full of stockings in my haste. A maid brings Mistress Lucy's summons.

I follow her down to the Lady's Parlor, passing through several rooms, each seemingly grander than the last.

Compared to the rest of the manor, the Lady's Parlor is cozy, sporting red satin pillows on chaise lounges and a delicately carved wooden mantel. There are portraits here, but none of them as overbearing as some of the vast ones I glimpsed in the ballrooms or the imposing ancestral portraits of the halls. A mirror with a gilded

Cockatrice's head is perhaps the most intimidating thing here. That, or the Yeti skin rug. I recognize the shiver of magic as I step past the rust-red fur.

Lucy sits on one of the chaise lounges, dangling yarn in front of a gray cat.

She looks up and smiles. "Ah, you've found me at last," she says. Something about the way she says it makes me feel guilty that I didn't find her sooner.

I curtsy.

She waves her hand at my nonsense. "What did I say about formality when we're in private?"

I look around at the maids. There are at least three of them in the room.

"Oh, they don't count," Lucy says. "Most of them are Tinkers. They probably barely understand what we say." She reaches toward an alabaster bowl full of grapes so purple they're almost black. She pops one in her mouth as she stands, pulling her skirts away from the questing kitty.

I think of the poor Tinkers I saw in the Imperial Refinery and of Syrus, the Tinker thief. There's no doubt *he* understands every word, glance, or gesture. But I keep my thoughts to myself. Maybe the Tinkers don't want the gentry to realize just how intelligent they are after all they've suffered from them.

Bayne said Syrus would be here to take me to the Manticore. I hope we find each other soon. Keeping the Heart from Charles is the only thing left to make me feel good about myself. Lucy doesn't know or suspect anything about me and Bayne, and she never shall. But how will I bear seeing the two of them together? I suppose it's just punishment for what I've done. I imagine a little room at the back of my brain and stuff my feelings about Bayne deep inside it.

"See here," Lucy says. She shakes a slender envelope trailing ribbons and seals in my face to get my attention.

I take it, hold it lightly.

"Go ahead," she says.

I open it. It's from Lord Grimgorn to Lord Virulen. An offer of marriage from his son to Lucy. A request to have potential bride and groom meet with the Imperial Matchmaker to determine whether their marriage pleases the saints.

I feel like I might faint and instantly hate myself for the feeling.

"You did it!" she says. She slips the proposal out of my hand, and takes my fingers in hers. For one second, I think she's going to dance me around the room in her happiness.

I don't know what to say. All I see is Bayne tearing the mask from his face, his eyes like brilliant blue suns. All I hear are his thoughts cracking with the strain of my enchantment. *What have you done?*

"Aren't you happy, Vespa?" she asks.

I look into her black eyes and somehow manage a smile, but I imagine it doesn't look at all happy.

She squeezes my hands. "My, you are a somber thing. But I've brought something at the request of your father that's likely to cheer you up."

For some reason, my stomach turns.

"He reminded me that your birthday is coming soon, yes?"

I nod.

"We thought a little something from home . . . or someone,

shall I say, would be a pleasant surprise." She gestures to the servant waiting at the door.

My stomach hits the floor when The Wad enters, wearing a fussy new frock coat and shoes with floppy ribbon laces. "Ladies," he says, bowing in our direction. He doesn't look at all like the murderer Bayne accused him of being. He looks like little more than a tarted-up chimney sweep, but looks, as I've found, are often deceiving. I know now that he is deadlier than I ever imagined he might be.

I swallow. "Mr. Waddingly."

"Miss Nyx."

Probably only I can hear the hiss of hatred as he says my name.

"Your father asked me to deliver this," he says. He hands me a letter and I take it as though he's given me a poisonous snake.

I open it, willing my fingers not to tremble.

Dearest Vee—

I hope this letter finds you settling in well. In honor of your pending birthday, I've sent Charles to bring you an early gift. He'll also be staying at Virulen to work on the control portion of our experiment; Lord Virulen has graciously offered us space to complete our work at his estate.

I'm sorry there wasn't time to tell you before of this arrangement. I sense you dislike Charles, but I hope this will be an opportunity for you to understand him better, darling. If all else fails in your endeavors, keep him in mind. He is, for better or worse, the heir to my work.

Your aunt and I look forward to hearing how you're getting on when you can spare a moment.

Your loving,

Father

I can't say anything in front of Lucy, but I know Charles must have put Father up to this. The thought is chilling. But what's more chilling is that he's here now, watching my every move. He's looking at me with a sliver of malice in his horrid eyes, enjoying my discomfort immensely. Then he slides a tiny box out from his waistcoat. For a terrifying moment, I fear it's an engagement ring. I can see by Lucy's feline smile that she's thinking the same thing.

"Go ahead," he says, pressing it into my palm.

My tongue is thick with fear as I open it.

My little jade toad stares up at me, its carnelian eyes winking.

"My toad," I whisper.

I look up at Charles. He's smiling, a genuine smile that I can't quite comprehend. As far as I know, he's never done anything except for his own gain. Why would he return this to me? Where did he get it? Has he had it all along? I realize in a flash that Syrus was telling the truth, that he wasn't keeping it from me. I blush.

Lucy is nonplussed.

I hurry to explain. "This is the only thing I have left of my mother. It was stolen from me a month ago. . . ." I stop. I feel uncomfortable calling Syrus a thief.

"I understand," Lucy says. "And now Mr. Waddingly has some-how found it and returned it to you. How very kind!"

She gives me a look which is easily read. She thinks he's in love with me.

Darwin and all his apes!

Charles bows, smiling, but his eyes cut viciously to me. He wants her to think he admires me. Can things get any worse?

I close the lid of the box without touching the toad. I'll need to investigate this further, to see if he's done any damage. There's an old saying: Beware of Gremlins bearing gifts. I think this certainly applies.

I once again force myself to smile and say, "Thank you."

Charles nods. "I sincerely hope that we can let bygones be, Miss Nyx."

"That is much to be desired," I say, hoping my voice doesn't shake.

"And now, ladies, much as I would like to stay in your delightful company, I must see to my work. Good day to you both." He bows again to Lucy, and she inclines her head.

She squeezes my arm once he's out the door. "Looks like you have a true admirer!" She claps her hands together. "And he's perfect for you! Perhaps we can be married at the same time!"

It's all I can do not to scream in terror at that suggestion, but I bite it back and say more calmly than I believe possible, "Oh, I don't think that's the case, Lucy. Besides, I wouldn't want to dull the shine of your day."

She giggles and bats at me, much like the cat playing with yarn. "Don't be silly. I think he likes you. And rumor is, he's on the up-and-up. Or did you have someone else in mind?" She narrows her eyes at me, as if I've been keeping secrets.

"Let's just get you married and settled first," I say. "No need to be matchmaking just yet for me, eh? I'm not even properly out yet."

"Very well, then," Lucy sighs. "Spoilsport. Help me reply to Lord Grimgorn for my father."

She leads me to her writing desk, where servants help us ready the everink and seals, but my mind is gnawing on what Charles has planned and what trap he must be setting for me. And how I will keep my heart from breaking every day I see Bayne by Lucy's side.

Chapter 20 ─

When Syrus had presented himself at the kitchens a few days ago, he'd been worried that Cook might not take him on. But Bayne had been right that the great estates always needed kitchen help. Cook had ushered him into the kitchen's sweet-scented hell with barely more than a growl and a gesture of her hammy hand.

He had been put to work, first on a spit with a broken pulley system, then arranging trays and carrying them out, then flinging the kitchen offal to the Virulen hounds, and so on. Syrus wondered why the Virulens didn't have more kitchen wights, as was the fashion these days. He'd heard rumors that, for all their finery, the Virulens were rather poor. It was hard to believe, looking around, but the state of the kitchens, the lack of wights, made him think perhaps the rumors were true.

He was sore today, and his foot ached. But the fever that Truffler had nursed him through showed no sign of returning. It was just the craving he couldn't seem to banish. Every night since the bite, he woke with it—the urge to be in the Forest, to roam its dark byways, to discover things he'd never even thought to seek.

Bayne had asked him if he felt any ill effects from the bite, and he had said no. And Truffler thankfully hadn't needed to ask. Syrus couldn't bring himself to admit his fear—that somehow the were-hound's bite was slowly changing him into one. He'd realized there was just too much at stake for his fears to overcome all that needed doing.

I won't let it happen. It can't happen again. It became his touchstone saying as he hoisted the joints of meat, stirred and kneaded the giant buckets of bread, sliced and gutted the still-gasping river carp. *Nainai* had been fond of touchstone sayings, but he doubted she'd ever wanted him to have one like this.

Because last night was the first night he'd actually changed and knew it for more than a fever-dream.

He'd woken at dawn, curled in the low window of the communal servants' quarters, stark naked. He'd found his clothes all around the room and had collected them red-faced before anyone else was awake. In the process, he'd nearly stepped in a relatively fresh pile of dog turds.

The door was bolted from the outside. There was no dog here. He'd looked frantically around again, but everyone was still asleep. He'd gotten the mess into the chamber pot as best he could, but the fear still lingered.

Syrus was certain he must have changed. It couldn't have been anyone else. And certainly no dog could be hidden in the gallery that passed for a room, unless it had been smuggled in and out during the night.

Cook grabbed him by the collar, shaking every thought out of his head. Her giant arms were lobster-red, one of them tattooed with an anchor. "Get out there!" she yelled over the roar of the roasting fire. She slammed a tray of jellied calves' feet, pickled eels, and salmon roe, among other things, in his hands and shoved him toward the dining hall door.

He recovered himself from stumbling just before the door swung open and spat him into the dining hall. The maitre d' coughed and gestured discreetly toward his hair. Syrus smoothed it with one hand as best he was able. He straightened the jacket of his itchy new uniform. He longed for his Tinker clothes, but they had been taken from him almost as soon as Cook dragged him into the kitchen. Luckily, he had hidden his darts and knife outside Virulen before he'd walked up to the servants' door.

One of the ladies nearest him saw his fidgeting and frowned.

He set out his dishes, looking for the witch.

She was farther down the table, exchanging pleasantries with a man twice her age. She looked pale and uncomfortable.

How to get her alone?

Syrus moved around the table, setting out the little salvers and dishes of roe, jelly, and eels. A woman leaned across the table and snatched up the dish of eels almost as soon as he sat them down. She very nearly caught her hair on fire in the old-fashioned candelabra.

He leaned between the witch and the gentleman she was speaking to, causing the old man to harrumph in consternation. He caught her eye, heard her swift intake of breath as she recognized him.

For once, she didn't scream at him about her toad. She just looked at him, her eyes full of words, her fork hovering above her plate.

WC, he mouthed.

She nodded almost imperceptibly.

He continued down the table, not looking in her direction again, hoping everyone was too busy in their food to have noticed. He stiffened when he passed Charles Waddingly, but the warlock didn't look at him or give any indication that he knew who he was. The urgency of his mission nearly made him drop his tray, grab Vespa's wrist, and run for the Forest. If Charles was here, that meant it was only a matter of time before he pressed Vespa into getting the Heart for him. Syrus didn't even want to think about what he would do to achieve that.

Syrus snuck back into the kitchen, sliding the tray onto a table and looking around before slipping toward the corridor exit. Cook was screaming at one of the scullery maids who had cracked some of the fine plates in the washing tub, and the maitre d' was outside the door, his hawk eyes on the table. If Syrus didn't go now, he probably wouldn't be able to.

He snuck out into the corridor, making for the ladies' water closet. He waited a few minutes, his every sense on pins and needles. If he was caught here before he had a chance to speak with her . . .

The witch tiptoed out in her fancy shoes, her skirts whispering along the stone floor. Her hair was done up fancy too, so high that it seemed to double the size of her head. He liked it better down.

The look in her eyes made Syrus back up a step. "You're not going to pull the alarm again, are you?" he asked.

For an answer, she shook her head and opened her palm. On it sat the jade toad.

"How did you—?"

"Charles Waddingly returned it to me," she said.

Syrus frowned. Granny Reed had said the toad was terrible bad luck. He'd been only too happy to sell it and now here it was again, having survived the burning of Rackham's hexshop. Charles must have taken it when he took the cursed jar. "Get rid of it," he said, his voice rising in fear.

Vespa looked around. "Come," she said and dragged him by his elbow into the WC before he could protest.

It was a large, spacious water closet with its own sink and even a fainting couch, but it was still a ladies' water closet. Syrus shrank against the door, wishing he hadn't suggested it. A toilet wight offered them a towel and a mint and looked perplexed when they refused both.

The witch peeled him off the door and latched it.

"Syrus," she said. "That's your name, isn't it? You can just stop now, because I'm not getting rid of that toad. It belonged to my mother. It's the only thing I have left of her."

"Miss Nyx . . ." he began. He scratched his head; he was still thinking about how and why Charles would have returned Vespa's stolen toad to her. Charles seemed the sort who would want to withhold things from people who wanted them, just for the sheer pleasure of tormenting them. Syrus was worried that this boded very, very ill for what they were about to do. He resolved to steal it back from her again at the first opportunity and dispose of it once and for all.

"Now, let's not speak of this toad thing further. You've tried several times to speak to me and I've not listened," Vespa said. "But Bayne said I should, so . . . I'm listening."

Syrus swallowed. He eyed the wight hovering by a basket of toiletries. Would it report their conversation? He'd never heard of such a thing, but he was beginning to understand that one could never be too cautious.

"I realize this is a most inconvenient place for conversation, but don't be tongue-tied," she said. "We haven't long!"

He cleared his throat. "Well, like I said before, the Manticore wants to see you. She says she needs a witch to help free the Elementals and I'm to lead you to her."

"Apparently, everyone needs a witch for something." Her smile was tight. "She won't eat us, will she?"

"Well," he offered. "She didn't eat me when we talked about my bringing you to her."

"Could that be because she wants to eat me instead?" It was becoming warm and swampy in the closed room. She opened her fan and fluttered it in front of her face.

He considered. "Well . . . I suspect maybe it has something to do with what Charles was trying to get from Arthur Rackham before he killed him."

She snapped the fan closed. "The Heart of All Matter? Charles killed Rackham over it?"

Syrus nodded.

Vespa was silent for many moments, her gaze turned inward, as if remembering something too horrible to speak aloud. Bayne must have told her of the murder of all the Architects.

Syrus thought again about the last story Granny Reed had ever told, about Athena and the Heart and how her father the Emperor had put her to death for giving it to the Manticore.

"But why?" Vespa asked.

"Charles needs it for his experiment—something about catalyzing a power source. I don't know. Perhaps the Manticore knows some spell you can use to help stop him," Syrus said.

All this thinking and talking was giving Syrus a headache and making him irritable. He longed to run through the dark alleys of the Forest, his nose to the ground, his paws . . . He grabbed Vespa's hand. "Well, then, let's go!"

He tried to pull her toward the door but she dug in her heels and refused. She was taller and heavier, and like a mule, couldn't be budged.

"Not now!" she said. "We've been gone long enough as it is!"

Syrus scowled and was about to retort, but she followed quickly with, "Look, I'll meet you, say, in a week. It would be too obvious if we disappeared now. We don't want to arouse suspicion. Will you lead me there and back a week from today?"

"Yes." He wasn't pleased that they couldn't go right away. He had no intention of returning here once his mission was complete, and one less night spent in the servant's gallery was one less night of worrying that someone might discover the truth about him—if, in fact, he'd become a werehound, which he still couldn't bear to believe.

And then the door to the water closet rattled.

Vespa's face was already white with powder but her pale eyes glittered with terror.

"Open the door, please!" a lady said.

The toilet wight drifted forward uncertainly.

"No, no, don't," Vespa ordered in a low voice. It hovered between her and the door, confused, its hand rising and falling as it tried to decide whom to obey.

"Quick," Vespa said. She helped Syrus into the cabinet under the sink. He crammed himself between towels, baskets, and bottles of scent, glaring at her.

"In the garden in a week," she whispered, as she closed the door tightly on him.

He heard her straighten and then he heard the door unlock. There were murmured apologies, sniffs of disdain, and after an ominous silence, the most horrid sound Syrus had ever heard.

The noble lady had unleashed a gigantic fart.

The smell came next, washing over him in an eye-watering, throat-gagging wave. He couldn't stay here. He couldn't breathe!

He crawled out from the under the cabinet. The lady, still enthroned, screamed. The wight moved to apprehend him, but Syrus scrambled away and out the door.

He ran back to the kitchens, gulping fresh air like water. Next week couldn't come soon enough.

CHAPTER 21 ━

O ver the course of the next week, there is much fluttering and consternation. I can't find a single moment to steal away and the looks Syrus gives over the dinner table have gone from hopeful to terrified. I'm caught up in the middle of everything as Lucy's Companion, from planning the wedding banquet to soothing her nerves nearly every night. At last, the day comes when the Imperial Matchmaker and the Grimgorns will arrive for what will hopefully end in a successful matchmaking party. The Matchmaker must approve the marriage based on the Church star charts and with the Empress's input, since every noble match must receive her blessing before it can proceed.

It is also my birthday. But since the mention of it when Charles arrived, no one else has remembered. Perhaps that's just as well. I am up to my eyebrows in a seating chart, the nuances of which will all depend on the Matchmaker's final pronouncement. Not to mention steeling myself as to how I will react when I see Bayne for the first time in weeks. Or Lord Grimgorn, I should say. My mistress's fiancé.

I'm getting a headache from thinking about all of it. Or perhaps it's because I tried opening the magic books and still couldn't read them. They resist my opening them, and when I manage to force them open, everything is gibberish. I feel immediately nauseated just glancing at the strangely slanting letters. Furthermore, there's no sense of power anymore. It's as if it's all drained away, leaving the world dull and gray and familiar as it was before. It's as if now that I've finally accepted I'm a witch and am willing to live with it, the power has been completely taken away.

I set the plan aside and try the books again, to no avail.

I'm feeling rather desperate, because Charles is frightening me. If what Bayne and Syrus said is true, then I need to be able to protect myself. Every night once Lucy has released me, I lay in my bed wondering what to do if he comes to kill me. There's no one to help me now. Lately, Charles has been very kind—too kind. He's often not at dinner, and if he is, he's unusually respectful and quiet. This Charles is almost more disturbing than the openly hostile one I'd gotten used to at the Museum.

Piskel is watching me, clucking softly and trying to hold the pages down for me. *Try again*, he urges.

I try to focus. For one second the letters resolve into something familiar and then melt away.

"It's not working!"

Piskel sighs, his little face drooping.

Lucy bursts into my parlor.

"I've been searching high and low—where have you been?" she says.

I frown. Piskel dives under a pillow on the settee.

"I told the maid I would work here on the seating chart. My apologies if you weren't informed," I say.

"Oh, seating chart be hanged!" she says. Her dark eyes are wild and her usually well-coiffed hair looks rather disheveled, like she's been out in a windstorm.

She starts pacing back and forth in front of the fire. She rings the bell by the door for service.

We've been through this routine nearly every day for the past two weeks. It's gotten monotonous, but at least I know what to do. Or I think I do, anyway.

"Lucy, whatever is the matter?"

She paces back and forth between settee and hearth for a few moments.

"Assure me again that this will work," she says finally.

Every day I've reassured her, again and again. But today, my own confidence is wavering. I feel that it's only fair she knows my fears, that magic isn't as easy to summon as it may seem.

"I can't," I say, before I can stop myself.

She stops her pacing and stares. "What?"

A maid enters with the tea tray. We're silent until she deposits it on the table by the settee. I pour her a cup, but make no move to have any myself.

"I just don't know how this will go. I can't turn people's minds to my every whim."

"But you're a witch!" she nearly shouts.

"I . . ."

"What?" she asks. Her tone is dangerous. I've seen her angry off and on again this week, but never directly at me. I'd take back my sudden desire to confess, except that I can't.

"I seem to be having trouble with the magic," I say. "Something's wrong and I don't know what."

"Well, you had better figure it out before dinnertime," she snaps.

"This match must go forward or all these pretty little things you see around you will go away in a flash. As will you! How's that for magic?"

If I didn't know better, I'd say Miss Lucy is a witch herself. Of the very unpleasant, baby-eating variety.

I swallow. So much for truthfulness.

"I understand," I say.

"Good," she says. "I expect you to attend me at two o'clock."

I nod and she flounces out without ever having touched her tea.

Piskel creeps out from under the pillows. He makes a few twittering motions, sashaying toward the door in clear mockery of Lucy.

"I've had better birthdays," I say to him. Yes, indeed.

At two o'clock, after all the cinching, powdering, and pinching I can stand, I meet Lucy in her parlor. She's calm and collected now, and she takes my arm with a flurry of bergamot and rose-scented lace.

"Oh, Vespa," she says. "I do apologize for my manner earlier. I'm just so distraught over everything."

I take the initiative to pat her hand. "It's all right." I smile as if I'm confident, though inside my stomach is full of fluttering sylphids.

She returns it with that winsome smile of which I'm so envious. Her face has been artfully painted and there are glittering butterflies affixed to her towering hair. She looks dazzling, so dazzling as to seem almost inhuman.

"All is well, then. You figured out how to . . ." She doesn't say it out loud. Despite her earlier remarks, she knows the servants hear things.

I nod. It's a bald-faced lie, but it's better than incurring her wrath. She squeezes my hand. "Wonderful," she whispers.

I escort her from the parlor and to the Lord's Sitting Room, where the matchmaking consultation will take place.

"You know," she whispers in the hall, "despite your coloring and those Tinker cheekbones, you really do dress up nicely."

I blush, whether with embarrassment or anger I'm not certain. Perhaps a little of both. How does she manage to compliment and offend simultaneously? It's a trick I hope I never learn.

And then I think about the poor Tinkers trapped in the Imperial Refinery and my heart hurts.

There's no time to say anything in reply, for we are at the door. Lord Virulen, who has been away on business until today, is already in the room. The silver werehound head on his ebony cane gleams near his chair. Firelight makes shadows of the seamed scars on his face. It's still hard for me to believe sometimes that this shattered man was responsible for killing the Manticore's child long ago. However he managed it, he certainly has paid the price.

Lucy enters, leaving me to stand outside the door. There are some things, even as Companion, that I'm not meant to witness.

The Grimgorns come down the hall—Lord and Lady and, last of all, Bayne. His wig is unobtrusive, his frock coat olive velvet, but his shoe buckles gleam. He wears no glamour and I see him fully as he is, as I never quite could when he was hiding out as Pedant Lumin at the Museum. He looks distinctly uncomfortable and sad.

And then he sees me.

His entire expression changes. That glacial cold comes into his eyes as they flit away from me; he raises his chin as if I'm no more than an ant under his heeled shoes.

I drop my eyes and curtsy deeply, trying not to feel the icy knife of his disdain twist in my chest.

When the door closes behind him, I lean against the wall, limp.

One of the maids grins at me. She's missing some of her teeth. "Handsome thing, ain't he?" she lisps.

I don't answer her.

CHAPTER 22 ━

It had been a bit of a trick avoiding being swept up with the other boys and locked into the gallery for lights out. But Syrus had managed, hiding behind the enormous pie safe. He had learned his lesson hiding in the water closet; never again! The manor didn't have regular security wights like other houses he'd heard of, so it was relatively easy to slip down the corridors and out into the garden once everyone was asleep. It was so cold that Syrus longed for his Tinker dart pipe and knife, but there hadn't been time to retrieve them from their hiding place outside of the estate. If Vespa would just hurry, they could make it before they were discovered.

He felt that itch again, that craving. The moon was rising and soon the Forest would be flooded with silver and shadows. He rubbed his hands along his arms, trying to warm himself. If she would just hurry . . .

Then he saw something creeping low and hesitant along the hedgerow. He moved toward it, hoping it was Vespa. He smelled her before he could quite make out her face—the sharp sweetness of lavender and lemon soap.

"Syrus?" she whispered.

"Here," he said, leaving his hiding place.

She sighed in relief. She wore men's trousers and a too-big old greatcoat, and her hair was stuffed into a bowler. A long knitted scarf was wrapped several times around her neck.

He snickered. "Where'd you find that getup?"

"In the trunk in my room," she said. "I wasn't sure what the proper attire was for meeting a Manticore, but I figured trousers were best in case we need to leg it."

"True." He was glad she couldn't see his face. She'd probably slap him.

"All right, then," he said. "Let's go."

He was relieved that they were finally on their way.

A strange scratching sound made him turn.

Vespa's hand was in her pocket. She lifted her hand and showed him the toad and a pebble, which she'd been rubbing together in her nervousness.

"You really must get rid of that thing," Syrus said.

She glared at him in the moonlight, looking more like a Tinker girl than she ever had. If she'd had darker hair and the checkered headband . . . He betted there was something about her family history she either wasn't telling or didn't know.

They started along a side path that Syrus knew would lead them out of the garden and into the surrounding pastures that bordered the Forest.

Light flared. Syrus stopped and turned and Vespa tripped on his feet. They caught each other from falling.

"Well, well, what have we here?" Charles Waddingly said. "The darling witch and her accomplice. Off for a moonlit stroll, are you?"

Syrus glared at the rogue warlock.

Charles was surrounded by men carrying everlight lanterns. A few of them carried heavy silver chains. Syrus's teeth chattered, and not just because of the cold.

"Charles—" Vespa began.

"No," Charles said. "I have no time to bandy words with you. I know what you're on about. You're going to the Manticore."

Syrus and Vespa were silent.

"You will lead us there. We will capture the Manticore and bring her back as a wedding gift to Mistress Virulen and Master Grimgorn. And you will give the Heart of All Matter to me."

"We will never do that!" Vespa said.

Syrus looked around. While they'd been talking, more men had filed silently down through the hedges. All of the escape routes were cut off. He could probably slip through a guard's grasp—it was what Tinker pickpockets were good at, after all—but he was quite sure Vespa couldn't. And she was what the Manticore needed.

Charles came down the steps. He stood inches from Vespa. Most of his face was in shadow, but Syrus could just make out his sneer as he said, "You will do everything I say to the letter. To the letter! Do you understand?"

"Or?" she said, raising her chin.

Syrus wanted to hide, remembering the last time he'd dealt with Charles in the Archives. Her impudence would likely get them both killed. He stepped a little away from her, hoping to get enough leverage to bolt, but Charles's hand shot out and held him in a grip of stinging iron.

"Where do you think you're going, Tinker imp? Your latest stunt in the caves hasn't been forgotten. There is much I owe you for, it seems."

Syrus's brain was ablaze with anger. He growled.

"Do you remember this?" Charles said. He patted the jar another man held for him.

No one said anything. He gestured for one of the men to come closer. He was a Tinker, someone who had left his clan to work for the Virulens a year or so ago. He refused to look Syrus in the eyes.

Charles flipped open the jar, and Syrus would have sworn the jar groaned like a starving animal.

Charles lifted his free hand and *tugged*. A white mist rose from the man's head, streaming from him to the jar with barely a sound. Syrus watched his eyes go white and his shoulders slump, just like the dead Architects around the table.

He took his soul. A creeping horror shivered along Syrus's limbs. And an anger so great that for a moment he was blind. Then, he felt it. The change rippling along his arms and back.

Charles shifted his grip to seize Syrus by the throat.

"Charles!" Vespa's cry was strangled.

"Ah . . . how amusing! So the werehounds did get a taste of you. I had wondered the last time we met. How rich! Almost better than what I'd planned."

He pulled Syrus to him. Syrus closed his eyes, clenching his teeth against the change. Charles's breath was so foul he thought he might faint. Whispering moans from all the souls trapped in the jar made Syrus want to cry. How many of those were people he'd once known trapped within?

"No, no. I'll not take you just yet. And you'll not change now, do you understand?" A slow, deadening energy numbed Syrus's senses, smothered his anger to a bare spark. "I have work for you to do that requires more consciousness than a wraith's."

He released Syrus, pushing him toward Vespa. She put her hands on his shoulders protectively. He wanted to sink back against her, as if she were one of his long-lost aunts, but he didn't. "You will lead us to the Manticore now," Charles continued. "And you, witch, will lure her to me. Or into the jar both your souls go." He patted it before capping it.

Vespa stared at him. "You took that from Rackham, didn't you?"

Charles's grin looked ghastly in the half-lit shadows. "I can't see how it matters, but yes."

"Why, Charles? Why are you doing all this?" Vespa said. "My father has always been good to you. In time, he would have—"

The boy's face hardened. "You will not interrogate me, witch. I will reveal my business all in good time. Enough talking. Move. And if you try to lead us into difficulty, Tinker boy, think again."

He pushed them forward. The wraith who had once been a man shuffled along with the rest, as mindless and in thrall as the Tinkers at the Refineries.

CHAPTER 23

Syrus leads us out of the garden, across an old pasture, and into the eaves of the Forest. He hesitates a moment before choosing a path. The moon weaves odd shadows through the naked branches. There is much creaking and scraping, and far off, a lonely howl that sets Syrus shaking.

Charles is an ever-present menace behind us with his cursed soul jar. I'm reeling with what's come to pass, even as I'm angry at myself for not being more careful. We should have waited longer or I should have tried to go alone. But since Charles infiltrated the Architects and has known everything all along, perhaps it never would have mattered. He has us all at his mercy.

I rub the toad and pebble together in my pocket. They make a sound like a cricket singing. I've been trying since the moment the Wad revealed himself to summon up energy of the sort Bayne used to rescue me from the Imperial Refinery, wondering if I could transport Syrus in the same way.

But there's nothing inside me. I don't know how to make the magic work. I am so angry and frustrated I could scream.

I don't know exactly what Charles means about the werehound bite, but after a while, Syrus is limping.

"What happened?" I whisper.

"I broke into the Lowtown Refinery. A werehound bit me." There's pain in his tone deeper than just the fact of the wound.

"Why did you go and do a foolish thing like that?"

He looks aside at me. "Because you wouldn't help me. I had to try to get my family out somehow."

I blanch, glad for the cover of darkness. I pull the old scarf closer about me. "Your family is locked in the Refinery?"

"Yes. With a bunch of other Tinkers. They turned my people into werehounds, too."

His words clip off like there's more that he just can't bear to say. It strikes me how vulnerable he is. I can't bear to tell him what I saw in the Imperial Refinery—the Tinkers being shoved into the boiler and made into wights. What if those people were his family?

"You're very brave," I say, "to have gone in after them like that."

"Thanks." He wipes his nose. I see the glimmer of snot or tears.

What he says next stabs me to the heart. "If you have so much power, why don't you use it now to get us out of this?"

I realize he is just questioning the truth as he sees it, just as I did with Bayne many a time. I swallow an angry retort. "I'm trying. It's just . . . I really don't know how."

Syrus snorts. "Figures."

"Quiet!" Charles says behind us. "I have ways of stitching your mouths shut, you know."

I very nearly turn and run back to punch him in the face, but I don't. Yet it's as if he hears my thoughts for, suddenly, Charles yanks me backward and closes his fist around mine.

"Enough of that," he hisses.

I pull my hand from his grip.

"Be assured I can turn you to dust if I choose," he says in my ear.

"Well, why don't you?" I say. My destiny seems to be dust, no matter what I do. The stench of his breath makes me want to gag. "Why all the games? Just do it and have done!"

He releases my hand and steps back, far enough out of reach that I can't punch him as I'd like.

"Whether I like it or not, I need you. But only for a little while longer. After that, you're of no further use to me. Now move along."

I turn and continue behind Syrus. We're on a narrow part of the trail, so I get as close behind him as I can without stepping on his heels. "When the time comes," I whisper to the back of his head, "you run like mad and get Bayne."

He nods slightly, enough to show me he's heard.

The rest of the walk is a grim march through moonlight. The wraith stumbles over roots and breaks limbs, his breath as heavy and ungainly as his shambling, and it makes me sick to the core. Though I joked that Charles was capable of much evil, I never guessed that he would be far more powerful or dastardly than anything my vivid imagination could conceive. He was always a nuisance, a thief of my father's attention and time, but the sheer malevolence of his designs astonishes me. And what is the ultimate goal? To build some Engine that will take him back to Old London? Whatever for?

At last, Syrus stops at the edge of a clearing.

"Here," he whispers.

I can see a bit of a mound, covered with bracken and tumbled flint that glows softly in the moonlight. A ticking sound, a little *tick tock tock* that reminds me of the clocks whirring in the Empress's Tower, scurries under the noise of wind in the branches. My cheeks are so cold now that I press the scarf against them. I can't feel my ears. I allow myself to wish for only a brief second that Bayne could be here with me.

I stare into the darkness of the Manticore's den. Charles tells his men to surround the clearing, and they go stomping off. I can't believe the Manticore isn't awake and already ripping out their throats.

"Now," Charles says to me, "it's your turn. Lure her out and the men will chain her and bring her back to Virulen."

I'm about to protest, but Charles grabs Syrus by the collar. He's fingering the lid of his horrid jar with the other. "You don't want to be responsible for a boy wraith, do you? Summon the Manticore!"

I think wildly about our options. If I could get the jar from Charles, could I use it on him? If I can summon the Manticore, can I convince her to kill him and not me and Syrus? I don't know.

Charles shoves me out of the trees. Faintly from somewhere behind me, I hear singing—a boy's voice. Syrus. I stumble for several paces before I fall to the ground on my hands and knees. Twigs and gravel and . . . bones? . . . dig into my palms. The ticking grows louder and there's a glow like the sun come to earth. My heart slams into my mouth. I crouch in a ball, all my vicious anger at Charles draining into a terrifying déjà vu. I am as I was before the Sphinx and this time there is no one to save me.

I look up and the Manticore smiles at me.

There are three rows of iron teeth behind that smile, but it's the ticking that draws my eyes. Her clockwork heart burns with a spectral fire in her chest.

The Manticore's voice is a chiming bell. In her song, I hear the shape of words, but they wash over me in waves of liquid silver. I cannot understand them.

The men creep forward with their chains. I've betrayed her. I've betrayed everything that I'm just beginning to believe in. I sob.

"I'm so sorry, I'm so sorry." I babble it over and over as if I'm only seven instead of seventeen.

And then her eyes look into mine. By the light of her heart they are blue, bluer than any ocean or sky or flower I've ever seen, bluer even than Bayne's eyes just before we kissed. And I can't hear anything. All is still.

Fierce compassion washes over me, a feeling I always expected to feel during the long masses to the saints, but never quite did. She understands me with a deep knowing that I can't even begin to fathom.

"Why?" I whisper.

Syrus's voice breaks through the stillness. "She says you must return the Heart to its rightful owner," he calls.

"What?" I say. "How can you understand her but I can't?"

"I understand their language," Syrus says. "All the Tinkers used to be able to do it, but now I'm the only one left." I hear a bit of a scuffle that involves Charles cursing and then I hear Syrus retort, "Do you want the Heart or not?"

I daren't look back. The Manticore's smile grows.

Then, Syrus is next to me. "Just because you know magic doesn't mean you know everything," he says, grinning. I suppose he's right about that.

"So, what is she saying?" I ask.

He tells me quick and low about the Beast in the Well, Tianlong, whose empty chest is just below the Museum observatory and to whom the Heart rightfully belongs.

I think of that iron-gated stairwell that leads deep into the bowels of the Museum and the breathing I once heard there. A place I've never been . . . where I thought the Grue might be hiding.

"Under the Museum observatory, you mean?"

The Manticore dips her head. "Then, let's go now and give it back," I say.

She shakes her head.

Syrus listens and says something in a low, musical language in response. "She has a score to settle at Virulen," he whispers to me.

A score to settle? Ah, yes. Virulen killed the Manticore's child.

Charles's men are trying to creep closer while we're distracted; the chains clink coldly in their hands.

The Manticore's tail lifts, and the barbed tips drip with poison. "Stop!"

The men do, but Charles orders them to move on.

Syrus shouts: "She will not hesitate to kill you if you come closer. She says she will be led only by Vespa."

"And why is it no one can hear this conversation but you?" Charles says. "Take her!"

The Manticore stands protectively over us and before I can even blink, I hear the *snick-snack* of poisoned barbs launching themselves at the men. Several of them fall dead, including the poor wraith.

I use the distraction to my advantage.

"Run!" I scream at Syrus. He leaps away. I see a brief tussle through the trees, and then a white werehound streaks away faster than a limping human should be able to run.

Charles strides up to me and slaps me so hard I fall to the ground.

I can't understand why the Manticore doesn't kill him.

"Kill him now!" I say. "Then you can go free!"

But the Manticore just shakes her head.

"What? Why?" I ask. I'm seeing stars and my mouth goes all coppery with blood.

"She won't kill me," Charles says, smirking. He opens the jar just a little bit. The Manticore's grin becomes a grimace.

"I can take her soul before you kill me," he says to the Manticore. "And if I die, you will never be able to retrieve her soul again. You will lose your precious witch, which we both know you sorely need for your misguided plan."

The Manticore growls like a lion.

"Charles, just let me lead her back to Virulen, please?" I say. I am horrified at the thought that all the people he may have stolen souls from might never get them back. Somehow, there has to be a way. Somehow, there must be a way to free them and give them peace. I just hope I have time to find out how.

Charles doesn't want to cave to me, but we are at an impasse. I shiver against the cold ground and stand up slowly. He throws a chain at me and turns away.

"I suppose we'll have to find our own way back now that your Tinker brat has deserted you," he says.

"I suppose," I say.

My mouth is swelling. It's hard to talk around my swollen cheek.

"Don't think he will bring some miraculous salvation. There is none."

I don't say anything.

"Lead the way." He gestures that we should go forward. I lift the chain to wrap it around the Manticore's neck, and I nearly sob again when she bows her head and lets me do it.

We walk together, she and I, with Charles and his dark jar coming behind.

When we finally reach the estate, Charles lowers the nullwards just long enough for the Manticore to step into the garden. Then he directs us to the old Refinery doors.

I lead the Manticore inside, afraid he'll shut us both in together, half-hoping that he will. I'd rather await my doom with the Manticore than have to go inside and pretend to smile and curtsy. Stars wink over the broken dome, and faint moonlight rustles the dark ivy that's crept down inside the walls. Crumbling catwalks circle the upper level. A blasted boiler and its pieces are strewn across one end of the floor, and the sunburst motif in the center of the floor is broken and blackened almost beyond recognition.

Silver bolts have been driven through intact parts of the tiles.

"Chain her to the floor," Charles says. He's almost purring with satisfaction.

I look to the Manticore for confirmation, and she nods in assent. The chain is heavy and nevered and I worry that it will burn her, but she crouches low and allows me to slide the chain over her velvet fur. She smells of rosemary where she passed through the garden.

"I'm sorry," I whisper to her. "Are you sure there's not another way?"

Again that shake of her great head and that swelling of compassion and assurance.

I try to make the chains as loose as I can without bringing down condemnation from Charles. But he's so satisfied with himself, he doesn't notice. He escorts me out of the dilapidated Refinery.

Before I can get away from him, he grabs my arm with his free hand.

I try to shrug him off, but he holds me fast. My limbs deaden; I can't move. My heart jumps around like a panicked rabbit.

He leans so close to me that I smell the carrion of his breath.

"I have known about you for a long time, Miss Nyx. Your misfortune is most certainly my gain."

"You pushed me through the field that day." Bayne had been right.

Charles nods, smiling at his own cleverness. "It seemed the proper thing—if you were a witch, you would survive and be of great use. If not . . ."

"You would be rid of me," I finish through gritted teeth.

"I sometimes wish I had been wrong about you. Then, I'd have been rid of a nuisance a long time ago. But that is all by the by now, I suppose. And I will soon be through with you."

"Once you have the Heart?" I ask.

"Yes," he almost hisses. His flat eyes appraise me, and I'd almost swear a serpent's tongue passes over his lips.

"You aren't . . ." *Human* is what I want to say, but he shakes me, hard, before I can.

"Ah ah, not yet, little witch. Not yet." He draws himself up, and when he speaks I recognize the cadence of magic in his voice even if I can't feel it. "You will remember everything, but you will speak of it with neither your lips nor your hands to anyone."

And then his lips are on mine, sealing them shut with the stench of death.

Tears of fury leak from my eyes, but the kiss is mercifully brief, though it can never be brief enough. It is as different from Bayne's kiss as day is from night. My cheek throbs with pain, as though he's just hit me again.

"Believe me," he says, when he pulls back, wiping his lips on his shirtsleeve, "I didn't enjoy it either. Only way to make the spell work."

"You . . . you . . ." I try to curse him, but I can't. I can say nothing evil against him, not even a filthy name.

He watches with a slow-curving smile.

"Now, off you go," he says.

I run into the house and all the way to my room, scrubbing at my lips until they bleed. I don't know if I'll ever feel right again. I can't understand where my magic has gone, and now it seems, Charles has also stolen my will.

All I can see in my mind is the Princess on her dais, her lips sewn shut by a powerful spell—seeing all, knowing all, but unable to say a word.

CHAPTER 24

Syrus ran until he thought his lungs would give out. His back paw was sore, and his heart even sorer, but he drove toward New London like a phantom arrow. The Forest parted for him as if it knew the dire urgency of his errand.

He barely slowed when he came to Lowgate, which was just opening for the earliest Tinkers and other merchants to bring in their wares for market. The banshee alarms screamed as he passed, warning of magical intrusion, and the paralyzing pain of the nullwards nearly knocked him to the ground.

He expected the null magic to change him, to find himself stumbling through the crowd on two legs, naked and cold. But the change didn't come. He was still a ghostly white hound and the crowd drew back from him—Tinkers making warding signs and other people screaming in terror at the sight of his red eyes.

Then the sentry wights came, pelting him with stinging darts as they chased him through Lowtown. He knew the Raven Guard would come next and probably carry him off to the Refineries or to the Waste. If he could just get to Bayne before then . . .

He dodged through Lowtown and across the Night Emporium bridge. He lost most of the sentries there, but the Emporium wights crowded around him, asking if he wanted flavored ice or perfumes. He snapped at one and it shrank back with a shriek like a punctured balloon.

A shopkeeper screamed when he saw him and ran inside to sound his own banshee alarm. With the bridge alight with wailing, Syrus loped out of the tunnel and up into Midtown. The sentry wights found him again soon enough, stinging him with jabs of energy that made him wince.

Only a few more streets. *Please let the gates be open. . .* It became the only thing he could think. His hind legs dragged as he pulled himself through the iron gates and up onto the front stoop of the Grimgorn estate. A banshee alarm went off down the street. The sentry wights jabbed at him, but he was sprawled across the porch, too exhausted to do more than growl at them.

His relief when the door banged open was so great that his tail pounded against the stone seemingly of its own volition.

"Athena's Great Grimoire! I came down when I heard the alarms, wondering if it might be you," Bayne said. He was in his dressing gown, a teacup in one hand. He waded into the swarm of wights, banishing them left and right. "Begone!" he said.

He lifted his hand and whispered for silence. The banshee alarms ceased mid-wail.

Bayne drew Syrus in and shut the door behind him. Then he carried him upstairs to his bedchamber before anyone could find them. He set his teacup down on his bedside table.

"By the Founders, boy, but you do try your damnedest to get me into trouble, don't you?"

Bayne's fingers searched his head and shoulders where the sentry wights had stung him. Then he whispered a word and Syrus felt himself shrinking, his paws returning to hands, his tail disappearing, his fur shriveling until it disappeared into skin.

A maid came just in time to see Syrus standing naked in Bayne's sitting room.

"Saints alive!" she exclaimed.

"Make us more tea, Bet," Bayne said. His voice was deadly calm.

She threw her apron over her head and disappeared back down the hall.

Bayne put his dressing gown around Syrus's shoulders, and Syrus slipped into its warmth gratefully, though it hung off his small frame and trailed far past his feet.

"You lied to me," Bayne said, as he led Syrus to the fire.

The Architect went and looked out the front window. He looked odd and certainly not at all menacing or powerful in his pajamas.

"Well, you lied to everyone," Syrus said.

Bayne said nothing, his back still turned.

"I'm sorry," Syrus said at last. "I just didn't want to believe . . ."

Bayne faced him. "But if you had told me, I could have given you a potion that might have helped reverse the effects of the bite before the damage was done. It may be too late now, I fear."

Syrus nodded.

"I should probably just have given it to you anyway, as a precaution," Bayne said, "but it's a deadly nasty thing to have to swallow if you don't need it. Makes you deathly ill. Didn't want to risk that with the illness you already had." He seemed almost sheepish, as if Syrus's predicament was his fault.

Syrus squirmed. After the near-death experience he'd had, considering the rest of his life as a werehound was too much. "I promise I'm house-trained," he said. Then he thought of the night of his first change in the Virulen servant's quarters and blushed. "I think," he added.

Bayne blinked. Then he half-smiled when he realized Syrus was joking.

"No worries. We shall find a way to reverse it. There must be something left in the Archives."

Syrus nodded.

"But that isn't why you came here. Or is it?" Bayne asked.

Betula brought a tray with tea and meat, cheese, and bread. The smell made Syrus drool and he tried not to wipe his mouth on his too-long sleeves.

"Thank you, Bet," Bayne said. "And see if you can find more boy's clothes, will you? Our young friend can't wander around in my dressing gown."

"Yessir," she said. She disappeared, and a few moments later, Syrus heard footsteps exiting the estate.

Bayne handed him a cup of tea and looked at him quizzically, waiting for his response.

"No. That's not why I came," Syrus said. His hands trembled on the china as he stared at the food.

Bayne saw the direction of his gaze. "Hungry? Help yourself, by all means."

Syrus set the teacup down and lunged toward a plate of food. He ate as if the wights were after him again. He burped happily afterward, then covered his mouth in shame.

Bayne frowned. "So, were you successful in getting Vespa to the Manticore?"

Syrus ran his fingers through his tangled hair. "Yeessss," he said.

"What happened?"

"Charles," Syrus said. "That is, Charles caught us as we were going there."

"What do you mean?"

"He made Vespa capture the Manticore and he's holding her now."

Bayne set his china cup down so hard that he broke the handle.

"Damn it!" He dug at his eyes with the heels of his hands, cursing vehemently to himself.

Syrus shrugged. "He's taken them, yes, but he said something about giving the Manticore as a wedding present to you and Lucy Virulen. Maybe there's still time." Syrus eyed the last cream cake on the tray. Hunger eclipsed everything.

Bayne dropped his hands. "Why can nothing go as I plan? Why?"

Syrus thought of the clans at Tinkerville, of Truffler who had only recently cared for him so tenderly when he was ill. He'd left him thinking that he'd be safer in the Forest, and now that the Manticore had been captured, Truffler wasn't safe at all. He thought of Vespa and how she'd said something had happened to her magic. And then he thought of *Nainai* reading his face and telling him he was meant to do great things. A great person didn't sit around eating cream cakes or bemoaning his fate when destruction threatened.

"We need to help them," Syrus said.

Bayne sat very, very still, his jaw working with tension. He stared at some distant point below them, as if he could see through the floor.

"Yes," he said finally. "Yes, we do."

CHAPTER 25 ━

The Imperial Matchmaker advises that the wedding take place in a fortnight, else the stars won't be aligned properly again for another two years. I wonder how much Lucy paid her to say that.

My days are so filled with wedding planning that I should think of nothing else. But my terror and rage is uppermost in my mind, such that I seldom speak at all, for fear I will burst into tears. There must be a way. Every moment I can, I open the magic books to see if they'll reveal their secrets to me. I've even snuck into the Virulen library deep in the night, hoping some forbidden book remains there that will tell me what to do. But I found nothing. I carry the Ceylon Codex from the museum for comfort, but there's little else it's good for.

Charles and Lucy seem to have grown quite fond of each other. Every afternoon, he joins us for tea in her sitting room and he acts as giddy as a girl over invitation styles and wedding favors. Lucy will, of course, wear the ancestral wedding gown of the Virulens, but there is still much to decide—bridesmaid gowns, the buffet menu, musicians to hire for the wedding masque.

Charles is there through all of it. There's scarcely a time now when Lucy and I are alone together, despite Charles's earlier assertions that he is here doing an experiment for Father. The one time I've been alone with Lucy, I try desperately to tell her what he's done, but I can only stutter and stumble, as if my lips had truly been sewn shut. Lucy, of course, thinks I'm having fits and sends me to my room with a posset and strict admonitions to see to my health.

No utterance against Charles can I make, nor any warning of the desperateness of my situation. One day, in sheer frustration I manage to pour tea on Charles's hand. I watch in horror as the skin parts for a moment, revealing only to me the dark, scaly second skin beneath. Definitely not human. But what is he?

No one is amused, and I'm banished to the corner to knit doilies with the other maids, still unable to say a single word.

And every night, the Manticore's silver song rises through the broken Refinery and pierces my heart.

Today, I try again to write a letter to Father. I can speak about the weather, the wedding plans, even inquire about his work. But the moment I begin to beg him for help or to speak against Charles, the ink runs away across the page in meaningless dribbles. I can no more write the words than I can say them.

I throw the pot of everink against the wall in frustration and watch it bleed down the faded wallpaper. What can I do? How can I help myself? I've waited in vain for Syrus to return, but there's been no sign, no word. I should have known better than to rely on him. I swallow, realizing that I'm only thinking these things because I can't accept the fact that Charles may have gotten him, after all. Syrus's soul may already be in that nasty jar.

I must attend Lucy soon, for the Grimgorns will arrive tonight. I wish there was some way to magically fortify myself against the sight of Lucy and Bayne together, but the magic seems to have gone away as fast as it came. I am a witch without spells.

The maids come to dress and powder me. Only Lord Virulen has a wardrobe wight—they're extraordinarily expensive. I'm glad enough for that. I don't think I could stand for a wight to touch me again, knowing what I do about their origins. I endure their ministrations, but all the while I'm thinking about what I can do, what I must do, to break free. I consider that if I could somehow wrest the neverkey from Charles, I could get in to see the Manticore. But Lucy has kept me close by her late into every night, and there are men watching everywhere.

I will figure this out.

In the parlor, I serve tea to Lucy, Lord Virulen, Lord and Lady Grimgorn, and Bayne. Charles is thankfully absent; I would guess he's afraid of what Bayne might do to him. Bayne watches my every move. I look up once to see Lucy frowning, and after that, I keep my eyes lowered. I must pretend that I've never seen or spoken to him. They talk mostly of the wedding tour, and how delicately that must be achieved considering the growing Waste between New London and Scientia. Bayne doesn't involve himself in any of it, but lets his parents, Lucy, and Lord Virulen sort out the details.

I slip over to the window seat while they continue to talk. I slide the Ceylon Codex out of my pocket and turn its old pages. Although I can't make out the symbols, at least my eyes don't sting when I look at them. The strange Dragonlike creature has a golden heart. I'd never noticed that before.

"What is that you're reading?" Bayne says.

He's come up behind me without my realizing it. I twist to look up at him, and see his eyes on the book.

I pass the book to him, trying to modulate my voice as if I'm speaking to someone I barely know. "It's called the Ceylon Codex. It's full of Dragons. My Father used to study them at the Museum."

He takes it very delicately, as he once took my hand. He turns the pages with the very edges of his fingers to keep from smudging them. "Fascinating. What do you think of it?"

"I think . . ."

Our eyes meet. "Bayne . . ." I whisper. My voice trembles.

Just at that moment, I turn and see that everyone is looking at us. The room has fallen deathly silent.

"Vespa," Lucy says, her voice snapping with frost, "remove the tea things, please."

I take the tray and head toward the kitchen. I hear Bayne excusing himself. I try to hurry and disappear down the kitchen corridor before he can catch up to me, but to no avail.

"Miss Nyx," he calls after me. I haven't heard him call me that since the first day we met.

I stop, but I don't turn.

He comes up beside me. "I beg a word with you."

"My lord." I bow my head. "I have errands for your impending wedding." I close my eyes. The tray is so heavy my arms shake.

He takes the tray from me and sets it on the floor. "I do not know why you did what you did," he says. "I want to believe that you didn't understand. But you have bound me now with shackles tighter than any signed contract or brokered promise."

"If you had only told me," I say. "If I had only known, I would never have—"

"Release me, then. Unbind me from this charm. Only you can undo this. I cannot break this spell on my own. Your strength, unschooled as it is, is greater than any I possess."

My teeth chatter with tension. "I can't! I—"

The door opens, and his mother pokes her aristocratic nose around the door frame looking for him.

"Bayne, we need your signature now," she says, eyeing me.

He turns away without another word or look.

I make my face as cold as I can. I bend and pick up my tray and say icily, "Good day, my lord," as I make my way to the kitchens. But it is as though I am walking on a thousand teacups all made of the pieces of my heart.

On the day of the wedding, I am up before dawn being trussed and pinched and perfumed. My hair is so tall I'm afraid I won't be able to get through the doorway. I'm exhausted because I haven't slept at all between Lucy's tantrums over a fault in the wedding favors, avoiding Bayne and Charles, and thinking about what I might do to free myself of these wretched, wretched spells. Short of trying to sneak away after this wedding, I have no solutions. And somehow, with both Charles and Lucy watching me like hawks, I have the feeling I won't get very far.

The maids cluck at the circles under my eyes, my puffy eyelids. They powder my face even whiter than usual to account for it; I look like a ghost.

But there's no time to worry over it. I must help Lucy in her chambers with the ancient Virulen wedding gown and escort her down to the chapel, as she has no mother of her own to do so. We have this loss in common, but with so many maids at her disposal, I'm hard-pressed to see why Lucy even has need of me. Except that I'm the reason she's getting married in the first place.

I sigh. Last night, a note was slid under my door, eversealed with the Wyvern seal of Grimgorn. I threw it in the fire unread. It's bad enough that I am a witch without magic, but even the accusation of being my new lord's mistress, whether true or false . . . I shudder at how fast Lucy would most likely have me sent to the Waste for that, despite all her charming smiles. I can't bear to read whatever accusations he might levy against me, or even kind words. Nothing can happen between us.

And yet, as I hurry up and down stairs and through everlit corridors packed with servants and guests, I wonder again if perhaps somehow Bayne would still help me, if I could only explain to him what happened, if I could make him understand that I literally have no magic to free him. Would he understand and forgive me? Would he put aside his hurt to help me free the Manticore? Could he, bound as he is by a spell I can't release?

I find Lucy holding tight to her bedpost and cursing the maids cinching her into the corset that looks more like a torture device than an undergarment. Her black hair straggles around her shoulders and her cosmetics still aren't on.

Lucy is determined to have an eighteen-inch waist because she is eighteen, for reasons that elude me. But all the rich cakes with tea have taken their toll. Though she looks natural and healthy to me (and my waist size hovers above hers—though only just), she has had many a tantrum over the failure of the maids to cinch her properly these last few days.

"Ah," she gasps, "there you are! Help the maids with the dress, will you? Where is that saints-bedamned hairdresser?" she shouts to no one in particular.

I hurry to help with the ancestral wedding dress of Virulen. It has been used by every Virulen woman since the New Creation, and is so ancient that its once-vermilion silk has aged to deep claret. It was spun from the silk of a now-extinct shadowspider. We've a few preserved at the Museum—ghastly, leggy, shriveled things. But their silk is flawless and beautiful as none other. This dress alone is worth a fortune.

It's so heavy that it takes three of us to lift the thing over Lucy's head. It smells of musty roses, but it slides on with a sigh, as if it knows the blood of its mistress.

Lucy can barely breathe, much less sit, when the hairdresser finally enters and waves her over to her vanity. He is foppish and odd.

Lucy stares at me in the mirror. The hairdresser is teasing her hair upward—soon it'll be even taller than mine. He affixes hot-house blood roses into the weave and across the shoulders of her dress.

"I've noticed something has been awkward about you lately. You're so quiet . . . and clumsy. What is it? You can tell me, I assure you," Lucy says.

But I know I can't. My lips are still sewn shut.

"I haven't asked anything further of you, you know," she says. "I should think you'd be grateful."

She pouts a little, fidgeting with the roses about her bodice.

I nod.

"Now," she says, "when the time comes for heirs, that might be a different story."

The hairdresser's lips quirk. He pulls her hair and she yelps and glares at him. "Do that again and your fingers will never touch hair again. Or anything else for that matter," she says.

A bright spot appears on his cheek, but he murmurs, "Yes, my lady," in a voice as smooth as the pomade he applies.

I hope that I will either be dead or far from here before I'm called to conjure up heirs for Lucy and Bayne.

At last, the hairdresser finishes his work and we carefully install the shadowspider veil over Lucy's hair. I lead her from her chambers and down the back stairs to the family chapel where her father waits for her. She says nothing further to me about heirs or magic or my demeanor.

Because of the large number of guests, the wedding is to be held in the Great Hall. A makeshift altar is draped in cloth-of-gold on the Lord's dais. The bishop waits in his white robes beneath the oriel window of the Saints praising the Ineffable Watchmaker's winged clock. At the sight of us in the chapel, the musicians strike up the procession, and everyone goes silent. I snatch the bouquet of flowers waiting for me and march down the aisle. Bayne is already waiting at the altar. He turns when I arrive. I look away from the mute appeal in his eyes.

From the crowd, Father and Aunt Minta catch my eye. Lucy invited them as a special favor to me. I smile, but I know my smile is strained. Then I see Charles. He's staring at me, a slow smile growing on his lips as if he knows my thoughts. I turn my attention to another window, the one in which Saint Pasteur smites the Demon Byron for his licentious poetry. I stare at it until the image is burned behind my eyelids—the great Saint in his armor piercing the loathsome Dragon-tailed poet. My stomach growls for want of food.

Lord Virulen limps down the aisle beside Lucy. He brings her to me, and I take her up on the dais because it's too difficult for him to manage. His shuffling gait reminds me of the poor wraiths—all those souls stolen by Charles for his hideous jar.

Then, Lucy weights me down with her giant bouquet. I pass both hers and mine to the maid nearest me, and then escort her up to Bayne. Her gown slides like a heavy, red snake behind us.

The line of his shoulders is tense as he takes her hand from mine. Our fingers touch for just a minute. What I see in his eyes makes it difficult to breathe. But I lay her hand in his, and I turn and go back to my place. I barely hear what the bishop says nor their responses in return. I seem to hang somewhere suspended beyond it all, drifting above the ceremony like a little, dark cloud.

The end comes before I'm ready for it. Lucy's train slides by me and I realize I must pick it up. I direct the maid nearest me to grab the other end; we follow the couple down the aisle, showered with blood roses and good-fortune ribbons. My ears buzz with the ringing of the chapel bells. I stand in the receiving line, while person after person congratulates the newlyweds. I'm itching to get out of this dress, even though I know I will just be exchanging it for a ballgown for this evening's masque. I greet people mechanically, a smile so false plastered across my face that it's a wonder my lips don't fall off.

At last, though, familiar hands press mine.

Father and Aunt Minta come to tell me how beautiful I look, to chastise me for not writing more often. Lucy allowed me to invite them as a special favor to me, for all that I've done for her, she'd said. I look at Father, my throat full, longing to tell him everything, sure that if he only knew the truth, he'd change course or at least banish Charles from the Museum. He's looking at me with consternation, as if trying to read my thoughts and wondering why he can't. I open my mouth, but then comes that stumbling block, the stuttering.

"You will come to see the unveiling of the Grand Experiment, won't you?" Father says. "Charles here says you're getting on splendidly. Surely they'll let you come away for a day?"

And then there he is, The Wad himself, decked out in all his ridiculous finery. I can't figure out how a mere Scholar like him could afford such, but I'm sure a person who can suck out people's souls has no trouble finding the resources to procure a fine suit. He's wearing more brocade than Bayne!

"I'm certain I can manage to steal her away. But she's such a busy little thing, aren't you? So busy in so many things. Hopefully soon she won't have to be quite so busy," he says, leering. Again, that terrible odor washes over me. I can't figure out how anyone can endure the smell, but no one else seems to mind. He's making fun of me. I back up without getting too far out of line and nod.

They're swept along down the line, but not before Father gives me that worried look again.

After the receiving line, I'm called to attend Lucy as she's changed into her ball gown. Late afternoon sunlight blinds me from the end of the hall as I hurry through the wing reserved for the Grimgorns. My ankle caves and my shoe goes flying just as I mount the stairs toward Mistress Lucy's chamber at the end of the hall.

Bayne comes down the winding stairs, ostensibly having escorted his new wife to her chambers, just as I'm bending and sliding my foot back in my shoe.

"My lord," I murmur.

"Miss Nyx," he says, moving past me. And then I catch at his sleeve.

He stops, presenting me with a glacial, lordly gaze.

"I'm sorry," I say, the words scraping from my throat. I drop my hand from his arm as though I've touched a neverdoor. He nods and sets his foot on the next stair, but my voice pulls him back.

"Must it be this way between us?" I ask. "I wanted . . . that is . . . I had hoped . . ." I frown and shake my head. "I didn't know it was you, I swear it!"

The sorrow in his eyes hurts. I have no idea how I've managed to cause so many catastrophes in such a short period of time, but this is almost the worst of them. He looks down at his shoes.

"I did not do this to hurt you," I say.

"Then, why . . . ?"

I try once more to say the words, to tell him what Charles has done to me, but all that comes are tears.

He pushes away from me clumsily, saying, "My lady, I must beg your leave. My new wife awaits you in her chamber." My face burning with shame, I curtsy and hurry up the staircase until the turn shuts him from my sight.

Mistress Lucy is shedding her wedding dress and petticoats like a musty chrysalis when I enter the room.

"So?" she says, catching my hands. "What do you think of him?"

"Hmmm?"

"Come, come now," Mistress Lucy says, collapsing on the bed in her chemise while the chambermaids struggle to pull off her stockings. "I want to know!"

"What do *you* think, my lady? You're the bride, not me."

Mistress Lucy crooks her arms behind her and stares into the puffy canopy overhead. "He seems a bit shy . . . rather inept, as if he'd never been around women at all."

"He does have three sisters," I say, casting about for something to occupy me. I start by picking up bits of wedding finery from the floor.

"Yes, but that's not the same thing. Oh, leave all that, will you? Come sit for a moment." Lucy raises on her elbows, patting the bed beside her.

I comply, though my stomach may crawl up my throat and betray my nervousness at any moment. For once, I am glad of not having had any breakfast.

"I mean, I wonder . . . do you think he kisses well?"

I choke, but instantly cover it with a fit of coughing.

"Oh, dear," Mistress Lucy says. Her head nods under the weight of its coiffure like a listing ship. "You're not taking ill, are you? I suppose you have been forced to exert yourself a good deal lately. You're terribly flushed."

I shake my head and manage what I hope is not a weak smile. "Just so much excitement! Your wedding and . . . the masque . . ."

And remembering past kisses with your husband. I choke again in absolute horror at myself.

"Oh, I know. It is terribly exciting, isn't it?" She flashes that radiant smile, and my heart aches.

She gestures me to come closer, and when I hesitate, she puts her arm around me and draws me close. "I'll let you in on a little secret."

I'm terrified that she somehow knows what's just transpired between me and her husband. But what she says is even worse. "Charles has said he has special plans for you after the masque, your clumsiness at tea notwithstanding."

I stiffen. I think I know exactly what those special plans are.

"I think he would make a wonderful match, don't you?" she asks. She lifts her head to look at my face.

"I d . . . don . . . I don't . . ." I stutter.

"Oh, come now," she says. "I think Charles would be perfect for you. He shares your interest in those unnatural creatures, saints know why, and will probably be in charge of the Museum once your father's gone. A marriage between two Unnaturalists seems quite . . . natural, don't you think?" She giggles at her own pun.

I sit up and try to hold back my tears. I sincerely doubt that Charles has any intention of marrying me, nor do I want him to. I'd rather he sucked my soul into the cursed jar than be his wife. Once, I would have had no problem speaking my mind about such a thing. The irony now is that I literally can't say a thing in my own defense.

"Oh." Lucy sits up and hugs me as I rock and hiccup at the edge of her voluminous bed. "My goodness, I never took you for a girl given to hysterics."

She pats me on the shoulder and stands up, stretching.

She brings me her silver snuff box. She sniffs a bit of *myth* herself and then offers it to me. But I can no more bring myself to sniff up fairy bones than I can unseal my tongue.

"It's all right," I gasp. I pull the handkerchief from my bosom and dab at my face. I'm sure my cosmetics have been utterly ruined. Lucy confirms this when she orders a maid to touch me up. She looks at me as if she doesn't quite know what to do with me, but I pull myself together as best I can and help the maids dress her for the ball. Lucy has gone back to her usual love of feathers with this gown, and she sighs happily when the maids remove the roses in her hair and affix a bejeweled spray of kingfisher feathers instead.

I try not to see the maids laying out her negligee for her wedding night as we leave the room in a cloud of scent and feathers. I am not going to think about it anymore. There is more important work I have to do. I have made up my mind. When the Manticore is brought out of the Refinery, I will free her and take her to the Beast in the Well. I'm not sure how I'll fare without magic, but perhaps she'll be able to protect us long enough to get us there. I pick at my gown as we descend.

Nervousness translates into hunger for me and by the time we're allowed to proceed to our places, I'm so hungry I feel I could eat an entire horse by myself. Luckily, the feast will be held before the ball, in the same Great Hall where the wedding took place earlier in the afternoon. We shuffle around, waiting to be allowed inside, and the smell of exotic foods is close to making me either faint or scream. I chatter aimlessly with Father and Aunt Minta, only half-listening to what they say, when suddenly the herald's trumpet rings.

"Her Most Scientific Majesty, the Empress Johanna! Her Heir, the Princess Olivia!" he cries.

I freeze.

Though the Empress had been invited as a matter of course, none of us expected her to actually attend. She hadn't responded to the invitation. She never leaves the Tower. So, why has she left now?

It can only be one thing—the Manticore.

Places are made for them hastily. The entire seating chart will be thrown off, and, more importantly, House Virulen has lost face for not being prepared for the Empress's surprise arrival. Lucy's dark eyes glitter against her pale face. She's livid. Her smile is terribly forced as she curtsies low before the Empress.

The Empress says a few words to my mistress and then she and the Princess lead our procession into the banquet. I watch Olivia follow her mother like a ghost. I can no longer see the spell that binds her lips, but I feel a kinship with her nonetheless. When her eyes find mine as we're settling ourselves, we gaze at each other in wordless sympathy.

Dish after dish is brought in—roasted peacock recovered with its original gorgeous skin and tail fanned out, suckling pig with everlights in its eyes and a golden apple in its mouth, a whole python coiled around a towering pastry. There are other cuts of meats that shimmer with their own light as they're carved—haunch of Satyr, tentacles of Kraken. I had heard that the Lords sometimes still eat Unnaturals at high feasts, but I never really believed anyone would, as fearful as they are of all things Unnatural.

What comes next has made me ill from the first time I heard of it during the wedding planning. A fleet of servants bearing glass-covered dishes with napkins carefully placed over the top file out along the table. I watch one eager lady whip the napkin off, and the stricken form of the flambéed fairy under the glass makes me gag. I think of Piskel hidden safely in my room and hope he remains so.

I know what comes next, but I watch helplessly as one person after another drapes the napkin over their heads, spears the tiny form on a silver fork, and lifts it to their mouth under the napkin. The sound of tiny bones crunching is almost more than I can bear.

I am just about to hurry my poor appetizer into my napkin and shove it under the table when someone takes me by the arm and drags me from my seat.

Charles.

"It's time," he says. "Let's go."

I nearly stumble as he pushes me out of the hall, out onto the veranda, and toward the old house Refinery.

"What are you doing?" I try to turn and kick him in the shins, but get tangled up in my dress and the sliding of my shoes.

"The Manticore is being uncooperative," he says. "I am guessing she will only allow you to bring her into the Hall."

"I won't," I say. "I won't do it."

"You will do it, or I will force the bishop to wed us right now. I think you know there are worse things than having one's soul trapped in a jar."

"No," I say. "I don't care what you do!"

He shakes me. Hard as he did the night he silenced me with that wretched kiss. I can't figure out how a boy who's only a few inches taller than me and slender as a snake can have such strength. "I can make you, you know. And it will be far more unpleasant than the spell I used to seal your lips."

I open my mouth to speak, but then he puts his hand over my lips and says a word, a single, vicious word. My lips fuse into a solid piece of skin. I cannot say a thing, and I cannot open them. I can hear my own muffled screaming in my head as he drags me to the Refinery doors and unlocks them one-handed.

"Now, unchain her and make her follow you to the Hall!" He pushes me so hard that I trip over the broken marble and fall to my hands and knees again before the Manticore. My reticule slides from my wrist and tumbles directly between her paws. The steel hoops of my skirt bite into my knees, but I daren't move. She's crouched over my neck, growling.

I can't say anything as her iron breath makes goose pimples of my flesh.

Pleasepleaseplease, I think at her. Hoping that she can release me. Hoping that she knows how to bring the magic back or can at least show me the way.

Her teeth are at my throat and for one moment, I'm afraid perhaps this has been her intent all along, that she'll dupe everyone and their hopes for me by eating me alive here in the twilight.

Then my lips split and I can open them and breathe through my mouth. And speak.

"Thank you," I whisper.

She laughs a low, feline laugh.

I stand and bend to unhitch her chain. In one swift motion, she lifts my reticule. The silk dissolves and I see a mirror, a pot of lip stain, and my handkerchief slide down her throat. She clamps her iron teeth around my toad.

"No!" I cry.

She bites down on it hard, and it dissolves with a sharp green flare. I'm suddenly lighter, as though I've sloughed off a heavy skin. The Manticore smiles and winks at me.

Charles, who's lurking in the doorway, laughs. "I see she disposed of the dampener. Doesn't matter, though. Your powers won't help either of you."

"What are you talking about?" I say. I'm still looking into the Manticore's eyes, wishing I could speak to her.

"It's a dampener," Charles says. "Families with known witches or warlocks in their bloodlines use them to suppress the gift."

"You mean . . ." I whisper, more to the Manticore than to him.

"Your father has known all along what you are."

My gut wrenches. I feel like I might fall down again. Memories flash with ever-increasing clarity—Father's concerned looks, being expelled from Seminary, whispered conversations outside my door, Father telling me to carry the toad with me as a good luck charm, all those sylphids singing to me in that exhibit long ago . . .

The Manticore nudges me as if to remind me we have work to do. I inhale as deeply as I'm able. "Yes," I say.

She gazes at me with her great eyes and silver smile. I understand now why Athena went to her death bold and unrepentant for what she did. If it comes to that, I will do the same. Energy dances all around the Manticore and in and out of the ivy—threads of nearly invisible light—and I know I have but to reach out and weave it into whatever shape I need.

I nod, leading her through the door. Her claws click on the marble, then go silent on the mossy steps.

Charles turns. I see the dark thing inside him; it's curled around his heart, an evil homunculus gnawing through his chest.

And at that moment, as I watch the last shreds of his humanity disappear, I understand. "You fool," I whisper to him. "You let the Grue eat your heart in exchange for its power."

He raises his hand to cuff me again, but thinks better of it when the Manticore growls.

"The witch is clever," he says. "Charles offered me something I could not refuse. And we will both soon have what we desire."

"What?" I ask. "What is worth destroying everything? For that's what you'll do if you let her die."

I turn to the Manticore. "Why should you abide by the Law if he doesn't?"

She stays silent.

He looks at us with dead eyes and a truly gruesome smile. "Not so clever," he says. "Come." He turns. I consider leaping on him and trying to kill him with my bare hands. But even though I have the magic back, I've no idea how to use it or if I'm strong enough to overcome him. I'm pretty certain I'm not. The Manticore paces behind me, the ticking of her heart like a metronome counting out my steps. Her iron breath is colder on my back than the oncoming night. She needs me.

I turn and follow the thing that was Charles.

When we enter the warmth, light, and noise of the Great Hall, we're met with a few shrieks that fall away into fainting and silence. The Empress stands so abruptly that she knocks over her chair and the crash echoes all the way to the domed ceiling. I follow Charles to the dais and the Manticore follows me. She settles behind me, her spiked tail scraping the steps, lashing like an agitated cat's. I glimpse the true redness of her fur for the first time; it's crimson and plush as fresh-spilled blood.

"What is the meaning of this?" the Empress asks. Her voice is gritty and ancient beyond her supposed years. The way she moves, the way her eyes are like holes in her heavily made-up face make me wonder how old she truly is. It's strange to stand higher than her; it feels almost sacrilegious. She is so very small.

Charles bows deeply to her. The golden ribbons on his shoes are one of the most ridiculous things I've ever seen. "Have no fear, Most Scientific Majesty," he says. He raises his voice so that all can hear. "I bring the Manticore as a wedding gift to the new Lord and Lady Grimgorn, and as a salve to Lord Virulen's longstanding wounds incurred from this deadly Unnatural. I know your Majesty has some quarrel with the Manticore, as well."

Charles gestures to someone at the back of the Hall, and I see them slowly wheel in a collecting unit.

"No," I whisper. I think of the Forest and all her people, the Waste creeping close. I know with a certainty as sure as my ability to properly identify a rare sylph that the Manticore's death will spell disaster for the Tinkers and all the creatures who rely on the Forest. By morning, the Waste will be at New London's back gate.

Lord Virulen struggles to his feet and limps over to the dais. He looks up at the Manticore with his one good eye. It's difficult to read his expression because of his perpetual leer, but I see fear gleaming in that eye. Fear and gloating.

"A worthy gift, Scholar Waddingly," he says. "Quite worthy indeed."

I'm holding the chain loosely, too loosely. I hear it slide almost before I feel it.

The Manticore leaps. Lord Virulen's thin scream evaporates beneath her razor claws. I'm dragged down the stairs after her, my elbows knocking the stairs, my knees scraped by steel.

The Hall reverberates with overturning chairs and screams, not least of which are Charles's screams of rage.

But the Manticore looks at me. The light around her heart is so bright I can barely see.

For the first time, I understand her words: *Take this Heart, Vespa. Take it back to the Beast in the Well. You alone can heal this world.*

Low percussion threatens my ears. The everlights dim as all energy in the Hall rushes to surround the Manticore's burning Heart. The Manticore's grin bursts in waves of dizzying light. Her paws, her spiked tail, and the chains melt white-hot as she dissolves in a towering blaze of magic.

My hair crackles and I shut my eyes against the heatless blast. Something rolls against my hands—the ticking Heart. I cup it and feel its steady beating, even as the everlights shatter one by one, as the oriel window bursts in stars of colored glass. Raw *myth* glitters on wigs and eyelids, makes silver shimmers of gowns and coats.

People who understand what the dust truly is scrabble frantically for it, heedless of shattered glass. The rest stand with their mouths open or faint away in shock.

Three points of attention hone in on me at once: Charles, the Empress, and Lucy. The Empress screams: "GET THAT GIRL AT ONCE!"

The garden entrance door is open to admit air. I can just make it, if I hurry.

But the guards are quickly surrounding me and I'm too unsteady on my feet. In my frustration, I kick off my shoes, heedless of the ribbons of glass slicing through my stockings and skin. I run, hearing the Manticore's last words. *You alone can heal this world.* I slip the Heart into my bodice and it nestles there, ticking its soft song against my handkerchief.

I see Father's face in his hands. Bayne's round eyes and open mouth.

I'll never make it in time.

A terrified turtledove that the bridal couple were to release on the terrace tears free of its perch and rises toward the dome.

Barely knowing what I do, I gather myself to follow it. Midstride, I'm borne aloft. My fingers turn to feathers. The Heart sinks under my skin as my dress sloughs away. I flex my talons and cry out. My voice is fire and my words are no longer human. I rise on unsteady wings, following the dove through the shattered oriel window, the Manticore's Heart ticking frantically under my skin in time with my own.

Far away in New London's everlit night, I can just make out the shadow of a mighty Beast curled alongside the river, its head crowned by the Empress's ridiculous Tower. There is a hole where its heart should be, right under the Museum.

That is where I must be, where I belong.

And then the night has wings and red eyes of its own. Mighty talons grip me with such force I'm sure my wings have snapped. Pain bleeds to absolute darkness.

CHAPTER 26 ——

yrus was half-woken by something tickling at his nose. He swatted at it and settled back into his quilt, grumbling about pesky flies. Then whatever it was bit his nose. Hard.

He sat straight up and hit his head on a root. He yelped, rubbing at his head and glaring at Piskel, who buzzed and hopped about the old fox's den like a manic firefly.

"What?" Syrus growled.

Then he noticed that it was morning and that he was, once again, naked.

He had to find a way to get Bayne to make sure he transformed with his clothes *on*.

Bayne! Confused memories piled in upon him. He'd led the sentry wights and Guard on a merry chase getting out of the City a few days ago, but he'd finally made it to the river. The swim had been unpleasant and nearly drowned him, but he'd made it under the wall. After that, he remembered only flashes—the forest, howling at the moon, racing through a line of hobs mourning at the Manticore's den . . .

Piskel jumped up and down so much it made Syrus's eyes hurt trying to follow him.

"Wait. Slow down, please," Syrus said.

The sylph came to rest on Syrus's palm. "Now, slowly. What happened?"

Piskel pantomimed what had happened. The Manticore had died. Vespa had been taken by the Raven Guard and imprisoned with the other Elementals in the Refinery. It had been very painful to slip out through the nevered bars and nullwards, but Piskel had managed. He didn't know when Vespa would be taken to the Waste, if that was what was meant to happen.

Syrus put his head between his knees. He had sincerely hoped and believed that if anyone could save Vespa, it would be Bayne. He'd tried to get back to her before the wedding, but had obviously failed. Now it looked as though the wedding had already taken place and Vespa had been captured. What had happened to Bayne after the wedding? Had he been captured too? Syrus certainly hadn't expected that it would all fall to him to save the witch. They'd made no plans for this kind of emergency. Bayne had said that if they were all caught, Syrus should go as far away as he could.

Piskel tugged at his arm, urging him to get up, but Syrus shook him off. Thankfully, Piskel refrained from biting him again.

"What am I supposed to do?" he said, head in his hands. He felt very sorry for himself. Small and alone and forever forced to shift his shape at every turn of the full moon until one day he would never change back. How could he possibly do anything?

Piskel trumpeted. It sounded like he was telling Syrus to get help.

"From who? Everyone who could help is imprisoned!" Syrus said.

Piskel puffed out his chest and drew his shoulders up. He marched tall and proud around the burrow, looking at Syrus with brooding eyes.

Syrus shook his head. "I don't know who you mean."

Piskel pointed off in the direction of Virulen. He grabbed Syrus's collar and tried to pull him bodily from the den. Then he took up his pantomime of the brooding person again. He took two roles, pretending first to be a simpering girl and then the brooding man again, looking at her.

"What? Do you mean Bayne?"

Piskel nodded so enthusiastically it looked like his head might wobble off. He tugged at Syrus again.

Finally, Syrus gave in and crawled from the den.

It was as though a great fire had swept through the Forest while he slept. Though there was no smell of smoke, little bits of ash— no, black sand—drifted here and there. The trees, already leafless, now seemed to lack substance, as if whatever held them firmly knitted together had fled. Pounding and pattering and squealing filled the air as a wave of animals surged up over the rise. Syrus watched in horror as white stags and does fled through the floating dust, as squirrels and skunks and chipmunks, greenmen and hobs and sylphs flitted alongside them. They spared not a glance for him and Piskel but thundered off to the east.

Silence stretched under the failing trees until a sizzling noise drew his gaze westward. Sharp light rode a wave of darkness through the once-dense forest. Distant trees collapsed into dust and realization dawned.

The Manticore was truly gone.

And now the Waste was devouring the Forest. He didn't know if it could leap the River, but it would devour the remaining clans in Tinkerville. He had to warn them. . . .

He started off in that direction, but Piskel frantically dragged and pushed at him, trying to force him east toward Virulen like the other animals. Soon, the Waste would sweep this part of the Forest and him with it.

Cursing in frustration, he shifted into werehound form and ran toward Virulen as fast as his paws would carry him.

Syrus was afraid that getting into Virulen would be nearly impossible, but he needn't have worried. Animals and Elementals were trying to flee the onslaught of the Waste as quickly as possible, and in typical fashion the Lords were taking advantage. As Syrus neared the pasture, thinking to slip in under the garden boxwoods or at the kitchen midden, he heard guns firing. He shifted back into human form, clenching his fists and wishing that he had the magical power of the Architects so he could smite them for their stupidity. He retrieved his dart pipe and knife from where he had stashed them on the lip of an old cistern near the back gate before slipping through it.

Bayne stood a little off to the side. He leaned on his musket watching the others with a look of deep displeasure on his face. Syrus watched him dispatch his servant for something. Alone, Bayne half-turned toward the manor as if he'd rather be indoors than witness this hunting charade.

Syrus threw pebbles from the hedge to get Bayne's attention.

"My lord," he called.

He tried not to cringe when he found the barrel of the musket pointed at his chest.

Bayne lowered the musket, but raised a brow. "Where have you been?" He drew Syrus out of the hedge, cloaking him in his hunting jacket.

Syrus coughed in embarrassment. "Bayne . . . the Waste . . ."

Another musket fired and a stag went down in the field.

"Vespa's been captured," Syrus said. Piskel floated around them. That got his attention.

As did the black sandstorm coming over the hill.

"Into the house," Bayne shouted. He grabbed Syrus's shoulder and dragged him along. He shouted at the other lords. Some of them heeded him, but others didn't. As they ran toward the garden gate, the Guards turned down the wards enough for them to pass. Those who waited too long became pillars of salt on the dark tide. Syrus looked over his shoulder as he ran. The Waste flooded right up to the gate, stopping only at the wards. Little puffs of dust flew up as if testing the field.

Bayne took Syrus by the shoulder. "In here," he said.

He directed him upstairs and into his private chamber. Word was already spreading among the staff; there were whispers down the halls. One maid sobbed as she stared out a window at the black desert crouching at the back door.

Bayne shut the door and told the manservant to make sure no one entered. He put his musket by the door and loosened his cuffs.

"What happened?" he said, turning to Syrus. "I thought you would have returned here by now, if you'd survived."

"I . . . got lost."

Bayne raised a brow, then tossed him some clothes. "You're in luck," he said. "My bath boy just quit yesterday."

Syrus waved a hand. "Look, that's not important. We're all in grave danger—"

"Well, that's rather obvious . . ." Bayne gestured out the window.

Syrus ignored his sarcasm and finished, "But if we can just get Vespa out and get the Heart away from Charles, maybe we can return it to its rightful owner." He struggled into his shirt and trousers.

"Us and what army? Do you not see the Guard everywhere?" There was an odd expression on Bayne's face, as if he was only saying the words so harshly to convince himself there was no hope. He went to the window and stared out at the eye-stinging expanse of the Waste.

Syrus didn't know what more to say. He stared at the lord's back, the stillness of his ruffled sleeves. He felt like he was in a game of tiles. He had played his last one, his finest one, and now was just waiting to see if his opponent had anything left.

"I tried to stop the wedding, you know," Bayne said. "But she put that spell on me. And my father . . . he . . ." He trailed off.

"Maybe it's time you stopped doing what your daddy tells you," Syrus said.

Bayne turned. Syrus couldn't see his eyes, but he worried now that he'd gone too far. Piskel squirmed inside his coat sleeve.

"You're probably right," Bayne said at last. "Now, what do you propose we do?"

"Piskel and I can find us a way into the Refinery, but you're going to have to get us out. And then, we'll just have to hope we can get the Heart where it needs to be." He grinned.

A knock came at the door.

"What is it, Boswick?" Bayne asked, opening the door a sliver.

"Your lady wife, sir. She requests that you pack hastily and meet her in the family carriage. All who can are evacuating the estate and retreating to the City."

"Is there a way still clear by carriage, I wonder?" Bayne asked.

Boswick shrugged.

"Well, go find out, man!"

Boswick hurried off.

Bayne gestured to Syrus to help him and together they pulled a sizable foot locker out from a little room behind a tapestry.

Bayne threw it open. "In you go." He smiled.

Syrus stared at him.

"How else am I to get you to my town house without Charles finding out?" Bayne said. "If we are to do this, I must conserve every bit of magical strength I still possess."

Bayne packed a few coats down and then Syrus crawled inside. Bayne threw in a few more things, and then the Architect closed the lid and strapped him in. The inside of the trunk smelled of scented paper and shoes. Syrus sneezed.

Bayne thumped the lid. "Best not do that again," he cautioned, his voice muffled through the trunk lid.

Piskel crawled out of Syrus's pocket and clambered up next to his face. He didn't exactly look pleased, but there wasn't much either of them could do about it until the trunk opened again.

After what felt like hours later but was probably more like thirty minutes, Syrus felt someone lift the trunk, grunting and protesting under its weight. He was carried out and strapped to the back of a carriage, presumably. He just hoped the Waste hadn't reached the road or Tinkerville. He also hoped no one would toss the luggage to help the carriage go faster.

It was a long, cold, bone-shattering ride being jounced along in the dark behind the carriage, but at last the carriage came to a stop. Syrus prayed that Bayne's new wife wasn't in charge of opening the trunks or they would all have a nasty surprise.

Then he was lifted and carried. He heard shouting following feet that ran upstairs.

Bayne yelled, "This farce of a marriage will be annulled, I swear by all the saints!" before the door slammed.

Then he heard the straps being unbuckled and the lid was thrown back.

Bayne's furious expression greeted him.

Syrus gulped a breath of fresh air. "Honeymoon not going too well?" He remembered how his people always made fun of a new married couple. They'd give them the clan car all to themselves one night, but they'd sure make it difficult—singing and hooting outside the window all night long. He thought it was odd that Cityfolk didn't do the same.

"That woman is an absolute shrew!" Bayne said.

Syrus couldn't help but chuckle. Piskel was laughing so hard that he fell out of the trunk.

"Tell me first," Syrus said. "Is there anything left of . . . of the trainyard by the city gates?"

Bayne shook his head. "All that's left is a narrow strip of road that's nullwarded between the city and Virulen. It was the only way we managed to get through. Everything on the west side of the road is gone. We don't know how long the road itself will hold before the Waste breaks through."

Syrus went to the window and looked out between the drapes. They were in the Grimgorn Uptown house. The sloping crest of Tower Hill came down virtually into the back garden. It was an ugly, thorn-tangled view, but he barely saw it. All he could think of were his poor people sleeping, unaware that the Manticore was dead, unaware that the wave of the Waste was about to destroy them.

"I'm sorry, lad," Bayne said.

Syrus didn't know how much Bayne knew about the train-yard and his people, but he realized with a sinking heart that the enslaved Tinkers and werehounds in the Refineries were probably all that was left of his people now.

A single tear trickled down his cheek. He felt Piskel catch it on his tiny hand. The sylph turned it into a bit of glimmering crystal, which he gave to Syrus with great ceremony. Syrus said words of thanks in the old language and slipped the crystal into his pocket.

Syrus drew a deep breath and then said, "We must get them out. Vespa, my people, the Elementals—all of them. We must."

He stared at the hill and the shadow of the Tower above. Just beyond it, the silhouettes of the Imperial Refinery's smokestacks were edged in glimmering, noxious smog.

"If only there were a door into the hillside—how much easier that would be than storming the Tower!" Syrus said.

Bayne was silent. Syrus glanced back at him and saw a startled, dreaming look pass like a cloud over his features.

"You know," Bayne said, coming to stand beside him. "I think there just may be a door. When I was a child, we summered here often. I remember playing in the garden alone once. I looked up and a Raven Guard had appeared out of nowhere. I was terrified. I remember him looking at me and then turning around and marching back into a black hole that went into the Hill. I ran inside screaming to my nursemaid. Of course, everyone thought I was being fanciful. I came to believe it was all just fancy, too . . . but . . . I'm not so certain now."

He stared down at the deserted garden, bare and winter-gray.

"Can you find out, Piskel?" Syrus asked the sylph. "How were you able to get out, anyway?"

Piskel made gestures as if he'd moved an entire mountain just to escape.

Syrus rolled his eyes. "Look, never mind. Just . . . go scout around and see if you can find something that looks like a door, will you?"

Bayne pushed the window up and Piskel fluttered out. Syrus watched him go, a tiny light flickering through the afternoon gloom.

There was a banging at the door. Lucy Virulen's voice sawed through the wood.

Bayne sighed. "You'd better hide in the trunk. And try to sleep. It may be a long night."

Syrus did as he was bid, though he chafed with impatience to be doing something. He heard the door shut and Bayne's voice warring with Lucy's until he drifted back off to sleep.

Syrus woke to the sound of the trunk thumping open again. A candle shone in his eyes, momentarily blinding him. He sat up, stretching his sore neck and cramped limbs.

"What time is it?" he asked, as he climbed from the trunk. He hoped after tonight there were better sleeping accommodations. And then he shivered just a little, thinking that if tonight didn't go well, he might end up nothing more than a pile of salt on the desert floor.

"Nearly dawn," Bayne said. He handed Syrus a greasy packet of cold sausages and crumbling crumpets. "All I could steal from the kitchens," he said.

Syrus nodded his thanks and scarfed the food down, saving a few crumbs for Piskel.

"Come. I think Piskel's found the door. Everyone's asleep, but I've no doubt they've got nullwards set here and there."

Piskel swam into view, pointing toward the garden and grinning. He was obviously proud of himself. He took the crumbs Syrus offered him with a tiny bow.

Bayne was deciding between two coils of rope as Syrus dusted his hands on his trousers. He already had a pistol and sword. "What does one take to a prison break? I've rope, weapons, and . . . these." He held up rusty bolt cutters almost sheepishly. "Will we need these to cut chains?"

Piskel giggled between his fingers.

"We'll probably need a neverkey or some other kind of nulling device," Syrus said. "Hopefully, Vespa can help us with anything more than that once we free her."

Bayne nodded and patted a pack next to the trunk. "I have those already." He decided on the rope and threw it in.

"And a few pebbles in case there are illusion mines."

"Illusion mines?" Bayne swallowed.

"Yes. The Lowtown Refinery has them. I don't see why the Imperial Refinery wouldn't," Syrus said.

"We'll get pebbles in the garden."

"Then, let's go," Syrus said.

Bayne blew out the candle and led the way out of the room and onto the landing. Piskel ducked up Syrus's sleeve so as not to give them away with his light. One creaking step at a time they went down the stairs. Syrus saw shadows of palms at the corner of the staircase. The handrail was satiny-smooth under his fingers.

They sneaked past an ancient grandfather clock and the cigar smoke–laced doorway of what must have been Bayne's father's study. At last, they were through the kitchens and Bayne was letting them out into the garden.

Syrus scooped up some gravel as they went. Piskel crawled out from under his sleeve and led them down through the boxwood border toward the thorn-tangled slope of the Hill.

The sylph disappeared among the wicked spines for a few minutes. When he emerged, he motioned them forward.

Bayne used his sword to hack through the thorns, but it was rather ineffective and Bayne muttered about dulling the blade.

When the vague outline of a door was visible, Piskel pointed them toward the keyhole.

"Let us pray this isn't warded such that the Empress knows when her fortress has been breached," Bayne said, as he slid the neverkey inside.

The door swung open with the faint scent of the Refinery and ordure. They stepped into the tunnel, and the door scraped shut of its own accord. They listened to the sound echo down the corridor for a long while. Bayne waited to kindle the magic flame in his palm until they were well inside and nothing seemed to have been alerted to their presence.

Syrus tried tossing a pebble down the long expanse, but it triggered no mines. He sighed in relief.

The tunnel wound around until it came to an odd, corkscrew-like chamber. They had to step over delicate stone sills and around edges of stone that reminded Syrus of a giant snail shell. They were about to step through to the other side when they heard something that was not the drip of water or the crunch of their own feet on stone. It sounded like coins dropping. Or armored feet trying unsuccessfully to creep toward them.

Syrus eyed Bayne's sword. It was the obvious choice. If the pistol was fired now, it could bring the entire fortress down on them. They needed more time. "You do know how to use that thing, right?" he whispered, even as he remembered the day at Rackham's when Bayne had fought off the rookery leaders.

Bayne snorted at him. "Of course." He unsheathed it slowly and blew the flame up into the air so that it danced above them. Bayne pinned Syrus with his gaze. "Stay here," he said.

Bayne slid around the odd folds of rock.

"Halt! You will come with me to the Empress," the Guard croaked.

Syrus poked his head around in time to see Bayne engage the Guard's pike. He feinted toward the wall, forcing the Guard to swing at him. Syrus watched in admiration as Bayne ducked the Guard's next cut; the force of the blow stuck the pike straight in the wall. Bayne spun close enough that the Guard had to release the pike or else be rendered nearly defenseless.

Bayne rained blows around the Guard's head and shoulders, but they bounced off with green sparks. Obviously, the Guard was protected by some kind of field. Syrus didn't know how long it would take to break through, or if the Guard would soon call his fellows to help deal with this troublesome human.

And then the Guard clapped his hands on the sword blade.

Bayne twisted this way and that, unable to swing the sword free of the Guard's grasp. They struggled like that for several seconds until Syrus heard a fatal ringing snap. Bayne tried punching at the Guard's shielded face, but got sizzling knuckles for his pains.

Bayne came away with the hilt. He cast it aside and, before the Guard could grab him, dropped and swept his armored legs out from under him. Overbalanced, the Guard fell heavily to the floor.

Syrus watched in amazement. He'd only ever seen some of his Tinker uncles fight like this hand-to-hand. Where had a spoiled lordling learned such tactics?

Then, all other resources exhausted, Bayne took the already loaded pistol out of his belt, cocked the hammer, and fired.

The explosion thundered down the tunnel with a burst of feathers.

"Should have done that to begin with," Bayne said. He removed the cap from his powder bag with his teeth and reloaded the pistol with powder, patch, and another silver ball. "Best hurry now. They know we're coming."

Syrus followed him.

Bayne tore the Guard's pike from the wall with a grunt. He kicked the useless sword blade aside. "That was my favorite sword, too," he muttered.

"Why didn't you make a sword of magic like you did at Rackham's?" Syrus asked.

"I'm trying to save as much magic as I can until we reach the main chamber," Bayne said. "Pity that we no longer have the element of surprise as our ally. Come on."

They raced down the tunnel, trying to get out of it before more Guards came. All they could do now was move forward.

Bayne reached out to stop Syrus before they ran out into empty space. They were on a narrow landing. A metal catwalk to the left went down toward the Refinery floor. Syrus looked out over the cages and swallowed. To see so many Elementals held captive, to imagine so many spaces in the world devoid of life because of their absence—it was almost too much to contemplate.

Beyond the cages sat a strange throne on a raised dais, but there was no sign of the Empress or any other human. Where was Vespa? Syrus wondered. Only one way to find out.

The sound of feet coming up the metal stairs severed his thoughts. Syrus drew out his pipe.

The first few guards—regular humans, rather than Raven Guards—fell to his fairy darts.

Bayne looked back at him. "Why didn't you just do that in the tunnel?" he asked.

Syrus shrugged. "You told me to stay back!"

Bayne glared at him. "If you have that much skill with a weapon like that, don't listen!"

Syrus blushed.

Bayne turned to the next wave of guards and pushed them down the stairs with his pike. Fortunately, none of these had guns, nor much skill at fighting, either, when it came to all that. Syrus supposed that the place was so charged with magic that a gun might not even fire properly in here. He just hoped Bayne's wouldn't suddenly go off and take off a foot or bit of his leg.

Syrus leaped into the fray with his dagger, trying not to remember his cousin Raine taken down by his own hand. Piskel also bit and confounded and rained curses down on the guards.

When at last they made the ground floor, the Elementals in the cages were going wild. Singing, screaming, hooting, chanting—all begging for one thing in a myriad of voices . . . *Free us . . . Free us!*

Bayne looked around wildly as a lull came in the fight. He had a gash on his forehead where a thrown dagger had nicked him. Hordes of wraiths and guards—human and Raven—poured down the stairs after them.

Syrus hardened his heart against the wraiths. They might have once been his people, but the most important thing now was to find Vespa.

"Piskel, where's Vespa?" Syrus yelled.

He and Bayne raced down the aisles of cages and things reached through the bars, crying out in pain. In the great, cloudy aquaria, water Elementals beat the glass with suckered arms and brilliantly scaled tails.

Piskel fluttered and floated, trying to get answers from his brethren above the din. At last, he came back shaking his head.

"She's gone, isn't she?" Bayne asked. "What have they done with her?"

A nearby dryad clutched at Syrus with twiggy fingers. "Do you seek the witch?" she asked. Her voice was the murmur of dry leaves. "They've already taken her down to the Museum for the Grand Experiment. That's why there are so few guards. The Empress has gone down with them for the viewing."

"So few?" Syrus laughed hollowly.

The dryad's green eyes pierced Syrus as perfectly as one of his fairy poison darts. "Let us out and we will help you free her. The control panels are over there by the throne. Just take all the fields down. Hurry!"

Syrus and Bayne nodded. So much magic in one place made Syrus's skin curdle. He was afraid at any moment he might find himself changing and be unable to stop. He gritted his teeth and raced across the floor toward the strange throne.

A Guard led wraiths to meet them. "Go!" Bayne yelled, lifting the heavy pike. Syrus pushed himself past them, diving for the control panel beneath the Raven Guard's swinging ax. He had one last dart left. He'd try to hold off using it as long as he could.

He stood in front of the control panel, as the Guard loomed behind him. He tried pulling levers and turning dials, but beyond some hissing sighs in the tangle of hoses above him, he heard nothing.

Except for the swinging hiss of the ax.

He dodged just in time, and it came crashing down on the control panel right where he'd stood.

Then he heard the flicker and murmur, the stuttering sound of paralytic fields dissipating. The nevered cages sparked and steamed, and then the bars dissolved entirely.

A Thunderbird rose toward the dark ceiling and when it shook its wings, lightning flashed and echoed around the entire chamber. A Giant uncurled from his cramped confinement and stretched high above; his shadow drowning everything in the flashes of lightning.

Syrus yelled triumphantly. But there was still the Guard to deal with. He brought his ax up again and swung. Syrus just barely jumped high enough to miss being severed in two. Piskel fluttered around the Guard's eyes, trying desperately to distract him.

And then the Giant lifted his foot. There was a gust of wind, and the Guard disappeared in a puddle of metal and feathers under huge, cracked toenails.

Syrus fell back, sure the Giant would crush him, too, but the Giant seemed as uninterested in him as he would have been in a mayfly. With a great roar, he smashed both fists down on the throne, sending sparks and smoke flying. The concussion knocked Syrus head-over-teakettle toward the cages, from which Elementals of every kind and description were pouring in a golden tide across the shaking stones.

"Syrus! Syrus!" Bayne called to him through the smoke.

Bayne lifted him from the floor. "Come on, let's help them get out."

"But . . . my people . . . they're trapped somewhere in here too. We must help them!"

Pain convulsed Bayne's face. "I know they are, Syrus, but look there—" He pointed up the stairs. Refiners, wraiths, and more Guards were pouring in, some of them toting thunderbusses whose humming charge carried under the sounds of the melee. "If we go that way, deeper into the Refinery, we and all the Elementals are doomed."

"But . . ." Syrus reached toward the Guard-infested tunnel. He pushed away from Bayne, tottering toward the wave of onrushing guards.

"Syrus!" Bayne yelled. Before the boy knew what was happening, he was upside down over the Architect's shoulder. Bayne raised a hand and sent a current of magic behind them, creating a great, glowing wall that nearly blinded Syrus with its light.

Then he saw a low, roofed tunnel and the Giant, stooping so he was almost crawling as he led them through it.

Bayne carried Syrus down the tunnel in a flood of Unicorns and Amphiteres, bugbears and dryads. A Kraken thundered by them at one point, desperate to get to the River. The Giant punched a hole into the living rock. The roof shuddered overhead as if in pain.

Soon enough, the winter sun shone on Syrus's face, but all he could do was reach back toward the dark tunnel, reaching for the people he knew were still imprisoned there, even as the Elementals rejoiced in their freedom all around him.

CHAPTER 27

When I wake up, I ache all over as if my bones have been broken and hastily reassembled. Something is breathing under me. At first, I think I'm lying on a great, billowing bed. Something takes slow, steady breaths, breaths that inhale the world and let it back out again. The Beast in the Well sleeps deep beneath me. For a moment, I think I might have reached my destination after all, that everything is safe, that victory is assured.

Then, I smell something familiar—the must of old books, dust, forgotten displays. My eyes don't want to open, but I sense the light going by in a circuit. I manage to peel my eyes open. I'm in the storage basement in the Museum, that room where Bayne and I first kissed. I'm lying on a pallet and an old blanket from Father's office.

The illusion of breathing remains just for a moment. Even the walls stretch and snore. Then the light passes the door and a paralytic field glimmers, the wards snug inside the door frame. Everything returns to normal. Except nothing is normal anymore.

A tall shadow passes, so familiar the cry is out of my throat before I can hold it back. "Father!"

He looks in at me through the shimmering field. His eyes are sad, so sad.

"Father, let me out!"

He shakes his head. "Charles told me you would try to use your witchery against me in any way you could. I can hardly believe it of you, my little girl."

There's so much sadness in his voice that I get to my feet and go to the door. I walk as if I've never used my feet before. I look down. I'm still in my torn stockings. My gown is tattered and streaked with dirt and blood. And I remember. I remember the Manticore's death, changing into the Phoenix with the Heart safely in my own chest, the Guard coming after me in a twisted cloud.

The field is so strong that it snaps and hisses at me the closer I come. There's definitely no way I'd be able to trip this field as I inadvertently did with the Sphinx's field. This one is a hundred times stronger. I stumble back, but I put out my hand toward Father.

"Father." I swallow the sharpness that rises in my throat. I won't apologize, nor will I beg. Charles—or rather, the Grue inside him—has been the puppet master all along. The puppet, even if he is my father, won't suddenly grow a will of his own. But I try to appeal to the inner recesses of his heart. "Father, I may be a witch, but I am still your daughter. I'm still your Vee."

He puts his hand up—the mirror image of mine, only larger, more gnarled. For a moment, for a single breath, I think he might free me. But instead he shakes his head. "Minta warned me you would turn out just like your mother. I tried to dampen your abilities, tried to shelter you from them while giving you at least some rein to enjoy what you loved. But Minta warned me. And I wouldn't listen."

"What does that mean?" I ask. "Father? What do you mean?"

He comes back to look at me through the glowing field. "Your mother was a Tinker witch, an opera singer who managed to hide her true origins behind the beauty of her voice. I didn't realize until I was so deep in her enchantment that I couldn't find my way out. I thought I could make you different with her gone. I thought if I just brought you up Logically, you would never stray. You were my Great Experiment, my attempt to prove, if to no one else but myself, that Tinkers could be normalized into Society. And I've failed. I've failed utterly."

I can't think of any Doctrine of Logic that could save me. Not that I believe in it anymore, anyway. It's not that the news is so very shocking—why else would they hide everything about my mother but the one thing that took away her power?—but the perspective is so very skewed. There is no language to express the wrongness of it. I don't even want to think about what must have happened to my mother, trapped as I am in a society that feared and reviled her gifts.

There is nothing more to say.

Father slouches off down the corridor, back toward the main stair.

I pace until my feet remind me that they're incapable of such abuse. I return to my pallet, thirst turning my throat and mouth to nettles. They haven't left any water or food for me. This is not a good sign.

I think about what he said about my mother, how Aunt Minta never wanted to discuss her. I was told she died in childbirth, something which is still all too common. Aunt Minta had moved in to help care for me and Father had never remarried, his heart too broken. But now I'm sure there's more than I will ever know.

I press my hand against my chest. The Heart ticks under a thin layer of skin. When I touch it, the skin dissolves and the Heart rests in my palm, singing out its ancient song. I look at it, trying to understand who made it, where it came from, how it came to be. There are characters I can't read incised into its metal chambers. All I know is that it, like me, yearns to be in the place it most belongs.

Ironic that I thought the Museum was where I belonged and now I'm imprisoned here. I frown, remembering how I soared toward New London, as I looked down and saw my purpose laid out so clearly before me. And now I know I'm only a few feet from the goal. A powerful field and a rusting iron gate are all that separate me from it, but they're enough to allow Charles to win and everyone else—the people of New London, the Elementals, the Tinkers—all to lose.

A slurring step. Charles. I press the Heart against my own again. My skin moves to accept it. Power surges through my limbs and I wonder . . . I wonder.

He is there in the doorway with his cursed jar.

The field dissipates.

I try one more time.

"Charles,"—I can't help but keep addressing him that way, even if he's not really Charles anymore—"what is it that you want? Is it really worth destroying everything for?"

He half-smiles. "Amusing that you should ask. We want the same things, little witch. Adventure, exploration, a means for our legacy to go on. It's only just circumstances that Charles found me in my lair first and offered me a bargain I couldn't refuse. In exchange for his body, I give him power. And soon, when he's cut that Heart out of your chest and placed it in the Etheric Engine, he'll give me what I crave."

"And what is that?" I say. The Grue's words coming through Charles's lips and tongue make me shudder. His menace and cunning are darker and more ancient than any Elemental I've ever come across. I curse Pedant Mervold in the back of my brain for ever thinking he could contain this thing.

"New worlds. New bodies. New powers. A place free of the machinations of my kin, where I will no longer be confined to some stinking marshland eating muskrats in the dark."

"But in your greed you are destroying everything!" I say. Charles's hand closes on my upper arm like cold iron.

He nods. "Some things must be sacrificed. It was a shame to destroy my sisters, but their energies were necessary to increase my power. You are not the first, little witch, and you certainly won't be the last."

I start to summon energy to defy him, but he sends a deep, cold shock down through my arm.

"Naughty, naughty," he says, rattling the jar to make sure I see it. I hear the Grue laughing underneath his words and I feel sick. "Up you go, now." He pushes me before him. I don't try to dissuade him any longer. I must figure out how I'll get the cursed jar out of his hands so that it's no longer a threat to any of us, how I'll be able to run back down and get through the gate on my own.

The Heart whispers in me that I have the power to do all things. I'm comforted by that knowledge, even if it turns out to be ultimately false.

We enter the old observatory. The Empress is there with her daughter. I take one look at Olivia and her sealed lips. This at least is something easy I can do.

Open, I whisper. The threads unravel and fall as dark dust from her mouth. Though she still says nothing, her eyes are shining as she watches Charles push me toward my doom. I look at her mother and then I understand completely.

Hiding inside the Empress's skin is a shriveled old man barely holding onto life. A warlock so ancient he saw the dawn of the New Creation with Saint Tesla. John Vaunt. The First Emperor and father of Athena. He is still alive, hiding inside a woman's skin. And he wants his Heart.

And this is why the girl, the Princess Olivia, has been bound from speaking. She saw early on what hid behind the Empress's stiff skirts. Is she truly the Emperor's daughter? Whether she is or not, I see her heart. And she is far more fit to rule than that wizened thing ever was.

My Aunt Minta is there and Lucy and other people I don't know—Pedants, Refiners, Lords . . . But why is the new Lord Grimgorn not with his wife? Perhaps he's still so angry at me that he's glad I'll soon be gone.

The Etheric Engine looms over me like a great octopus. Its tentacles lie quiet beneath the dome; the Waste stirs inside its nevered beaker. I stop.

"Give me the Heart," Charles says from behind me. "And we can end this ridiculous charade."

"No," I say softly.

Charles's lips curl. The Empress's dead eyes glint.

"If I have to, I will strap you to that table and cut the Heart out with my own hands. I know you're hiding it under your skin. Give it here or else prepare yourself to suffer."

"Do what you like," I say. "Just know that the Waste will sweep through this place faster than it did at Virulen. All will die if you use the Heart in this Experiment, I promise you." I'm stalling, hoping something will occur to me. If there was a way to control the Waste, to stop it from leaving the observatory and swallowing all of New London, I might be able to stop Charles and the Empress at one go.

"What are the promises of a witch?" Charles laughs. "I will have the Heart. And your soul. And everyone's in this room if I so choose."

Then he begins to chant. The Waste whirls; the tentacles of the strange Engine rise. There's a noise like a clap of lightning and then a fan of light opens just under the mouth of the Engine. Things move in it—ribbons of roads, people in odd clothes. A peal of bells from some distant church echoes underneath the dome. I smell the breeze from an ancient world I've only heard of but never visited— Old London.

Charles laughs. "And now the Heart to speed me on my journey!" He reaches for me.

I hear the sound above the wildly ringing bells before he does. A thundering . . . the sound of hooves and wings and . . . song.

I want to laugh as the dome breaks above us. Tiles rain down and a huge, blocky face peers in at us. I glance at the grains of the Waste stirring, stirring, stirring in their beaker.

Charles's gaze moves upward to meet that of the Giant glaring down at him.

And that's when I do it. I reach forward and grab the horrid jar out of his slackening hands. Before I can think, with all the power coursing through my veins, I throw it to the ground.

Charles's gaze returns to me, his eyes nearly white with terror. He screams.

It's an echo of that day long ago when I unwittingly freed the sylphs with my growing magic. I don't hear anything else because the release of souls nearly deafens me. They rise in a ghostly whirl-wind, singing, screaming, crying, mumbling . . . so much noise I clap my hands over my ears. Their sound breaks the glass in the Engine. Together, the souls and the Waste whip up in a devilish dance. They sweep up people like matchsticks—I watch in horror as Lucy, Charles, my father, the Empress . . . all are thrown through the air like dolls. Olivia crouches under the orrery, holding to it for dear life. Aunt Minta I can't see at all.

The portal to Old London sucks Charles and hordes of whis-tling souls toward it. I watch, horrified and helpless, as Charles grabs Lucy's arm and drags her in before the portal claps shut like a fan.

The Giant sneezes above me like someone inhaling pepper. He frowns and retreats from the smashed dome.

And then Syrus and Bayne are beside me. Bayne's grabbing my elbow and forcing me to run as the Waste begins to devour the observatory.

The last thing I see is Father lying and staring up at the falling cloud, his mouth open in terror before Bayne pushes me down the corridor and toward the stair.

"You must wake the Beast now," he says. "He's our only hope of stopping the Waste from spreading."

"Father . . ." I say.

"He'll have to find his own way. The best thing you can do now is return the Heart to its rightful owner."

I nod, too breathless to form words. The Wyvern and Dragon hatchlings, freed at last from their long confinement in the Exhibit

Hall, bow as we pass. But the sad plinth of the Sphinx remains empty. I still cannot believe the Grue destroyed her. Evidently, there are all kinds of greed.

We are down the stair and at the gate faster than I thought possible. The Heart beats out the time through my entire body. The Waste follows us in a black wave.

Bayne gets us through the gate with a burst of magic. "Into the tunnel!" he shouts.

I run until I can't anymore. The jagged rock simply hurts too much and my feet refuse to move. Bayne scoops me up as if I weigh no more than a sylph. I'm embarrassed, deeply embarrassed, but I put my head against his neck for just one moment. I smell his wonderful smell and my heart, my true heart, aches at my own foolishness for casting that spell.

I feel the line of his shoulders and neck tense under my cheek. "I'm sorry," I whisper. My throat is so dry I can barely speak.

"I am too," he says.

"Will you ever forgive me?"

"If you will forgive me."

I lift my head and look at him, but we've come to the stairs above the great pit. The breathing is so loud now, I can't speak over it.

The stairs just end in a great open space that would terrify me if the Waste behind us didn't terrify me more. Pipes run this way and that, but I can see the glimmer of golden scales petrified by time far beneath them. There's a well, a space where the breathing hitches. And it's below us, far, far below. Far deeper than any of us can reach.

"Down there," I say.

Perhaps if I could be a bird again . . .

Bayne looks at me and shakes his head. I haven't noticed how terribly pale he is until now. "I'm using all my energy keeping us safe from the Waste, blocking the tunnel against it," he says. "You must get there yourself."

Syrus says in a small voice, "I can do it. I can climb down and put it there. If you'll give me the rope."

I smile, remembering a day long ago when he started this whole mess by stealing that seemingly harmless toad.

I pass him the Heart. My chest, my whole body, feels hollow without it. I understand why everyone wants to keep it; its tremendous power is alluring. But it's not mine. It has never belonged to any of us who stole or borrowed it. It belongs here, in this world, with this Beast.

Syrus shows me the characters incised on the heart. "Endurance," he says.

I am stunned. He can read it. And if he can read that, I wonder what other mysterious texts he can read. I long for the Ceylon Codex with its strange Unnaturals, but it's probably still in my room in Virulen, if it's not been swallowed by dust.

I say what the Manticore said to me, "Heal this world."

We take the rope that Bayne hands us and secure it to the railing. It falls down into the abyss. Syrus climbs down it like one of St. Darwin's most agile apes. Bayne sinks to his knees, gritting his teeth. I can feel the pressure of the Waste bearing down on us, everything above dissolving—the push and pull between Unnatural forces and the dread disease of the black sands. I put a hand between Bayne's shoulders, offering what power I can to hold the Waste at bay. I watch as Syrus vanishes into the well.

I close my eyes. The ticking sound of the Heart is lost under the weight of the building collapsing above us.

And then I hear it. Louder and ever louder. A chorus of clocks, as if the thousand clocks in the Tower were all ticking in unison in this one great chest. And then comes a great, belling chime.

It reverberates through the rock around us, driving it all back.

"Hold on!" Bayne shouts. And I only know what he means because I see him wrap an arm around the buckling railing.

The power courses under our feet and then we're falling. Beneath us, emptiness turns to golden-scaled skin. My breath whooshes out of me as I make contact with flesh solid as stone, and claws clutch me, carrying me faster and faster up through the air, twisting like a bucking horse. I glimpse the sun rising over New London below us, but it's no New London I've ever known. Streets are rising and being shaken off golden scales. The Tower teeters and falls from a great, horned head that turns and snaps at the Waste boiling over the walls and along the riverbank as if it's little more than an annoying cloud.

Color spreads from where the Beast rises, from where all the Unnaturals return to their native places. And where they go, they push the Waste before them, until it recedes utterly beyond the horizon in the West. Even though it's technically winter, it looks like spring.

But the bigger problem now is how to get off this ride before we die.

Farther up the bucking body, Syrus desperately clings to the metal chest, a stupid grin on his face at the sheer wonder of it all. I don't know how much longer we'll all be able to hold on. I see him put his cheek against the golden scales and whisper something.

A shudder moves along the great frame, and then the scales slide against the ground and the Dragon gently turns to allow us to disembark.

He bows his horned head to me over his shoulder. This is exactly the creature I saw in the Ceylon Codex—horns, beard, cloudy fetlocks, and golden scales.

"Tianlong," Syrus says softly. "Heavenly Dragon."

The Beast smiles at that and I see his long iron teeth. Then he rockets straight up into the air, his body rippling like a gold banner in the sun until he's out of sight.

"That would be one hell of a way to get back to Scientia," Bayne observes.

I elbow him in the ribs.

And then I stop, because I don't know if I have the right to do such a thing. Here at the beginning of a new world and the end of all the struggles of the last months, I find my heart is heavier than ever when I look into his eyes.

CHAPTER 28

It takes a long while before anything in New London even approaches normalcy. Everything that we knew is gone—many of the buildings, the Emporium Bridge, the Walls, and the Refineries are smashed to oblivion. There will be no *myth*power ever again. All the evered and nevered things—silks, pens, lanterns, locks—cease to function. Nothing that had once been powered by *myth* works at all, and though many of us agree it's for the best, there's much grumbling from some survivors.

We're forced to live like Tinkers. Syrus shows us how to build fires like them, how to tell which woods are inhabited by dryads and therefore off-limits, how to fix mechanical things that are broken and retrofit those things that had once run on *myth* if we can.

The predicament of the wights is perhaps saddest of all. Those whose bodies were still retained as wraiths in the Refineries were made whole again by the breaking of the Empress's power. Those whose bodies had not been retained were less fortunate. They wander as ghosts, and a committee has been formed to find understanding families willing to house them. Bayne still has hope that we might find a magical solution that will give them peace someday.

Bayne and I sort through the magical things the Architects and the former Empress had hoarded away. Since I have always been an excellent cataloguer, I dive into it like a natural. Syrus promises to help us translate the books written in the old language of his people.

And whenever we aren't rebuilding, we search for those who have been lost. Syrus was devastated when he searched the ruins of the Refineries and found his people gone. But where are they? He says they can't be dead, that he would sense if they were. One day, I fear, when the moon is full, he'll run away like a white shadow over the hills seeking them.

We don't find Lucy or Charles or Father. Bayne closes his eyes when I tell him about Lucy's fate. "A terrible way to die," he says quietly. I don't look at him and I try not to think beyond just the moment. We both of us need time to mourn, to adjust to this very new New London.

Hardest to bear is Father's loss. I still can't believe he meant to do evil; I'm quite certain Charles had tricked him into thinking he was doing good. I know the Waste destroyed his body, and it saddens me that I will never be able to even visit his grave. The Empress—or more correctly, the Emperor—is also gone, but we find Princess Olivia sheltered by dryads in Fauxhall Gardens. I must confess that we embrace and shed tears together for our shared trials when we meet. I believe Olivia will be the Empress we need to rebuild the realm in the coming days.

Aunt Minta we find one day in the streets babbling over a broken music box. She has no idea who I am and shrieks in terror when I try to touch her. She wanders away to a group of people who gather around the bishop of the broken Church of Science and Technology. He glares at me as he takes her in, but at least I know she'll be safe. And where to look in on her if need be.

Bayne's father and mother apparently took an airship out of New London not long after he went off with Syrus into Tower Hill. We're working together at a town house we've commandeered in Lowtown—not far from where Rackham's shop once was, oddly enough—when a letter arrives by a regular courier of the disheveled and disgruntled sort. The letter is damp and stained, the seals ragged. The courier drops them without a word and leaves.

Bayne opens it. I'm afraid to watch him, afraid of what it says, but I see that there are two letters inside, one folded within the other. He scans it and then lets them drift down on the scarred table.

Syrus looks up from where he and Piskel and Truffler are translating some of the old Tinker manuals by the hearth.

"What is it?" I say.

Bayne sighs heavily. He scrubs his chin, which is badly in need of a shave. "My parents have formally disowned me," he says at last. "They've stripped me of my titles and the Grimgorn name. I suppose I shall be Pedant Lumin after all." He pauses, rubbing his chin again. "They've also graciously included a dispensation letter from the Imperial Matchmaker, annulling my marriage to Lucy Virulen due to my 'change in status.'"

"Not to mention that she's also dead," Syrus said.

"Syrus!"

"Good riddance," Syrus says. "I never liked her anyway."

"I think it's awful," I say softly. The look in her eyes as Charles drew her with him through the portal still haunts me.

Bayne slumps in his chair, staring at the rough-hewn ceiling. I feel badly when hope flutters in my heart—the hope that perhaps we can forget all that has gone before. It's not fair to think this way. It's far too soon.

Another knock at the door. Syrus goes to open it, and in steps one of the new Imperial guard. His patchwork livery makes me smile. Our new Empress is behind him. Just yesterday, she stood before the grumblers and naysayers and reminded them quite plainly, "This is not our world. It never has been. We are guests and we must strive for balance with those who have been here long before we were. We have done great harm. It's time we set it right." Then she'd rolled up her royal sleeves and begun digging into a broken building with her shovel as willingly as any mason or farmhand. She will be long-remembered and well-loved indeed.

But today Empress Olivia is dressed in a simple cotton gown. She smiles and invites us out with a gesture. "I have something for you," she says. We go out to find her guards, plain human guards, unveiling a beautifully crafted wooden sign. Above a winged clock, our names are painted in gold and black: LUMIN & NYX, IMPERIAL UNNATURALISTS.

Piskel flits around it, making small noises of approval between bites of honey cake.

Olivia tells me in an aside that she'd wanted a winged heart, but her carpenter had scoffed at such a thing as unbecoming for Pedants. It seems she took his advice, though I don't know what he meant by Pedants. Only one of us is a Pedant. She unrolls a scroll with the Imperial seals stamped in beeswax upon it—simple parchment without everink or everseals.

"Let it be known that by this royal decree, I do declare Pedant Bayne Lumin and Vespa Nyx Imperial Investigators of Unnatural Phenomena with all the titles, privileges, and honors accorded thereunto. Together they shall act as our advisors on all items magical and heretofore deemed unnatural, liase with said Unnaturals, and generally"—here Olivia smiles—"help us to learn to live more wisely together throughout the realm."

She signals to her men.

"Vespa," she says, motioning me forward.

A robe is draped around my shoulders along with a hood and a braided cord; they must have foraged it from the rubble of the University. Olivia herself fixes the tasseled beret over my hair, fussing a bit with my chignon.

She hands me a scroll, sealed with tassels in University colors. Startled tears spring into my eyes.

"I bestow upon you the honorary title of Pedant of the Realm. Our second female Pedant in all of history. May you serve us well."

There is much shouting and cheering. I'm clapped on the back and then feel Bayne lifting me over the heads of the crowd and carrying me while my name is chanted all through Lowtown. I look over them all while his eyes, brilliant as suns, mirror my joy.

I am a Pedant; I am a witch. And I am proud.

Author's Note

Many things inspired this novel, among them a lifelong fascination with the Victorian naturalists and their propensity for collecting anything and everything from all over the globe during the late nineteenth century. Baroque fashion and sensibilities, as demonstrated in movies like *The Duchess*, *Dangerous Liaisons*, and *Marie Antoinette*, also shaped the culture and customs of New London. Tesla, while he isn't a main character here, is definitely so fascinating that I couldn't help at least making him responsible for everything. Not to mention the City of London itself. I'm indebted to the Society of Children's Book Writers and Illustrators (SCBWI) for making possible a trip to London as part of their Work-in-Progress grant. My visit to the British Natural History Museum was foundational for this and other books.

There are also many authors who inspired this book. I would be remiss not to mention Peter Beagle's *The Last Unicorn* in particular. I only recently saw the movie again, not having seen it since I was twelve years old. Those images must have been burned into my brain; we share a very similar mythological aesthetic. And of course there are also echoes of Mervyn Peake's Gormenghast, C.S. Lewis's Narnia, the tales of H.G. Wells and Jules Verne, and, of all things, *Dr. Who*.

I'm certain people will assume that the Tinkers are lifted from Rom or Gypsy culture. While perhaps there is a little of the Gypsy in the Tinkers, the true progenitors of the Tinkers are the Baima people of the Sichuan highlands in the People's Republic of China.

The Baima, or Duobo as they call themselves, are a Tibetan ethnic minority who live on the very edge of the Tibetan plateau. I spent a summer with the Baima and other Sichuanese while living with my husband at Tangjiahe Nature Reserve. I will never forget the kindness the Baima showed us when we visited their village. I was most distressed (though not surprised) to discover that the simple beauty of their culture was disintegrating under the weight of modern progress; only one ancient shaman still knows how to read their religious language and no one else is interested in learning. Their young people are fading away to the big cities in hopes of work.

In my own small and perhaps strange way, I hope at least to preserve some of their beauty in the pages of this book. While my Tinkers speak Chinese as their sacred language, it's only because I was never fortunate enough to learn the Baima language or alphabet.

They gave me a song that summer about the green hills of their homeland because I was missing my own. This is the song I give back to them.

ACKNOWLEDGMENTS

This book is a testament to persistence—mine and the many people who've shared the journey with me. My agent, Jenn Laughran, persevered tirelessly to make sure my equally tireless editor, Navah Wolfe, found this book the one she couldn't live without. It was a long journey, and I'd be lying if I said I didn't stumble here and there along the way. I also very much appreciate the dedicated staff of Simon & Schuster Books for Young Readers: production editor, Katrina Groover; production manager, Michelle Kratz; and the wonderfully talented designer, Chloë Foglia.

Though this book is dedicated to Tricia Scott, I also can't thank her enough for her abiding enthusiasm and support, sometimes given literally from what we all were sure was her own deathbed. I'm so proud of her for conquering breast cancer and so grateful every day she is still with us. If this story belongs to anyone, it's hers.

I must also thank other writers for their support, good humor, and friendship—Stephanie Burgis, Ying Lee, Lisa Mantchev, Gwenda Bond, Mark Henry, Richelle Mead, Caitlin Kittredge, Cherie Priest, Kat Richardson, Stacia Kane, and Nicole Peeler, to name quite a few! Early drafts were read by Tessa Gratton, Maggie Stiefvater, and Natalie Parker—I appreciate their excellent comments and suggestions. Thanks to J. Kathleen Cheney for the epigraph. I'm very grateful also to Jeff Mann, Kelly Fineman, Cheryl Ruggiero, and Sue Hagedorn for some damn fine poems and meals, to boot. Big hugs to Synde Korman for the beautiful and inspiring jewelry based on scenes from the novel. Thanks to my dear local friends—you know who you are. And of course for all years of unfailing love, belief, and devotion, endless thanks to my Jewel.